FATAL
INTENT

FATAL INTENT

A NOVEL

TAMMY EULIANO

OCEANVIEW (PUBLISHING
SARASOTA, FLORIDA

This book is a work of fiction. Names, characters, businesses, organizations, places, and incidents either are the products of the author's imagination or are used fictitiously. Any resemblance to actual events, businesses, locales, or persons living or dead, is entirely coincidental.

ISBN 978-1-60809-484-4

Published in the United States of America by Oceanview Publishing

Sarasota, Florida

www.oceanviewpub.com

10 9 8 7 6 5 4 3 2

PRINTED IN THE UNITED STATES OF AMERICA

For Neil, Erin, Matthew, and Catherine

ACKNOWLEDGMENTS

I'd like to thank everyone at Oceanview Publishing for believing in this project and bringing it together with such skill and professionalism. Also, thank you to my amazing friends, the Lake House Writers, who have believed in me since the start and encouraged me to stick with it even when I felt inadequate to the task.

I'd especially like to thank my parents and siblings for supporting everything I've ever attempted, including this encore career. For reading and loving my work and always finding something positive to say, even if they had to search for it. Thanks to my daughter, Erin, for her willingness to provide insightful comments and suggestions from the perspective of her generation. And, to Matthew and Catherine for continually asking how the writing is going and for loving the finished product.

And, finally, thanks to my husband, Neil, for accepting this hobby that became a passion and caused me to move my office into our empty playroom. Thanks for supporting everything, always, and for keeping me sane.

CHAPTER ONE

I DREADED WEEKENDS. That alone set me apart from my colleagues—from humans in general—even without all the rest.

Nights I could handle. By the time I ate dinner with Aunt Irm, took Shadow for a run, and played cards or read aloud with my great-aunt, exhaustion would claim me. But weekends brought spare time, the enemy of all who grieve.

On Saturdays, the few hours I spent in Jacksonville at my husband's bedside offered little comfort. Watching him waste away tore at my heart, at my conscience, but it hadn't been a year yet. There was still hope.

I woke Sunday morning earlier than I'd planned—or wanted. Pots clanged in the kitchen. For my great-aunt Irm, all days were the same; and sleeping in was as foreign as the idioms of her adopted country.

Shadow, my black Lab, pushed past me as I opened my bedroom door. "Good morning," I said to Aunt Irm, my voice gruff with sleep.

"Oh, kindchen, did I wake you? I have much to do before church this morning."

Aunt Irm had called me "kid" in her native German since I was a child. Even now, as I approached thirty, she almost never called me Kate.

I breathed in deeply and smelled not the aroma of Sunday breakfast, but an Italian restaurant. "What are you making?"

She pointed around the kitchen. "Lasagna, minestrone soup, and tiramisu. I am sorry, no time for breakfast."

"That's fine, but when did you become Italian?"

"Carmel gave me the recipes." She held up handwritten pages. "She does not have enough time before the wake."

"Wake?"

"Yes, I told you last night."

Oops.

"Carmel's next-door neighbor, Isabelle's husband's cousin, passed away."

And I didn't remember . . . shocking.

"Just like my Max," Aunt Irm went on. She jabbed a finger toward me. "There is no minor surgery. What you do, it is dangerous."

I'm an anesthesiologist. It's not dangerous for my patients, or for me for that matter, and ordinarily I would argue with her, but we'd long since pounded that dough to cement. Aunt Irm's brother, my Uncle Max, died two days after an operation to place a feeding tube. It's a common operation, especially in old, sick patients. But in her mind, the operation, or more likely the anesthesia, killed her beloved brother. Not his obesity, diabetes, heart disease, love of alcohol, or recent stroke. His doctor signed the death certificate, no need for an autopsy. The death was not unexpected.

"I'm sorry to hear about your friend," I said.

"Oh, I did not meet her." Aunt Irm turned back to the stove.

Only she would spend her Sunday morning preparing a feast to celebrate the life of someone she'd never met.

Pans and trays lined the countertops. "How many people are they expecting at this wake?"

"Oh, did I not say? Half is for the wake; the other half is for a funeral at Saint Mark's this afternoon."

"Tough week." When Aunt Irm joined a church, she joined a church. Less than a year since moving to Florida, she was on more committees than there are days in a week, including the bereavement committee.

"When it rains, it snows," she said.

"Pours. When it rains, it pours."

She gave her "whatever" shrug, along with instructions for constructing the tiramisu. Apparently, I was on the bereavement committee as well.

* * *

Ensconced in our usual pew, I asked my aunt the name of her not-quite-friend who died.

"Yes, please say a prayer for her. Dorothea McCray is her name." Aunt Irm knelt and folded her hands beneath her chin, eyes closed in concentration.

McCray. I'd taken care of a McCray that week. I held my phone low and pulled up the OR schedule. "Where was her surgery?" I whispered.

"Shhh. I do not know. And put that away." She snatched it from me with the look of shocked disappointment I hadn't seen since my teen years. I'd seen it a lot back then. After Mom and Dad died, Aunt Irm's visits were the only time my brother, Dave, and I attended church, and we were . . . rusty.

Chastened, I knelt beside my aunt and silently recited my standard pre-Mass prayers: for Aunt Irm, for my brother and his family, and for my in-laws. For my patients and for friends with struggles of their own. Finally, for Greg, my husband, whose prognosis grew dimmer by the day, and for Emily, our baby girl, born too early, who waited for us in heaven. The image helped, fantasy though it was.

I stayed awake, if marginally focused, and reflexively followed the sit, stand, kneel mechanics of Mass,—until I was jarred back to consciousness by the lector.

"What did she say?" I whispered to my aunt.

"To pray for those defending our country. We pray for them every week."

"No, before that."

"A Dr. O'-something, former president of the university."

A vacuum formed around me, no air.

"Kate?"

I pushed gently past her, grabbed my phone from the pew, and strode down the aisle, fellow parishioners a blur on either side, the priest's voice an echo in the far reaches of my consciousness. Dr. O'Donnell was dead. He was my patient, my VIP patient. One I cared for at the special request of my chairman. Holy crap.

Outside, the cool morning breeze contrasted with the warm church and helped regain my balance. My chairman's call early Thursday morning had come as a surprise. There were any number of faculty he could have asked to cover his VIP case, pretty much all with less baggage than I, yet he'd called.

"I fractured my hip on my son's skateboard yesterday," he'd said. "Word to the wise—don't try to jump a garden hose."

Unable to work clinically while taking painkillers, he asked me to take care of Dr. O'Donnell, president of the university during my freshman year. In such a small town, the university president's fame was second only to the football and basketball coaches'.

And now he was dead.

On my phone, I checked the medical record system. The last note in Dr. O'Donnell's chart was his discharge from the recovery room on Thursday evening. I scrolled back in the OR schedule and said a word one should not say on church property. Dorothea McCray had been my patient as well, the day before Dr. O'Donnell.

Maybe it was a different Dorothea McCray. I leaned back against the brick exterior of St. Mark's. Two Dorothea McCrays, with connections to Newberry, Florida, who underwent minor surgery last week. Nice try. It was her. Had to be. Two of my patients had died.

Having a patient die is never good. Having two die in quick succession is awful. Having two die in rapid succession when you're on probation? That warranted another unholy expletive.

No choice. I had to call my chairman.

"Kate, I thought I might hear from you," Dr. James Worrell said.

What could I say to that?

"I saw the paper this morning—about Dr. O'Donnell," he continued.

"Does it say what happened? Do you know?"

"The paper blames a 'long illness.' You know how lethal those can be."

"I should have admitted him."

"From the records it looked like he was doing fine."

Worrell had checked the chart? Of course he had. He'd taken care of Dr. O'Donnell multiple times in the past. I cursed his garden hose. "But if I'd kept him . . ."

"It was two days later; you couldn't have kept him that long."

He had a point, one I wanted to cling to, but there was more. I cleared my suddenly dry throat. "Another patient from last week died, Dorothea McCray. She had an uneventful G-Tube placement on Wednesday. I took care of her, too."

That brought a less committal, "Hmmm."

"I just found out this morning. She looked fine in the recovery room but had multiple sclerosis."

A keyboard clicked in the background. "Neither of them died on your watch. I know you're worried about the probation review, but if there are any questions, I've got your back."

All my anesthetics were subject to review, my job at stake. Could I hope those two charts wouldn't be selected? But both cases had gone fine.

"Should I tell Dr. Walker up front?" I asked. The chief of staff was not particularly fond of me.

"Of course not," James said. "Why look for trouble? If it comes up, I'll take care of it."

Tears threatened. I didn't try to talk. I'd disappointed the chief of staff once and was still paying for it nearly a year later.

"This kind of thing might not be uncommon," James said. "Unless our care was implicated, we'd never know about delayed complications."

"This is a pretty big complication."

"I don't disagree, but these are end-of-life-type cases. This could be a common occurrence."

Common occurrence? Really? It's true we rarely follow patients once they leave the recovery room. With eight or ten patients a day, it would rapidly become impossible. But the reassurance of that thought immediately felt wrong. Why should knowing other patients likely died be reassuring?

"Thanks, James."

"Kate, are you okay? This is not your fault." He emphasized the last words.

"I'm fine." Hopefully the lilt I added sounded less fake than it felt. This was not on me. Hey, a new mantra. A little pathetic compared to *carpe diem*, but my days had a habit of seizing back lately.

Still, common occurrence or not, I would find out why my patients died.

CHAPTER TWO

I RETURNED TO our pew in time for the Lord's Prayer, which I hoped would remind Aunt Irm to forgive me for sneaking out. I squeezed her hand at that part of the prayer.

After Communion and the Recessional, we exited through the main doors and waited our turn to greet Father Jeff. "You apologize to him," Aunt Irm said in an over-loud whisper as our turn approached.

I followed orders and then said, "I'm so sorry to hear about Dr. O'Donnell. I took care of him earlier in the week and he seemed fine." It would be a violation of patient confidentiality, but Father Jeff already knew.

"Yes," he said, "I prayed with the family that morning. Molly asked me to give him Last Rites."

"Last Rites?" Aunt Irm said. "Before he is dying?"

Father Jeff smiled at her. "Little known fact, but yes, with serious illness or before a major operation."

"But this wasn't—"

Father Jeff interrupted me with raised hands. "Molly was insistent, and it can't hurt. Last Rites can be administered more than once. When she called yesterday morning to say he'd passed away, I was glad we'd done it."

We thanked him and moved on to give other parishioners a turn. Aunt Irm gave a very uncharacteristic but very German-sounding harrumph.

I pulled her arm through mine. "What?"

"Last Rites before death. I did not know this was possible. My Max did not get this."

"You know if anyone deserves to be in heaven, it's Uncle Max." He'd taken in my brother and me. Two orphaned teenagers thrust on a sixty-something man whose parenting experience extended only to chickens and a really bad dog. When we were small, Max's wife left him, and he farmed a plot on Dad's land. When Mom and Dad traveled, which was often, he watched us, which was awesome. Uncle Max was a bigger kid than we were. He would have been an amazing father. He was an amazing father.

* * *

At home, while Aunt Irm put the finishing touches on her feasts, I read Dr. O'Donnell's obituary aloud from the front page of the newspaper. "Dr. Michael O'Donnell, former president of the university, died in his sleep Friday night after a long illness. He was eighty years old. Dr. O'Donnell is best known for pushing the university to the forefront of research, quadrupling income from licensed technology, and raising its national status. Current University President Bernard Thatcher said, 'He had a vision for this university and the skills to implement it. We will be forever in his debt.' Dr. O'Donnell is survived by his wife, Molly, three sons, two daughters, and four grandchildren. He is predeceased by his parents, a brother, and a granddaughter. Memorial services will be held at St. Mark's Catholic Church, Sunday at four p.m."

Dorothea McCray's obituary garnered less attention on the interior section. She'd been a professional violinist and then a "beloved violin teacher." The cynical side of me questioned the adjective. Was anyone not *beloved* in an obituary?

I helped my aunt deliver somewhat less than half the food to a small nondenominational church on the far side of town and the rest to the hall adjacent to St. Mark's.

Aunt Irm glanced at her watch as we climbed back into my Accord. "We just have time to dress and return for the memorial."

There was much wrong with that sentence, beginning with the pronoun, but I skipped that for the moment. "Are you serving at the reception? You already cooked."

"No, my work is done."

My questioning eyebrows came down low enough to limit my vision. Why would I attend church twice in one day? And a funeral at that?

"I don't do well at funerals," I said.

"No one does well at funerals."

"No, I mean I embarrass myself, crying even when I barely knew the person."

"Death is part of life, kindchen. We will all die."

"Yeah, I got that memo. But I don't have to celebrate it."

"We do not celebrate death; we celebrate life."

"You never even met Dr. O'Donnell."

"But you attended the university, you work at the university, and you took care of this man. Attending his memorial is a matter of respect."

Argument was hopeless. Once my aunt had a bee in her tight German bun, nothing I could say would change her mind.

Back at home, I took Shadow for a short walk, freshened up, and changed into the same simple black dress I'd worn to Uncle Max's funeral. Aunt Irm, already in the car, wore a tasteful black hat over her, hopefully, bee-free bun.

As I backed down the driveway, I said, "You explained why I need to go, but why do you want to come?"

"Father Jeff's comments about Last Rites. I wonder, could she be a *Schwarze Witwe.*"

"Bless you!" I giggled. "A what?"

"A Schwarze Witwe, a spider who kills her husband."

"A black widow? Oh, come on. First, at least in English, the term is for serial husband killers, and second, we have no reason to believe Mrs. O'Donnell killed her husband. If you embarrass me at this memorial . . ."

"Do not worry, kindchen. I only want to watch."

I shot her a warning look, but Aunt Irm just smiled serenely.

"Let's sit in the back and stay inconspicuous. Okay?" We didn't know the family, and, however unlikely, I didn't want them to recognize me.

Approaching the church, it was apparent how very many people in town respected Dr. O'Donnell or wanted to be seen respecting him. I dropped Aunt Irm near the entrance, then circled back to park in an adjoining field. Greg called it ChrEaster Field, used for overflow parking for the major-holidays-only Catholics.

I started looking for my aunt toward the back of our usual section. When she stood and waved, I cringed. Not only was she calling attention to me, she was doing it from the front frickin' row. Apparently "inconspicuous" meant something very different in German. At least the family was not yet seated. I genuflected and knelt beside her. "What are we doing way up here?"

"These were the first seats I found, kindchen. Now pray for the dead." I glanced over my shoulder at the smattering of available seats behind us, but arguing in church might be considered disrespectful, so I said another prayer for Dr. O'Donnell's soul and his family, and sat back in the pew.

There was no casket, but a large portrait of Dr. O'Donnell's much younger smiling face stood on an easel. Fortunately, I'd attended few funerals in my life—my parents', of course, and Emily's. The others were for elderly relatives and a friend of Greg's I'd never met, yet still, I cried. In that case it wasn't the death, but the grief I observed that cut into me and brought unbidden tears. It was embarrassing. I would be fine until someone else cried, and then up came the waterworks.

The processional began. Mrs. O'Donnell walked stiffly erect on the arm of one son and surrounded by the rest of her children. I turned away when one of the sons, Christian O'Donnell, looked in our direction. The morning of his father's surgery, he'd confided his mother had a premonition about the operation. I hated those. He introduced me to his father and invited me afterward for pizza around the bedside as they awaited his discharge. I wondered, irrationally, what Christian thought of me now. Whether he blamed me for his father's death.

The Mass proceeded . . . again. Twice in one day. I should get the next weekend off. The sons and daughters did the readings. One played a piece on violin while another sang, but she couldn't get through the chorus. It was beautiful, and heartbreaking, and I pulled out a tissue.

Next, Father Jeff introduced Christian O'Donnell, "who will say a few words about his father."

During his eulogy, he mentioned how grateful he was that his mother had convinced him to come up for the surgery. He attributed her sixth sense to an angel whispering in his mother's ear. That triggered more tears, but at the same moment Aunt Irm harrumphed a little too loudly. I pressed on her foot with the toe of my black heels and glanced around to see if anyone had heard. Embarrassing, but it halted the tear factory.

At the conclusion of the service, Father Jeff invited the congregation to a reception across the lawn at Father Walsh Hall. After the Recessional, Aunt Irm beat a path toward the door. I caught up to her. "Slow down."

"I want to pay my respects, and the line's going to be long. Come on."

I followed her across the lawn, skirting the crowded sidewalk, and wishing I'd worn flats as my heels sank into the grass. At the hall, I changed my mind. Aunt Irm could pay respects, or whatever she was doing, without me.

In the antechamber, I pretended to take interest in the announcements pinned to the bulletin board. As the throng passed, I reviewed the Pray-then-Play basketball schedule, the bowling league sign-up sheet, and the perpetual notice requesting volunteers for various activities. Someday I would find time to volunteer.

Out of news to peruse, I peeked into the hall to see Aunt Irm still twenty people away from the family. Dressed all in black, Molly O'Donnell stood rigidly in the center. She seemed almost regal, greeting her subjects as they approached, holding their hands in hers, nodding sadly at each in turn. She must be at least seventy herself and had just lost her husband, yet she stood poised and dignified in the receiving line.

It occurred to me I had no idea what Aunt Irm would say and prayed she knew better than to mention me. *Please God, don't let her mention me.*

Another table held flyers for various church outreach programs—the Knights of Columbus Easter program, a Habitat for Humanity fundraiser to build a home for a parishioner, and a hospice newsletter with a dove on the front.

The home health nurse I'd hired for Greg had gone to work for hospice. She had been working for us the night his trach clogged and the suction catheter wouldn't pass. By the time she woke me, his face was blue. His abdomen collapsed with each attempted breath, but his face betrayed nothing. Did he know he was dying? His neurologist didn't think so, but could we really know for sure? What would have happened if I hadn't taken over? If I'd been working that night?

"Kate?"

I turned to find my brother-in-law, whose calls and messages I'd been avoiding for more than a week. Not good. "Adam." I said it with all the lack of feeling it warranted.

"We need to talk."

"No, we don't." I spun on my heel and bumped directly into Christian O'Donnell.

"Dr. Downey?"

Flustered by Adam and surprised Christian recognized me, I fumbled for words.

"Thank you for coming," he said.

I mumbled something lame about being sorry for his loss. How I'd hated that phrase at Emily's funeral, and here I was using it. Add hypocrite to the week's resume.

"Thanks. Mom was right after all; it was his time. I'm grateful he went peacefully, and we were all here." Less lame but rehearsed. He was allowed. He glanced at Adam. "Did I interrupt something?"

Adam stepped forward, hand outstretched. "Adam Downey, Kate's brother-in-law. I know your brother, Mike. I'm sorry for your loss as well, but it must be nice to have closure. To know he's no longer suffering. That he's in a better place."

"Adam," I said, too loudly.

Christian looked from Adam to me. I guided Christian away from Greg's insensitive nutcase of a brother. "I am so sorry. Adam's mother is suffering with dementia." Though true, it was not his mother Adam referred to. It was my husband. "He's struggling a bit."

"Your form declines intubation and resuscitation," I said. "Do you know what that means?"

Mrs. Greyson nodded for both of them. "No tube in his throat, no ventilator, and no CPR." The couple stared at each other. A joint decision. Devastating, but mutual.

"Right, but did Dr. Dearborn describe general anesthesia to you? It requires a breathing tube and ventilator temporarily. We could avoid that by doing a spinal. You won't feel anything but can breathe on —"

"No." They interrupted in unison.

"He needs general anesthesia," said Mrs. Greyson with unexpected conviction. Likely she'd read much about her husband's disease, and knew the pros and cons.

"Okay. We'll remove the breathing tube as soon as you're able to breathe on your own again. So, to be clear, we're going to rescind the DNR during the operation, reinstating it once you're out of the recovery room."

Mrs. Greyson's eyes narrowed fractionally. "Alex has been through enough." Her voice broke. With considerable effort, her husband touched her shoulder.

"It's okay," he said to me in his soft voice. "I trust you. Do what you think is right." He let his arm fall back to his side, rail thin but still too weighty. Then his eyes changed, wider, piercing, imploring. "Just don't let me linger on a ventilator. It will be time soon enough either way."

"I promise, sir."

Mrs. Greyson leaned over the stretcher and kissed her husband as he struggled to embrace her in return. When she pulled away, a single tear tracked down the right side of his face. She caressed it away with her thumb, clutching a mascara-streaked tissue in her palm.

I nodded to Jenn and she released the brake, tugged the curtain aside, and pulled the foot of the stretcher into the aisle as I reassured Mrs. Greyson. "We'll take good care of him."

When we arrived in the OR, Dr. Ricken had not yet appeared. "I've called him," said the circulating nurse, holding up her hands defensively. With administration's emphasis on on-time starts, this wasn't the way to begin the day.

"I recorded the reason for the delay," she added.

While we waited, Jenn showed impressive maturity for a med student. She engaged Mr. Greyson in conversation, distracting him from the wait and impending surgery. Listening carefully to his soft voice, in ten minutes we learned he'd been married five years, had a three-year-old son who loved animals, and a golden retriever named Acadia, after the national park in Maine where he had proposed. They decided to have no more children after the ALS diagnosis. "This death sentence is not worth the risk. She will have more children, just not mine."

I thought about that comment. A sperm donor perhaps? But Dr. Ricken's arrival prevented further discussion, probably a good thing, as another tear formed in the corner of Mr. Greyson's eye. I handed Jenn a tissue and she gently wiped it away.

After Dr. Ricken and I confirmed patient and procedure, Jenn moved to the head of the bed and applied a clear mask over Mr. Greyson's nose and mouth. She continued to talk soothingly to him but forgot to turn up the oxygen flow. Justin took care of it. Though not her first intubation, the tremor in Jenn's hand betrayed her nerves.

I administered the induction drugs, and once Mr. Greyson fell unconscious, Jenn opened his mouth, slid in the metal laryngoscope, and lifted his lower jaw.

"What do you see?" Justin peered over her shoulder.

"Vocal cords." She slipped the endotracheal tube in with little difficulty. Justin attached the ventilator tubing and squeezed the breathing bag while we watched for a deflection in the carbon

CHAPTER FOUR

I STARTED MY other room with much less drama and returned to the Anesthesia Clinical Office, where I slumped into a chair before one of the half-dozen computers lining one wall. But I didn't log in, I just stared. Why would someone be so rude? How could it possibly be productive?

Strong hands squeezed my shoulders. In the dark computer screen, I saw the reflection of Sam Paulus. "Uh-oh, Ricken?" he said.

"He is not a pleasant man."

Sam sat and swiveled to face me. "What did he do now?"

"Yelled at my student while she tried to intubate and at me for letting her try a second time."

"Helpful."

"Sorry you got stuck with him," said Amal. I hadn't noticed her sitting at the long table behind me. "Sam, why are we putting up with his behavior? He should be kicked out."

"Won't happen. He's bringing paying patients," said a woman at the computer next to Sam. "It's all about the bottom line and you guys have an awful payer mix here, too much Medicaid and uninsured."

"Have you met?" Sam asked, looking between us.

I offered my hand while he made introductions.

"Cheryl, this is Kate Downey, one of our up-and-coming young faculty members. Kate, this is Cheryl Smith, a locums CRNA here to help us out for a few weeks."

"Welcome," I said as we shook hands. Several unexpected departures and sick leaves of our physician extenders necessitated the hiring of very expensive *locum tenens* nurse anesthetists. These travelers obtained hospital privileges quicker than a full-time hire and could come and go on short notice. Without residents and extenders, faculty would be unable to care for more than one patient at a time, and the hospital would have to close operating rooms.

"Want me to say something to Ricken?" Sam asked quietly.

"No, I'll take care of it."

"No, you won't."

He knew me too well, knew my aversion to confrontation.

"Any news on Greg?" he asked.

"Adam's fighting me over withdrawal of care."

Sam's face clouded. "I'm sorry, Kate. I can talk to him, too, if you want."

What might help is if Sam talked to me. Or I to him. He'd been a mentor to both Greg and me during training and had become a friend. He'd been at our wedding and was the first person in the department I told about my pregnancy. Even though he disagreed with me bringing my comatose husband home, he helped set everything up. And when he was proved right a month later, he helped me move Greg to a long-term-care facility without a hint of I-told-you-so. I could talk to Sam. But what if he agreed with Adam?

"No, Sam, I've got this." I stood to leave. "Don't forget I'm teaching at ten."

"Yep, I'll cover you."

He stared after her, then at Nathan. "I'd like to talk in private."

Nathan straightened and looked ready to argue.

"It's okay, Nathan." The young man wasn't going to attack me; he was probably embarrassed. Privacy might allow him to drop the tough-guy persona that kept him from participating fully.

Once the door closed behind Nathan, Robert's posture crumpled. He leaned back against a table, head bowed, and looked at me through over-long bangs. "I have to pass this class, but I don't do well with simulation."

I nodded. "We'll have to work on that. It's part of board certification. You can't avoid it."

"I try, but when I know I'm onstage, I just can't think."

I put a reassuring hand on his shoulder. "You'll be onstage your whole career. Stage fright isn't an option."

"I'm fine when it's the real thing. It's just in here." He lifted his head toward Stan.

"How do you know that? How many emergencies have you led?" I knew the answer. In the name of patient safety, the role of medical students in emergencies had been whittled to barely observer. "How about talking through a scenario? We could start there."

"Like an oral exam? That's even worse."

"Well, Robert, we have to figure something out, because I can't pass you until you prove you can perform in a basic emergency. How about I write out some scenarios and you think through them on your own, even write out what you would do, then when you come in here maybe it will be easier to recall?"

He shook his head slowly, resigned and skeptical.

I patted his shoulder again. "It's going to be okay. Is there anything else going on? You seem awfully down."

He rubbed his face. "My brother committed suicide last week."

Oh my. "I'm sorry, Robert." Such inadequate words. I was getting good at that. "Maybe you should take some time off. You can remediate this any time. Have you spoken to Dr. Duffy?"

The Dean of Students was a friend, and sensitive to students' needs.

Robert stood and turned away, shoulders slumped, and my heart ached for him. Medical school was hard enough without losing someone you cared about.

"I'm happy to talk, or help you find someone to talk to, if you like."

He nodded, but kept his face averted.

"I'll email you the scenarios, but no rush. Give yourself some time."

He nodded again.

I wondered about time to recover from the loss of a loved one. Did it ever happen?

The skin around the patient's eyes twitched, evidence the drug was taking effect, relaxing the spasmed vocal cords, unless I had the wrong diagnosis. The twitching spread to her arms.

Sam squeezed the breathing bag, and I felt some give in the mask, maybe. The patient's chest moved, maybe.

Sam felt it, too. "It's working." He gave another breath and the chest rose. I said a silent prayer as Sam gave rapid, deep breaths. We had lots of carbon dioxide to breathe off, and oxygen to replace.

The oxygen saturation began to climb, and the room let out a collective sigh of relief. The crowd who responded to the alert began to file out. "Thanks, everybody," I said and several people waved. The tracheotomy tray disappeared.

As my adrenaline surge began to wane, I saw Erin. Her shaking hands and red face tore at my heart. I'd been in her shoes once. We all had.

Sam saw her, too, and was still the attending of record. "She's starting to breathe on her own," he said. "Why don't I get her to Recovery while you guys go see your next patient?"

I guided Erin to the faculty locker room where we could have privacy. We sat on the bench and I waited while she collected herself. When she could speak, she said, "I almost killed her." She choked down a sob. "I froze. I didn't know what to do."

"It's okay. That's why residency is four years." I squeezed her shoulder. "Everyone has a first big event and you feel completely overwhelmed. In mine, I stood by and let everyone else take care of the patient. I felt useless and out of my league."

Erin nodded. "Exactly."

"And I wondered if I'd picked the right field, whether I'd ever be able to stay calm and focused during an emergency."

She nodded again.

"And here I am." Oh, the irony.

She was silent a moment. "I shouldn't have pulled the tube."

"Probably not. But most times, it would have been fine. Now, for your next hundred patients, you'll be waiting until they're doing higher math before you extubate."

She gave a small smile.

"Hang in there," I said. "You'll probably have trouble sleeping tonight, reliving every second, and thinking about everything you should have done differently, and that's okay. That's how we get better."

She took a deep, shuddering breath. "Thank you."

"You okay to finish your cases today?"

"Definitely. I need to get back on the horse."

"Okay," I said. "Go get a drink and relax for a few minutes, and I'll get the next patient ready."

Thirty minutes later, she looked back to normal, with only slightly puffy eyes. We got the case started and talked a while, until my phone rang.

"Are you okay if I step out?" I asked Erin.

She nodded.

I answered the phone as I left the OR.

"Kate, it's Pat Duffy. Can we meet?"

CHAPTER SIX

I MET DR. Duffy in the Surgery Lounge. Recently remodeled, its tiny kitchen area was stocked with coffee, Gatorade, crackers, and peanut butter. The meal of champions when we had no time for a lunch break. Computer workstations lined two walls, while sofas and tables with chairs crammed the remaining space. We sat in over-stuffed lounge chairs in the back corner.

"A student came to see me," he said.

That was quick. "Good." But Dr. Duffy didn't look like it was good. "Was it Robert Barton?" I pulled the roster from my pocket.

"He believes you have it in for him."

"What?" That was the sum total of words I could get out, since "What the hell?" seemed inappropriate in front of the Dean of Students.

"He claims you placed him in an impossible situation so you could fail him and then gave him extra work that you aren't requiring of the other students."

I stared, open-mouthed. "You've got to be kidding. I wrote up scenarios to help him prepare. To help him." *Had I made it sound like required extra work?* "He doesn't have to turn anything in. He just has to remediate the scenarios from today. The whole group does." I handed Dr. Duffy the current roster.

"Jenn Mason?" he said.

"Not her, she'd already left. She did a great job."

He nodded. "He says everyone else worked as a team, but you made him work alone."

Had I? I had sent Jenn away. Crap.

"Tell me what happened," he said.

I recounted the scenarios in broad strokes, including Robert's final inept performance and our conversation afterward. I wasn't sure whether the death of his brother was told to me in confidence so I said only, "He's going through some things in his personal life. I suggested he consider getting help and maybe taking some time off."

Dr. Duffy frowned throughout, grimaced toward the end, then seemed to deflate.

"Is something going on?" I asked. A student complaint generally warranted an email, not a face-to-face barely an hour later. "He's on probation, isn't he? He's afraid my evaluation will get him dismissed. I told him he can remediate."

"So you didn't treat him differently than anyone else?"

"Jenn left before his turn. She was blurting out all the answers, so I arranged for her to be called back to the OR. He hadn't participated at all, so I made him take the lead."

He winced. "Have you documented everything?"

"Not yet. If he improves, that's what I'll report."

He nodded. "Okay. You might consider having another faculty member present when you do the remediation."

"That would be treating him differently. Is that appropriate?"

"Yes, in this case, it would be appropriate, but you bring up a good point. Why don't you have someone present for all of them? We need to cross t's on this one." His eyes bored into mine, trying to tell me something without violating confidentiality.

All I read was gravity.

He stood and offered his hand. "Keep me posted on the remediation."

* * *

In preop holding, Jenn squatted beside an elderly woman at the bed-side of our next patient. The woman leaned into Jenn.

"Dr. Downey," Jenn said, standing. "This is Mr. and Mrs. Sander-son. They were my family for Interdisciplinary Family Health."

Mrs. Sanderson gave a watery smile. "Yes, Jenn and her friends take care of us." She tapped her husband's hand and said in a loud voice, "Remember they built you that ramp from the garage?" He turned his head, but his cloudy eyes seemed not to register. At a normal volume, she said, "And they had his medications switched to liquid, and so many other things." She patted Jenn's hand like a doting grandmother. "I'm afraid it isn't enough anymore. He won't swallow when I tell him."

That explained the scheduled G-Tube.

Mrs. Sanderson stood with some difficulty and pulled Jenn into an embrace. Over the young woman's shoulder, she mouthed some-thing to me. If there's anything I'm worse at than confrontation, it's reading lips, but I gathered she wished to share something outside of Jenn's hearing.

When they separated, I asked Jenn to check on the OR's readi-ness. Mrs. Sanderson watched her depart, then turned to me. "I don't want Jenn in there."

Not what I expected to hear.

"Please, I don't want her to be a part of this."

"Jenn is an excellent student," I said. "We won't let her—"

"It's not that. Sandy is like a grandfather to her. If something happens..."

"Nothing will happen." Did I say that out loud? "But I understand."

"Thank you. She's so special to us. Can you say it's hospital policy since we're so close? I don't want her to know."

"I'll take care of it," I said.

I headed Jenn off in the corridor. "It's best if you're not involved in the care of someone you're so close to."

"I understand," she said, but disappointment was etched on her face.

"Why don't you go up to Labor and Delivery for the afternoon? I'll let the attending know you're coming."

She brightened at this. "Justin's wife is coming in."

"She is?" So who was doing the Sanderson case with me?

I checked my phone. I'd missed a text from Sam Paulus twenty minutes before: Dearborn wife in labor. Sending you Jernigan.

I'd worked with Brad Jernigan the week before, another locums CRNA. Standoffish but competent.

I gave Jenn my cell number. "He asked me to place her epidural. Let me know how she's doing."

She hurried away as I texted the OB anesthesia attending, Dr. Wendley, to expect both her and the Dearborns.

Marcus Culpepper, the PA, arrived in the OR ahead of his boss. I pulled him back into the sub-sterile room. "What do you think happened to Mrs. McCray and Dr. O'Donnell?"

He frowned. "I've been wondering the same thing. Both operations were straightforward. Do you have any ideas?"

"No. The anesthetics went fine, and they both looked good at discharge."

"Frustrating."

No doubt. "I called their primary care physicians. I'll let you know if I find out anything."

"You think it's more than a coincidence?"

I shrugged. "Just don't want to miss anything."

He nodded.

"Thanks for your help with Ricken earlier," I said. "He's . . . volatile."

Marcus smiled. "Anytime."

All the time, more like it.

CHAPTER SEVEN

I RAN DOWNSTAIRS to grab a late lunch in the food court. In line, I pulled out my smartphone. No wasted moments on clinical days. I scrolled through my personal email comprised largely of junk and spam. Before I finished reading, I heard, "Dr. Downey," and turned to see Christian O'Donnell. "Call me Kate, please. How are you?" Stupid question. He'd just lost his father.

"We're hanging in there."

I nodded, searching his face.

"It was time for him to go, but it's still hard."

"I can only imagine." And it was true. My parents died unexpectedly, long before it was time, and Greg was still living-ish. "What brings you to the hospital?"

"To be honest, I'm getting Dad's medical records. My brother, the internist, had to go back home, so he asked me to get them." He looked sheepish. "We know you took great care of him. It's nothing to do with that. Luke's having trouble coming to terms with all this. He's not looking to blame anyone; he just wants to understand." Christian's expression was earnest, imploring, and apologetic. "Since I'm still in town—"

He was interrupted by the "sandwich artist" asking for my order: six-inch turkey on whole wheat, hold the cheese, load on the veggies. Christian ordered behind me.

CHAPTER EIGHT

JUSTIN SAT ON the far side of the bed, back straight, face tense, gripping his wife's hand in both of his. Shelley reclined on the bed, dirty blond hair arrayed in a messy halo on the pillow, eyes closed and breath deliberate.

"I did her preop, she's healthy," he said.

So much for not taking care of family.

"I figured you'd want to do the consent yourself."

Good call. Between contractions, I explained the risks and she signed the form without reading a word.

"Do you mind if a med student watches?" I asked.

Shelley shook her head, wincing and breathing hard. "Just make these contractions stop." With help, she sat on the side of the bed and the nurse corralled her unruly hair into a ponytail holder.

I explained the steps softly to Jenn as I slipped in the epidural and secured it. After repositioning Shelley in bed, I watched a contraction crescendo on the monitor. "How does this one feel?"

"I'm having a contraction?" She looked at the monitor, then up at Justin, and laughed. It was a laugh of relief.

"I love my job," I whispered to Jenn. My phone beeped. "I need to go start another case downstairs," I said to Shelley. "Call if you need anything."

The couple thanked me as Jenn and I left the room. "Want to do the next intubation?" I asked her.

"Of course."

We headed to the stairs. "Mr. Brighton has advanced Parkinson's and needs a G-Tube."

"Another G-Tube?" Jenn said. "We didn't do this many the whole month I was on general surgery."

"Yeah, I guess it's Dr. Ricken's specialty."

After we discussed the rest of his preop and the anesthetic concerns, Jenn said, "I wanted to ask you, I'm enjoying anesthesia more than I expected, but I've already matched in Family Medicine."

"It's never too late. How did you pick Family Medicine?"

"It's what I've always wanted to do. Same as my dad. When I got accepted to med school, he put my name on one of the doors at his office."

"No pressure there."

"It's what we always planned."

I used my fob to enter the OR suites. "Lots of kids come in with a plan, but until you experience all the fields, you can't know what fits."

"I know that now."

"You should do another anesthesia rotation."

"I really want to, but there's only one more month of electives and I'm scheduled to work with a private Family Medicine doc north of Atlanta. I would change it, but my sister just had a baby and she needs my help. Her husband is deployed for four more weeks and our mom is leaving this weekend."

North Georgia. I knew people in North Georgia. "A former resident is in charge of a group at Canton General. If your sister lives anywhere near there, I can see if he has room for you."

"Seriously? That would be awesome." Her bright smile faded almost as fast as it had appeared. "What will I tell my dad?"

That needed follow-up, but we'd arrived at OR12A, sneakily wedged between ORs 12 and 14. I reintroduced myself to Mr. Brighton and introduced Jenn to both him and to Brad Jernigan, the CRNA for the case.

Her pleasant aura of confidence evaporated at the sight of the CRNA. "We've met," she said in a clipped tone. I looked between them, but Brad was busy attaching monitors and Jenn started talking with Mr. Brighton.

"I'd like Jenn to manage the airway," I said to Brad. He handed her the mask and stepped back. The induction went smoothly.

"Good job," Brad said.

Jenn thanked him. Soon after, she followed me from the room. "He doesn't like students."

I stopped. "He what?"

"He asked me to leave while he gave Justin a break."

"That's not okay."

"No, it's fine. He said he's a temp and not used to having students. I'd rather go back to OB anyway, if that's okay."

I hesitated, but agreed.

In the recovery room, I checked on Mr. Greyson, our ALS patient from the morning. His breathing was rapid, shallow, and labored, definitely not back to his baseline. I instructed the nurse not to discharge him without my approval. Mr. Greyson's condition was too tenuous to risk sending him out prematurely.

A couple of hours later, the nurse called to say Dr. Ricken had written a discharge order.

Ricken? The recovery room belongs to anesthesia. The official name is PACU: post-anesthesia care unit. Surgeons don't discharge patients from the PACU, only anesthesiologists.

I examined Mr. Greyson, listened to his lungs, and watched his breathing pattern. Still not back to normal for him. "How do you feel?"

"Okay," he whispered, his face blank. No pain or anxiety, just blank.

"I'd like to admit you overnight," I said.

"Dr. Ricken said we could leave," his wife said, her face far from blank.

How to play this? "He and I look at different things. From a surgical standpoint, everything's fine. I'm worried about your breathing and muscle strength. It'll just be overnight, to be on the safe side." Who could argue with that?

"He looks fine to me."

Apparently, his wife could.

"I'm sorry. We have to do what's safe." I canceled Dr. Ricken's order.

"You go home with Billy," Mr. Greyson said to his wife, his voice barely audible.

She looked at him, then her obstinate posture deflated and she hugged him.

"The DNR?" he said.

"I'll reinstate it if that's what you want."

He nodded, not a large movement, but his intentions were clear.

I added that to my orders, but just as surgeons don't discharge from PACU, anesthesiologists don't admit to the wards. The primary service does. I called Marcus, Ricken's PA, rather than the surgeon himself. "Hey, this is Kate Downey. Mr. Greyson isn't back to baseline respiratory-wise. I want him to stay overnight."

"Oh, Dr. Ricken won't want that."

"Too bad. If he won't do it, I'll get Medicine to admit him."

"He promised the Greysons he would be discharged. They have a little boy."

"I already spoke to them."

Marcus groaned.

"The note is in the chart that he is not ready for discharge and will be admitted by Dr. Ricken." I didn't mean it as a threat, or maybe I did. If they ignored the note, and Mr. Greyson suffered a preventable complication, Ricken would have a serious problem defending himself.

"I'll be there in a second," Marcus said, resigned. Poor guy.

Moments later, he joined me at the bedside. "Show me his flowsheet."

Tamping down irritation, I logged into the medical record system. My decision wasn't going to change, and he could pull the information himself, but I needed him on my side against Ricken. I opened the graph of Mr. Greyson's vital signs since arrival.

"He still requires four liters of oxygen to stay above ninety percent saturated," I said.

"Okay," Marcus said, pulling his phone from his pocket.

Eager to avoid the conversation with Ricken, I logged off the computer, promised to visit Mr. Greyson in the morning, and left.

On the drive home, I answered a call from an unrecognized number. "This is Kate."

"Dr. Downey? This is Dr. Richard Black from Internal Medicine. You left a message for me regarding Dr. O'Donnell?"

"Oh, yes, thanks for returning my call. I took care of him during his surgery and was surprised to hear he passed. I wondered if you had any information about the cause of death."

"Unfortunately, no. Molly called the office to say he died in his sleep. She declined an autopsy."

This I knew. "Do you have any thoughts?"

"I don't. It took me by surprise as well. It seemed he was recovering fine, with minimal pain. Tylenol covered it. An autopsy would have been helpful, but she was adamant."

"Is that unusual?"

"No, not really. Not in cases like this."

"One other question—do you know how they ended up with Dr. Ricken as the surgeon?" I hoped it didn't sound disrespectful. Dr. Black could be great friends with the insufferable surgeon, though I seriously doubted it.

"I don't. Molly called to ask for a general surgery consult and had already selected the surgeon."

She chose Ricken. Why?

"She said the hernia had grown and become more difficult to reduce. I suggested she wait until the next bladder tumor surgery. He had one scheduled in a few weeks, but she was convinced he would suffer bowel entrapment by then. She'd read about it on the internet."

I chuckled silently at that. So many patients felt their internet searches obviated nearly fifteen years of training and experience.

"To my discredit, I filed the consult for her, without reexamining him myself. Perhaps the surgery could have been avoided."

"If you hadn't done it, sounds like she would have found someone else," I said.

As we disconnected, I considered her resourcefulness. She insisted on a possibly avoidable operation, then had a premonition it would end badly. Why not cancel it then? But how could I, of all people, judge?

CHAPTER NINE

WHEN I ARRIVED home, Aunt Irm kissed me on both cheeks as usual, but something was off, her smile not quite genuine, and her eyes darted to the junk desk by the door to the garage.

"What's wrong?" I asked, moving toward the desk, where a bright green card was attached to an envelope.

She grabbed my hand. "Later, kindchen. Let's eat."

Dinner—chicken Caesar salad and crusty French bread—was delicious as always. Too bad my aunt's cooking talents were wasted on my unsophisticated palate. We exchanged stories of our day. She'd played bridge and excitedly announced her winnings of three dollars and twenty-five cents.

It's the little victories.

I shared a watered-down version of my run-in with Dr. Ricken, anger still heating my core at the recollection.

"Is he the surgeon who hurt Dr. O'Donnell?"

"He operated on him and Dorothea McCray as well, I'm afraid."

"He killed two people in one week, yet he is still working?"

"He didn't kill them. We don't know why they died."

"But he cared for both, and they died."

"I cared for both, too."

She stared at me. "But you would not hurt people."

"Neither would Ricken, jerk or not."

Later, after I'd cleaned the kitchen and taken Shadow for a walk, we played cards. It was Aunt Irm's day. She skunked me at cribbage in five hands, or maybe six, I lost count with my mind continually floating back to the day's near-disaster, my dead patients, and the simulation fiasco.

I texted Erin, the resident with the lost airway that morning. She was coping.

Just before heading to bed, I remembered the envelope on the junk desk.

Aunt Irm caught my gaze and bowed her head. "It came this afternoon, from Adam. I did not want to ruin your evening."

Funny. Just when I'd thought my day couldn't possibly get worse. He'd threatened legal action to withdraw care for Greg. Looked like he made it official. "It can wait."

Shadow barked at the back door.

"What is wrong with him?" Aunt Irm asked.

I opened the sliding glass door and he flew into the darkness of the backyard, barking and growling. That wasn't like him, even for a really big squirrel.

"Shadow? What is it, boy?" As if he would answer. I took a step into the grass, following his bark, and heard thudding on wood. He wouldn't run into the fence. Movement at the top of the fence caught my eye, but it was gone before I could focus in the gloom.

Shadow returned. I petted his head. "Good dog." He came back inside proudly. Job done.

I flipped on the patio light, but it didn't illuminate out into the yard. Nothing seemed out of place.

"Everything okay?" Aunt Irm asked.

I reassured her as I turned off the light, locked the door, and said good night.

In my room, I got ready for bed, then invited Shadow to join me. Curled around him, I drifted off and dreamed about my husband. We were playing flag football. Someone collapsed on the sideline and Greg was resuscitating him. I wanted to help, but he insisted I stay in the game. Weird.

I woke just before my six o'clock alarm.

Shadow leapt down as soon as I stretched. Somehow he knew it was Tuesday, my day out of the operating room. I slipped on exercise clothes, but when I sat on the floor to tie my running shoes, Shadow rolled over in my lap for a belly rub. Not so conducive to getting out the door. Perhaps realizing this, he jumped up and started whining, running back and forth from the bedroom door to the closet. I pulled my hair into a ponytail, put in earbuds, and attached Shadow's leash.

This early, we stuck to reasonably well-lit streets and sidewalks. At the small village center, about two miles from home, Shadow strained toward the specialty dog store across from the coffee shop. Selling homemade dog treats and all manner of items beyond what even I would consider buying, the store always had a bowl of water on the doorstep "for local dogs out walking their humans."

As he lapped at the dish, I leaned back against the brick building and bent forward, not quite touching my toes, or even the tops of my shoes. Flexible I am not. At Shadow's deep-throated growl, I stood, to find Christian O'Donnell smiling at me.

"It's okay, buddy." He held out the back of his hand to the dog.

I apologized, pulled out my earbuds, and tugged Shadow's leash. "He's a friend."

But Shadow was already licking Christian's hand. Some guard dog.

"No problem," Christian said, petting Shadow's head. "Good song?"

"Obviously a little too loud." I wiped a sleeve across my damp face. "You're out early."

Christian squatted in front of Shadow and rubbed the dog's head and ears. "Speak for yourself. Job hazard?"

"Shadow takes me for a run if I don't have to be in early."

Standing, Christian said, "Can I buy you breakfast?"

Before I could decline, as he surely knew I would, he said, "I have the anesthesia records, if you have time to look them over."

I glanced at my watch—six thirty.

"I can wait if you'd like to finish your run. Wouldn't want to disappoint Shadow."

"And I need a shower."

"We can do lunch later, if you prefer. Or dinner."

Dinner? No. That sounded like a date.

"No. Breakfast works. How about The Mill in an hour? It's just around the corner."

"I know the place. It was Dad's favorite. Seven thirty okay?"

An hour to run home, shower, return. "See you then." I tugged Shadow's leash. "Let's go." We started down the street while I replaced my earbuds and turned on the music. I hoped he wasn't watching me, except a tiny part of me hoped he was. I ran faster, away.

*   *   *

The strip plaza showed its considerable age. Pockmarked, formerly white walls supported a flat roof without adornment. Single-pane glass doors separated large windows at intervals along the length. Small signs hung from the eaves, identifying each cheerless shop—a specialty music store, a nail salon, a natural vitamin supply. No chain stores here, just mom-and-pop retail establishments struggling to survive.

The Mill Restaurant, formerly occupying a high-rent property adjacent to the town's only mall, was now wedged between a barber and an alterations shop. I pulled in several minutes late. Normally punctual, dressing had required more than usual consideration. What would I have worn today if I weren't having this breakfast? Careful not to primp in any way, I consciously chose an outfit that was not particularly flattering, and pulled my hair into a ponytail rather than spending time with a curling iron. I put on mascara, but no other makeup—standard for me. Now, as I caught my reflection in the restaurant's glass door, I may have gone too far in the opposite direction. I scanned the small room. A pastry case lined the left side of the deep but narrow restaurant. Christian stood and waved from a table near the back. He pulled out a chair for me. "Good morning again. You look a little different."

I smiled as I draped my purse over the back of the chair and sat.

He leaned in a little too close. "You smell better, too."

"Always a plus." My voice trembled slightly, like my stomach. The door seemed far away.

Christian sat, handed me a menu, and opened his own. "What's good?"

I hadn't been here since Greg's accident. Why in the world did I suggest this place? I cleared my throat. "I usually get an omelet. My husband loved their pancakes." Had I used past tense? I fidgeted in my chair. Had they always been so hard?

His eyes darted to me over the menu, but he didn't ask. The waitress who took our order was attractive beneath all the tattoos and studs in her face. I ordered a western omelet and water. Christian was a bit less health conscious: blueberry pancakes with bacon and orange juice.

"You seem nervous," he said.

"Do I?" I rubbed the condensation on my water glass.

"Is it because I asked to talk about my dad's case?"

Not entirely, but I nodded.

"We don't have to if it makes you uncomfortable. It's just that doctor-ese is incomprehensible."

"Said the lawyer."

He gave a crooked grin. "Fair point."

"What kind of law do you practice?"

He held up his hands defensively. "I handle corporate financial dealings. Nothing in health care."

I couldn't help but smile. "You're forgiven." I pushed my water aside and leaned forward. "Let me see those records."

Christian pulled a thick folder from his briefcase and opened it on the table, pushing the service items back toward the wall.

The anesthetic record was on top. I explained the document's layout. The vital signs graphic showed he was stable throughout the case.

"Luke asked about narcotics; where would I find that?"

I showed him the rows near the top of the vital signs grid. "We used some fentanyl early on. That's a short-acting, very potent opioid."

"Sorry?"

"Narcotic."

"You guys have a different word for everything."

"More than one sometimes. Your dad received fentanyl during the case, not an excessive amount, and some Dilaudid before we woke him up, also a normal amount. But regardless, those would have worn off within hours, long before . . ."

Christian met my eyes. "I get it." He referred to his smartphone. "The other question was muscle relaxants. Did you use any and were they reversed?" he read.

I returned to the record. "At induction we gave him rocuronium, a relatively short-acting muscle relaxant, to paralyze him for intubation. Brad didn't record any more during the surgery, which took more than two hours. And here—" I pointed at a spot on the medications line—"just before emergence, he gave a drug to bind up any remaining relaxant. Also, we confirmed that he was strong and following commands before we pulled the breathing tube."

"Commands?"

"Simple things to confirm he was awake and strong: 'squeeze my hand, lift your head.' He did all those things." I pointed to the notes in the bottom comment section. "I also saw him in the recovery room. He was strong and even talked to me. So, long story short, the relaxant we used doesn't last long enough to be the culprit."

Our food arrived and we were silent a moment. Christian poured a generous amount of syrup on his pancakes. I asked for ketchup.

"May I ask about your husband?" he said.

That came out of left field. I reflexively rotated my plain gold wedding band with my thumb.

Christian broke the awkward pause. "Sorry, I don't mean to pry. Your brother-in-law made some unusual comments at the memorial, and just now you mentioned your husband in the past tense."

"Yeah, sorry about Adam. Greg's in the Army medical corps." I cut my omelet with a fork, but didn't lift the bite. "Last year, an IED exploded near his jeep and he suffered a severe traumatic brain injury."

"I'm sorry," he said.

"He's been in a coma ever since." When I saw the compassion in his eyes, I knew he understood too well. Only people in the "club" understood like that.

"That's a lot for you to deal with," he said. "I know this sounds trite, but if there's anything I can do . . ."

"Actually, there may be. My brother-in-law is threatening to sue me." I pulled the envelope from my purse. I'd planned to read it sometime that day, maybe.

Christian opened it, skimmed the letter, then looked up at me. "I'm sorry, Kate," he said again.

"What does it say?"

"It's a notification of intent to sue on behalf of Greg for unlawful life. Besides you, it names a hospital in Jacksonville and a couple of physicians." Christian cleared his throat. "He wants all life support withdrawn, allowing a natural death."

I blinked back tears.

He reached across the table for my hand. I resisted the urge to pull away.

I shook my head. "I shouldn't have put that on you. You just lost your dad."

"I offered." His voice was so gentle, I couldn't help but meet his eyes. "Tell me," he said.

I shifted uncomfortably and pulled my hand away to take a long sip of water. "Greg is in a persistent vegetative state. If he doesn't improve within twelve months of the injury, he's not likely to."

"Has he improved?"

I shook my head. "But there's no switch to turn off. He's breathing on his own. Adam wants to starve him to death. I can't do that."

He was quiet a long moment. "I have a law school buddy who practices in Jacksonville. I'll call him today. If he can't help you, he'll know someone who can."

It sounded so simple. "Thank you. And thanks for not judging me."

"It's a personal decision, Kate. One no one should have to make, but one no one can, or should, make for you."

We returned to our meals in companionable silence. The waitress seated an elderly couple at the next table. Christian rose to help the woman maneuver her walker. She looked up at him with cloudy eyes. "Joe, how good to see you. How is Ida?"

Without skipping a beat, he said, "She's fine. Thanks for asking. Good to see you, too. Enjoy your breakfast."

"How about if I go first? Luke and I both think something isn't quite right."

Obviously, since they requested records.

"We're not big on Mom's premonitions." He rolled his eyes. "How about this for a coincidence: less than a year ago, Mom had a similar premonition about her sister, and the end result is the same."

Breakfast forgotten, I sat motionless.

"Aunt Edith had a stroke. She ended up in a wheelchair. Mom went up to Pennsylvania to take care of her. Dad couldn't handle the new environment, and Aunt Edith refused to move down here. Mom wouldn't put her in a nursing home. Their parents were in one when I was a kid. Apparently, she and Aunt Edith made a pact back then, no nursing home for them." He rotated his empty juice glass back and forth, the napkin beneath spinning along. "Anyway, between my aunt needing almost constant care, and Dad getting worse, we tried to hire help. Mom refused. She said God wouldn't let Edith suffer much longer. A few weeks later, she died in her sleep soon after minor surgery." He caught my eye. "Sound familiar?"

My heart skipped several beats, but I kept my expression impassive. "What was the cause of death?"

"No autopsy. She was a sick old lady. Her death was not unexpected."

I recognized the truth in that statement and its recent frequency. "Where was the surgery?"

"Up in New Castle, Pennsylvania. I don't know which hospital." His glass stopped rotating and Christian stiffened. "Could it have been Ricken?"

My thought exactly, but what were the odds?

"I can get the records." Christian typed into his smartphone, then placed it facedown on the table. "Your turn."

I stared at my fork making designs in the ketchup on my plate. Sharing my concerns would be a relief, but telling him about Mrs. McCray would violate her privacy. Did the deceased need privacy? I had no evidence the deaths had anything to do with Ricken, but the similarities between them might help Christian and Luke figure out what happened to their father. Ugh.

Christian waited patiently, giving me time to gather my thoughts and redecorate my plate.

"Has Dr. Ricken done something?" he asked.

"No."

His head tilted, eyes narrowed, searching my face.

"Being a jerk doesn't make him a bad surgeon," I said. "At least not in this case. Anesthesia's as likely to blame as the operation itself." Did I say that out loud? Time to go.

"But you didn't do anything wrong."

"No, not intentionally, but the medications might have been contaminated, or something could have happened when I wasn't in the room."

"Something not documented in the chart?"

He caught me there. Our conversation appeared to be interesting other patrons. Not good.

"I can't talk about this. I'm sorry." I placed my napkin on the table and stood.

Work was all I had. The one dependable constant into which I poured the splintered shards of my life. If I lost my job, I'd be lost.

I opened my wallet and tossed too much money on the table. "I have to go." I strode outside, the cold air a slap to my hot skin.

He called my name and caught up as I reached my car. I stopped but didn't face him. He held out my cash. "Breakfast is on me."

I wanted to argue, but the need to leave was more intense.

"Thank you," I said, my tone neutral, desperate to hide the turmoil roiling beneath the surface.

"I'm sorry I put you on the spot," he said. "But Luke and I need to know what happened to Dad. I'm sorry if that makes you uncomfortable."

"Uncomfortable?" I blinked back tears. Tears. Where had they come from? "What makes me uncomfortable is being on the wrong side of an investigation of my hospital."

"The wrong side? How can finding the truth be the wrong side? What if other patients die the same way, and we could have prevented it?"

I met his eyes, the gold flecks burning a hole in my heart. "You're right, but I can't."

As I drove away, my mind spun. Thinking about my job was completely selfish. Christian was right. More patients could be at risk. Ricken might be incompetent, and more patients were scheduled for surgery this week. Should I go to my chairman? The chief of staff should be alerted, but that was not a conversation I wanted to have.

I had to learn why my patients had died, but I didn't have to collaborate with one of their sons.

The entire breakfast conversation replayed in my mind. I thought about Christian's sister-in-law saying God decided when it was time to die. It reminded me of a Sunday night shift as an intern. We cross-covered amongst services, and I was called to talk with the family of an unfamiliar patient. The elderly woman had suffered a devastating stroke a few days before. According to the notes, she was dependent on a ventilator and demonstrated no brain activity on multiple scans. The plan was to withdraw care the following morning. Three generations of her African American family, decked out in their church finery, were crammed around the hospital bed. A middle-aged woman, likely a daughter, sat on the edge of the bed holding the older woman's hand. Clad in a hospital gown and covered to her chest with a crisp white sheet, the patient's makeup was perfect, her hair carefully styled. When I introduced myself, a tall man, late forties, in black suit pants and a white shirt, directed me into the hall. Several family members followed. "Why do you want to kill my mother?" he said.

I stumbled right out of the gate. "This is something you need to discuss with her primary physician."

"Why do you get to play God?" said the son, undeterred.

Though an atheist at the time, I had an answer for that one. I spoke as kindly and gently as I could, twenty hours into my shift. "God gave us the ability to keep your mom's body alive almost indefinitely, but He also gave us the tools to recognize when the person inside is gone. Your mom's brain is no longer working. In a way, we're fighting God right now by keeping her on the ventilator. We won't be killing her, just allowing God to take her as He planned."

The rest was murky. I didn't recall what happened the next day, only the son's accusations. Odd I hadn't related that memory to Greg's situation. And I wouldn't now.

CHAPTER TEN

IT WAS AFTER nine when I pulled into the garage and hustled to my office. I hated arriving late. Not that I was late for anything in particular—it just felt wrong to show up after eight.

I dropped my bag in my office and checked on Shelley Dearborn on the Mother-Baby unit. Jenn was there, admiring Baby Dearborn as she rested on her mother's chest, wrapped in a hospital-issue baby blanket. She gave a sweet, contented coo, then a yawn. Shelley kissed her head through a pink and blue cap. My eyes became unfocused; jealousy sparked from somewhere deep inside. I forced it back to its hiding place and asked Shelley about her recovery. All was well.

"Thank you so much, Dr. Downey," Justin said. "The epidural was perfect."

"Saved my life," Shelley said.

"And my hand." Justin rubbed his right hand dramatically, then leaned down and kissed his wife on the cheek. "I'll be right back." He patted the baby's back.

"Enjoy your beautiful daughter," I said as we retreated out the door.

Justin closed the door softly. "Did you hear about Mr. Greyson?"

Jenn and I exchanged a look and both shook our heads.

"When he got to his room, he started bleeding, probably from his tonsils. He aspirated some of the blood and had to be re-intubated emergently."

"But he was a DNR," I said. I reactivated the order, unless Marcus canceled it.

Justin looked at Jenn. "Do you remember intubating him in the OR? Any trauma or bleeding? Were his tonsils especially large?"

"Not that I noticed. It did take me two tries though, remember?" She peered at me from beneath her bangs, her face stricken.

"Oh, yeah. That's when Ricken went ballistic." Justin smirked. "Apparently the intern wrote the cause was a traumatic intubation by a medical student."

"What?" I said, too loudly. The normally bustling nurses station quieted. I moved us farther down the hall. "That was written in the medical record?"

"I haven't seen the note myself, but that's what I heard." Caution replaced humor in Justin's voice.

"That's completely inappropriate." *Control. It's not Justin's fault.* "Where is the patient now?"

"Uh, he's in the ICU." Justin's posture collapsed a bit. For the first time in months, confidence seemed to elude him.

Jenn kept her face averted, blinking back tears.

I put an arm around her. "This is not your fault. We would have known at the time if you damaged his tonsils."

* * *

Rounds, shmounds. As a resident in the ICU, I hated interruptions that extended our already marathon rounds, now I was the interrupter. Too bad. In ICU Pod 2, I found the attending, Dr. Joe

"Okay. If you're sure," I said.

She nodded. "No one should die alone."

Truer words . . .

I went to Mr. Greyson's bedside, grasped his hand, and leaned close. "Mr. Greyson? It's Kate Downey. Can you hear me?"

His hand squeezed mine. Damn. I'd hoped he was unconscious, that he wouldn't know he was dying.

"I took care of you for your surgery yesterday. I don't know what happened, why you bled, but I'm sorry the DNR was not followed as I'd promised. I understand you want the ventilator disconnected, and we're going to do that in a few minutes."

Another hand squeeze. What do you say at the end? Why wasn't there an instruction manual? A burning in the back of my throat made talking difficult.

"I will keep you and your family in my prayers." I squeezed his hand one last time and stepped away, blinking back my own tears. I nodded to Jenn and explained the situation to Mr. Greyson's nurse. I gave her my cell phone number.

"I'll keep an eye on her." The nurse rolled one of the desk chairs to Jenn.

I stepped into the hallway, deeply unsettled. Would this experience scar her? Maybe I should stay instead. Suddenly, I couldn't breathe; my chest felt compressed in a vice. I leaned against the wall for support, eyes closed, chest heaving, but it wasn't enough. I started to squat down, less distance to fall.

An arm wrapped around my back. Joe Layton pulled me up and guided me into a consultation room across the hall and into a chair. "Put your head between your knees and take slow deep breaths. You're okay."

No, I wasn't. There was no air. I was suffocating. My heart pounded, faster and faster.

"You're okay," he said again, and kept repeating it.

Gradually, the terror subsided. Sweet air filled my lungs, my heart slowed.

"What just happened?" I said, raising my head.

"I'm no expert, but my guess is a panic attack. Never had one before?"

I shook my aching head.

"This whole situation is too close to Greg. You need to let me handle it."

"Jenn feels responsible. I should stay instead."

"Not a chance. Not this time. Let her stay. Dying is part of life. Part of medicine."

The adrenaline surge ebbed, replaced by shame. "Thank you, Joe. I'm sorry for all that. It was uncalled for, and weird." And selfish. This wasn't about me. Before he could offer some platitude, I asked about the note in Mr. Greyson's chart.

"I called the surgical resident and he says the attending told him what to write. Guess who?"

My mind cleared. "Ricken." What an ass. Worse than an ass. That note was completely irresponsible, inflammatory, a medico-legal nightmare. "He needs to be reported to the chief of staff."

"I called Risk Management, again," said Joe. "I'd already told them about the DNR cluster."

"It needs to go further." My face flushed; it had to be red-dye number whatever was most toxic. "I'll take care of it."

The chief of staff was not my biggest fan, in fact, quite the opposite. The thought of going to his office could spark another panic attack.

"Take a breather first. By the way, the bleeding has stopped and Mr. Greyson is breathing over the vent. He doesn't meet criteria for extubation, but he may not die when we disconnect support."

CHAPTER ELEVEN

BACK IN MY office, I tried to calm my frayed nerves. The right thing to do was to confront Ricken before going over his head. The mere thought made my hands clammy.

I apologized to the Greg in our wedding photo. His eyes, so full of love.

"You tried to toughen me up."

"You're stronger than you think," I heard in his voice.

"Not today I'm not."

I imagined his right eyebrow rising, always the right.

"Yeah, yeah, *carpe diem*. Seize the day because there may not be another." Greg's words. "Bite me." My words, back then. But he was right. It was time to put on my big girl pants and deal with the real world.

First step, information on my adversary, maybe something to humanize him in my mind.

Google informed me he graduated from a Caribbean medical school ten years ago, completed a general surgery residency at a community program in South Florida, and worked for a locums company. His employment at University was not listed. Was he a locums here, too? University had recently opened its doors to non-faculty physicians in an effort to attract more insured, read paying, patients. I wondered what the credentialing requirements were for these surgeons. The College of Medicine thoroughly vetted potential faculty, but Ricken wasn't faculty. He was an independent private guy who was allowed to use the ORs.

When I added "malpractice" to the search terms, nothing useful appeared, but did that mean anything?

A more general search found the obituary of Malcolm Ricken II, published on the front page of the *Miami Herald*'s local section eight years earlier. Must have been an important guy. According to the obituary, Malcolm Ricken II was "a well-respected surgeon and philanthropist" who had done much for the community in his retirement. That explained the high-profile obit. The article went on to say he was pre-deceased by two wives and survived by two sons, Dr. Malcolm Ricken III of Boca Raton, and Dr. Charles Ricken of Miami.

Out of curiosity, and because searches are too easy, I looked up older brother Malcolm Ricken III. He was also a "respected surgeon" according to his obituary published just four months after his father's. Tough year for my new nemesis, but that was long ago, not an excuse for current behavior. Malcolm III was fifty-one at his death, probably twenty years older than baby brother Charles. In addition to his brother, Malcolm was survived by a wife. No kids mentioned.

So Ricken was a middle-aged orphan with no family of his own. Otherwise, I'd gleaned little of use and couldn't put the meeting off any longer. I checked the OR schedule; he was between cases. "Wish me luck," I said to Greg's photo.

Dr. Ricken was in the first place I looked, the surgeons' lounge. He sat alone at a computer, checking email. Two men I didn't recognize sat across the room, deep in conversation.

I rehearsed my opening lines, then approached. "Dr. Ricken, I hate to interrupt, but—"

"And yet, you will."

I closed my eyes briefly. "Yes, I'm afraid so." I pulled out the chair next to him and sat. "I'm concerned that we've had three patients die in the last week—Mrs. McCray, Dr. O'Donnell, and now Mr. Greyson."

Hand still on the mouse, he spared me the briefest of glances, then returned his focus to the computer monitor. "Greyson was a cluster, as you well know. None of it would have happened if you'd let him go home."

"Except he'd still be dead," I said, immediately regretting it.

The next glance was more of a glare. "O'Donnell was no surprise. Brain pathology and anesthesia don't mix. I have no idea who Mc-Cray is." He continued on the computer, but his grip on the mouse tightened fractionally.

"You placed a G-Tube in Mrs. McCray last week. She had advanced multiple sclerosis." I waited for a nod, some evidence he remembered her. Nothing.

"She died the next night." Why would Marcus know and not his boss?

"Again, anesthesia and neurologic disease." Dispassionate, and blaming anesthesia? I checked to make sure the others weren't listening.

"Thirty-six hours later? Our drugs don't last that long." He had to know that. "Do you know Dr. O'Donnell's cause of death?"

Still he faced the computer screen, but the mouse no longer moved. "Only what was in the paper."

I pressed on. "What about autopsies? Have you spoken with the families?"

"The operations went fine. It is up to the primary care physicians to follow up."

"But don't you want to know? Maybe the suture is contaminated or someone on the team is inadvertently infecting patients. Two of them were G-tubes—maybe there's a contaminant in the tubes."

No response, though he finally released the strangled mouse and stood. "We're done here."

Done? I stood too, causing my chair to roll back and bang another. "Do you often have several patients die in a single week? Because I don't." Ill-advised, I knew, especially with others in earshot, but I couldn't help it.

Cold dark eyes met mine, his voice low and full of contempt. "Are you suggesting—"

"I'm suggesting nothing. Those patients were mine as well, and I'd like to know why they died."

"Well, perhaps you should look on your side of the drapes."

My heart threatened to choke me.

"I have a case to start. Old people die, Dr.—" he made a show of looking at my badge —"Downey, with or without surgery." As he strode off, his normally subtle limp was pronounced. The door slammed in his wake.

My face burned as I returned to my office, fingernails boring into my palms. How could he be so callous? Feel so little for his patients? What about their families? For the first time in my life, I wanted to yell or throw something. I stomped back and forth in my tiny office feeling Greg's disapproving gaze from his photo. I couldn't bring myself to place it facedown. Deep breaths, then I would visit my chairman. He needed to know what was going on with Ricken and with Greyson. When had everything spun out of control?

*   *   *

James Worrell, my chairman, was out of the office until the next day. I texted him anyway.

James: At physical therapy. Can it wait until tomorrow?

Me: Sure.

I didn't feel sure, but I also couldn't be needy when he was dealing with a broken hip.

My secretary, Mary, called. "The chief of staff wants to see you. That doesn't sound good."

"It's probably not." Had Ricken gone to him already? "When?"

"Two thirty. There wasn't anything on your calendar, but I can call back if you want."

"No, it's okay."

"What's the matter? You sound down." Mary could always tell. "Is it Greg?"

"Among other things. I'll be fine. Two thirty. I'll be there."

"Don't let him bully you," Mary said. She was channeling Greg now, too.

It might take until two thirty to calm down and figure out what to say. The chief of staff, Dr. Walker, was a former surgeon who no longer operated. We'd interacted only once, a memory I worked hard to bury. Like the principal in grade school, being called to the chief of staff's office was not for kudos, and it hadn't been last year. My intraoperative medication error ruined a heart intended for transplant and, though my chairman was supportive and concerned for my welfare, Dr. Walker focused on the hospital and its reputation in the transplant community. To mollify the recipient's irate surgeon, he concocted a probation, in which my records were subject to random review, with immediate termination looming should the reviewer find anything of concern.

"That's ridiculous," my chairman said at the time. "Unheard of." He attributed my lapse to stress. I had moved Greg home—another mistake. James offered to fight the probation while I took a leave of absence to get my life in order. I declined both, moved Greg to the nearest neuro-care unit, and lived with the knowledge my actions cost someone his life. According to Dr. Walker, the intended recipient died before another organ became available. It served as a constant boulder on my conscience.

And now I was being called to the principal's office again. What could possibly go wrong?

Then thoughts of Jenn and Mr. Greyson and his tearful wife brought my troubles into perspective. I texted Joe Layton.

He replied: Still hanging on.

My phone rang. I didn't recognize the number.

"Dr. Downey? This is Dr. Babcock. You left me a message about Dorothea McCray?"

"Yes, thank you for calling me back," I said. "I was her anesthesiologist last week and was surprised to hear she passed. I wondered if you knew her cause of death."

"No, unfortunately. Her husband declined an autopsy. She looked great Friday evening. They had an anniversary party, believe it or not. I encouraged her to postpone, but she insisted."

"Do you know whether she'd taken any narcotics? Or missed her MS meds?"

"She said she had no pain, and I reminded her about the meds." Dr. Babcock paused. I waited. "I was surprised when I got the call on Saturday. She died in her sleep."

After a soft knock, Mary appeared in my doorway, Diet Mountain Dew and Twizzlers in hand. I gave her a half-hearted smile. It was all I could muster.

"Forgive my ignorance," I said into the phone, "but doesn't an unattended death require an autopsy?"

Eyes wide, Mary put the cheer-up gifts on my desk, patted my back, and closed the door on her way out.

"Not if the funeral director on-scene thinks the death was natural. He called me to sign the death certificate. Dorothea had advanced MS. There was no reason to put the family through any more."

I wanted to argue but feared it would sound desperate—or guilty.

"If it's any consolation, I don't think it had anything to do with her surgery or anesthesia, and the family is accepting her death graciously. They have a strong faith. The timing was just an unlucky coincidence."

I didn't believe in coincidences, especially not when it came to patients dying.

An hour, and a whole pack of Twizzlers, later, the ICU nurse called. "It's time."

Dread weighed on me as I hurried down the stairs. I had to hold it together. I absolutely could not have a panic attack, or whatever that was, in front of Jenn. Or anyone else for that matter.

I arrived at the bedside just as the ICU resident, stethoscope in hand, confirmed time of death. Jenn sat silently, holding Mr. Greyson's hand, tears streaming, darkening her scrubs around the neckline. I gently guided her across the hall to the consultation room.

Though not foreign to me, consoling physicians after disastrous cases was not a particular skill. We had colleagues specially trained to counsel after unexpected patient deaths. I should have called them. Why hadn't I thought of that?

Jenn cried on my shoulder for several moments. I rubbed her back, feeling impotent. When her sobbing ebbed, she didn't want to talk about the experience.

"You know this wasn't your fault, right?"

She nodded, but I wasn't convinced. Death is difficult. Death in which you have some role can be overwhelming. We're taught to replay the case as an impartial observer, identifying what we could have done differently, much like my resident, Erin, yesterday. Learning, and ideally sharing, the hard-won lesson at a Morbidity and Mortality conference. But in reality, many physicians either become defensive, refusing to consider the possibility they erred, even to themselves; or the reverse, blaming themselves for missing a vague symptom or failing to order an additional test. Neither extreme makes a good physician, but the latter could create a paralyzing habit of self-doubt. Examination, yes; blame, no. How to get Jenn to understand this so early in her training, when I struggled with it less than a year ago.

"Many physicians find journaling helpful in these situations," I said. "Writing down your thoughts and feelings can help you understand them." I hoped Jenn would heed this advice. Classic "do as I say, not as I do."

CHAPTER TWELVE

I ARRIVED AT the chief of staff's office at two thirty sharp. Comforting Jenn through her distress rekindled my anger and provided clarity for the meeting. Nancy, Dr. Walker's secretary, offered me water and a seat. She looked apologetic.

"How's the baby?" I asked. I'd cared for her daughter when she delivered Nancy's first grandchild.

"She's great." A smile brightened her face.

Before she could pull up a photo, a red-faced resident in scrubs came from the office. He avoided eye contact and moved past in long purposeful strides, seemingly desperate to put distance between himself and the chief of staff. Great.

Nancy went to Dr. Walker's door and said something I couldn't hear, then nodded to me and held open the door to a different world. The health center building that housed academic offices was once the hospital. The cinder block walls, drop ceilings, and fixed windows complicated remodeling. My tiny interior office had threadbare flooring that might once have been carpet and plain white walls with little room to decorate beyond the framed print of our honeymoon spot at Emerald Lake Lodge in Alberta. Dr. Walker's office came from a different decade, not to mention a different funding source. Worthy of a modern office building, its large windows overlooked the tree-lined campus, and his dark furniture looked like real wood. No laminate for the chief.

His Harvard Medical School diploma hung above his credenza, together with various plaques I couldn't read. Through the blinds, the sun painted strips of orange across his enormous, cluttered desk. The door closed behind me.

He remained seated. "Dr. Downey, we seem to have a problem, more than one, in fact. And you are not in a position to have a problem, you understand?" He did not offer me a seat.

"Is this about Dr. Ricken?" I asked.

"We can start there. You accused a surgeon of malpractice in front of trainees."

"No, sir. That's not what happened."

A soft knock and the door opened. James Worrell entered, leaning heavily on a cane. "Sorry I'm late."

I glanced back at Dr. Walker, who covered his surprise, and maybe disappointment, at James' arrival.

"Let's sit," James said and offered me a chair. "What did I miss?"

"Dr. Downey made libelous allegations against a surgeon in front of trainees. Completely unacceptable. That's a fireable offense even if she weren't on probation."

"Kate, tell us what happened," James said.

I could have hugged him, if it weren't completely unprofessional. "Three patients cared for by Dr. Ricken and myself have died in the last week."

That got Walker's attention.

"Three?" James said.

"Yes, another one died today, and Dr. Ricken had a resident blame my medical student in the chart."

"What did the student do?" Dr. Walker asked.

"Nothing." My voice rose, and I forced it under control. "She took two tries to intubate, but there was no airway trauma, no bleeding at the time. I was right there, but Dr. Ricken started yelling in the middle of it, criticizing my management. It was completely inappropriate and upsetting to the student. Still, she did a great job."

"But last night he had an airway bleed," Dr. Walker said, "and was reintubated against his wishes because you rescinded his DNR."

"No," I said. "The DNR was reinstated, but the sign had fallen from the wall, and the ICU team was not informed."

"That's awful," James said. "But regardless, that note should not have been in the medical record. Has it been corrected?"

I nodded. "Joe Layton called the intern and had him delete it."

"Good," James said. "Back to the conversation with Dr. Ricken."

"All three of the patients who died underwent minor operations and then died the next night. I want to know why and went to their surgeon to discuss possible causes. I made no accusation of malpractice. He said that sick people die and blamed anesthesia."

James winced. Dr. Walker said nothing.

"Three patients," I said. "I took care of them, too, and one was Dr. O'Donnell. I thought it worth discussing, at least."

"I'm afraid your story does not agree with Dr. Ricken's."

It was obvious whom Dr. Walker believed.

"Ask the two guys that were there."

"There were witnesses?" James looked at Dr. Walker.

"I didn't recognize them, but apparently they were trainees. I made no accusations against Dr. Ricken." At least, I didn't think I had. I was pretty angry at the time.

James moved as if to stand. "Well, it appears we can get to the bottom of this."

"I'm not through," Dr. Walker said. "I received a call from the patient's family about the DNR."

"Dr. Downey already explained that. I'm sure you'll see in the chart that she reinstated the order." He looked to me for confirmation.

I nodded. "And Joe Layton found the sign on the floor."

"So, not her fault," James said. "Anything else?"

"I understand there is a complaint from a medical student, and a chart of yours to review regarding a lost airway yesterday. You're having quite the week, Dr. Downey."

I said nothing.

James pressed his cane to the floor to stand. "I'm sure you will find she took superb care of that patient, and the student is being handled by Dr. Duffy. Let me know when you want to meet with the witnesses so we can clear up the other matter."

Always the gentleman, James ushered me from the room. I pressed my shoulders back, striving not to resemble the resident departing earlier. Did everyone leave this office red-faced?

In the hallway, Mary stood with a wheelchair. James winced as he sat.

"How did it go?" she asked.

Confused, I looked from one to the other.

"Mary called me," James said.

"Nancy loves you," Mary said. "She called to warn me her boss was on the warpath. I'm sorry, but you didn't seem up for a battle today."

Should I be offended? No longer fresh out of residency, I should be able to mount my own defense. I shouldn't need my injured chairman to come in.

For now, I was eternally grateful for the support. "Thank you." I turned to James. "I'm sorry you had to come in, but I really appreciate it."

He angled his head, brow furrowed. "I'm not sure what's up with him, but I don't want him cornering you again."

I was relieved to hear he thought it odd, as well. "Will you let me know when you're going to interview the witnesses?"

He smirked. "I'd be very surprised if it comes to that."

So just a power play.

"I need to get you back downstairs to Gail," Mary said.

"Your wife had to bring you in?"

"We were at the orthopedic center. I had a little setback last night, but I'll be back tomorrow. Call tonight if you want to talk; otherwise I'll see you in the morning."

As Mary pushed the wheelchair toward the elevator, I was gripped with the overwhelming desire to flee. To get away from the hospital. To see my husband.

CHAPTER THIRTEEN

I CALLED AUNT Irm from the highway. "I'm sorry. I said I would be home on time, but—"

"It is okay, kindchen. Dinner can wait. You sound troubled."

"I need to see Greg. You go ahead and eat."

"Drive safely."

I made it to Jacksonville in record time, though five o'clock traffic began to build as I hit the outskirts. Fortunately, the veterans neuro-care unit sat on the western edge of the city. I parked near the covered portico of the four-story building that screamed *nursing home* with its red brick exterior and unimaginative rectangular architecture. I'd come to despise the building, never more than right now. I wanted my husband, needed him, outside, at home, not here in this museum of lost life.

Get a grip.

I entered through the sliding glass doors with "Veterans Administration" engraved at eye level. Bypassing the elevator, I climbed the three flights, slower than usual, and was surprised to see Glenda, the weekend head nurse, on the ward. "What are you doing here today?"

"Had a callout. What about you?"

I groaned but said nothing. Glenda understood. She didn't look down with pity like so many others; I appreciated that. But then Glenda did this for a living. The neuro ward housed only patients like Greg, alive in body only.

Quietly, I entered his room, pulled a chair to the bedside, and grasped his hand. Was it my imagination, or was his hand thinner today, withering, approaching skeletal? I spun his gold wedding band. Definitely looser. I did the math in my head for perhaps the millionth time . . . nearly twelve months. It had been a year since he'd moved his hands, even longer since those hands had caressed mine. Why wasn't this getting easier?

I looked past him out the window, to the gardens lit by a callous afternoon sun. Soon the weather would warm enough for walks in the garden. Last summer I brought Shadow once, in the naïve hope he would stir something in Greg, but no. The dog ran to him in tail-wagging bliss. But the wheelchair, the lack of response, the raspy breathing; something scared Shadow, and he stayed behind me for the rest of the shortened visit.

We both so loved Shadow, a love reciprocated unconditionally. Was it a blessing we had no surviving children? No. That was most certainly not a blessing. I stared at Emily's ultrasound picture on Greg's bedside table. My preterm labor had resolved, no need to worry him. If only I had. On family emergency leave, he wouldn't have been on the transport, he wouldn't have—

"Regrets are not useful," Greg would say.

I tore my eyes from Emily to scan the other photos. All showed Greg in health. Reminders of happier times, when life held meaning and joy, and a future.

I looked back at his thin face, still recognizable. How I needed his counsel right now. Never judgmental, he'd been my confidant since med school. He gave advice only when asked and didn't presume to solve my problems. He listened, with his ears, his eyes, his whole being, and asked questions to help me see clearly. What did I have to lose?

Sitting by his inert form, I held his bony hand and described the events of the week. Not to the Greg in my mind but out loud. I told him about the deaths, my run-in with Ricken, Jenn and Mr. Greyson, the simulator session, and the confrontation with the chief of staff. Only later did I realize I left out Christian.

I imagined Greg's raised eyebrow, his look-at-this-from-both-sides face. Might Ricken struggle with remorse and guilt? Doubtful. Might he have had a bad experience that shades his behavior today? Probably, but it's no excuse. Have you tried to talk to him? Yes. Really talk to him? Argh. Or maybe someone who knows him well? Like his PA.

And what response did you expect from the chief of staff? You're on probation and got into a row with an insecure, volatile surgeon. Meanwhile, something is killing these patients. Time to end the pity party and get your priorities in order. Okay, that last part came from me, never Greg.

I gave a slight smile. "Thanks. Even from wherever you are, you help me." My eyes stung as I rose. "Come back to me," I whispered, and kissed him on the forehead. When the Greg in my mind seemed ready to protest my request, I pushed him to the back. He'd given me enough food for thought.

I logged onto a physician discussion site and posted a vague description of the deaths, in case others had a similar experience.

It was not a restful night. Still, I reported to Labor and Delivery in the morning and presented a conference discussion on fetal monitoring. Jenn attended and contributed at least as much as the third-year residents.

After, I pulled up the spreadsheet again and simply stared, hoping something would jump out at me. It didn't. I called Ricken's PA. Marcus Culpepper agreed to meet me between his cases. Jenn's entrance barely registered while I was on the phone. Once I hung up, I felt her behind me.

"Did all those patients die?" she asked.

Shoot.

"I heard about Dr. O'Donnell."

"It's just something I'm working on." I minimized the spreadsheet. "How are you?"

"I'm okay. I started that journal you recommended. And one of my classmates and I went to the Sandersons' and planted new flowers in the front boxes. It took my mind off things for a while."

"How is Mr. Sanderson?"

"He was sleeping. Mrs. Sanderson said he was fine, but she was exhausted. We offered to sit with him for a while so she could take a break, but she didn't want to."

"That was kind of you." Before I could think better of the line of inquiry, I said, "What do you know about your classmate, Robert Barton?"

I smiled at the face she made. It resembled that of our patients after drinking the sour preop antacid.

"He came as a transfer this year, so I'm sure it's been difficult for him, since the rest of us already knew each other. But he hasn't tried very hard."

"Do you know why he switched schools?"

She shook her head. "Some of the kids say his father got him in here, but I don't know."

Teresa, one of the residents, entered. "We're ready to go with the first case in room three. She's healthy, fourth cesarean with a tubal ligation. No history of significant scar tissue. Placenta looks fine."

"Would this be a good first spinal for Jenn?" I asked.

"BMI is thirty, so sure."

Jenn's eyes widened, an expectant smile splitting her face.

"You can't do Family Medicine," Teresa said. "You should see your face right now."

An accurate observation. "I'll get the patient to the back while you go over the procedure with Jenn." I nodded to the back model and the extra spinal kits stored on the counter.

Mr. and Mrs. Gentry were all smiles, excited to welcome this fourth, and final, child, since she was having a tubal ligation. With the nurse's help, I pushed Mrs. Gentry to the OR and had her sitting upright for the spinal.

Teresa did a great job guiding Jenn through the procedure with a couple passes of the spinal needle, and soon the surgeons had the baby out and squalling on the warmer, surrounded by the newborn nursery staff. Jenn's eyes were glassy, staring at the baby. "How do you ever get used to this?"

"It gets easier to control emotions, but if you're lucky, it remains a miracle."

The placenta readily disengaged and the bleeding seemed about normal. I left the room while the surgeons closed and reviewed the labor board with my other resident. Everyone was stable for the moment, but things can change quickly on a busy obstetric service.

I returned to my spreadsheet and double-checked the medical records system for autopsy reports. Nothing.

forcibly resuscitated against his wishes . . . Of course." He put the phone on speaker and held it between us.

"Dr. Downey, are you intent on being fired?" It was the chief of staff. Crap. "As a hospital, we have put this family through enough."

"But—"

"*You* have put this family through enough."

"I—"

"You suspended his DNR. You overrode both the surgeon and the family's desires, requiring he stay overnight, which led to the undesired resuscitation and ultimately to the family's difficult decision to withdraw care. We have failed this family at every turn, and you now wish to put them through an autopsy against their wishes?"

"No, sir." He was right. They'd been through enough.

CHAPTER SIXTEEN

EMBARRASSED TO BE yelled at, especially in front of Ramsey, and not a little ashamed at my self-absorption, I returned to Labor and Delivery chastened and withdrawn. The nurses noticed, and a few asked if everything was okay. It wasn't, but as I told the residents, "Each new patient deserves your 'A' game." So I compartmentalized.

The next scheduled cesarean went fine. Soon after the baby was delivered, I received a call from my chairman. "I need to see you."

That couldn't be good.

"Dr. Walker called," James said, directing me to one of the comfortable rolling chairs at the overly large round table occupying half of his office. With blond wood furniture and a coordinated modern sculpture on the wall, the chair's office was easily the best decorated in the department, but didn't compare with the chief of staff's. He eased himself into the chair across from me. "You had words with Dr. Ramsey in pathology?"

I sat, but couldn't meet his eyes. James Worrell had been nothing but supportive of me, through Adam's troubles, through Greg's accident and my miscarriage, through my own medical error and probation, and still I caused him trouble.

"I asked for an autopsy on Mr. Greyson, my patient with the tonsil bleed. I should have realized it was overstepping."

CHAPTER SEVENTEEN

I WENT FROM the frying pan of meeting with my chair, into the fire of an RCA with Dr. Ricken, with just a few minutes in between for an attitude adjustment. I'd debated about inviting Jenn. She really should be there to review the system issues, but I didn't trust Ricken not to lay blame on individuals.

The decision left my hands when Justin arrived with Jenn in tow.

"Aren't you supposed to be on paternity leave?" I asked.

He gave a tired smile.

"How are Shelley and the baby?"

"They're both great," he said. "Shelley's mom has everything under control, and the program director thought I should be here."

I looked at Jenn, her young face too hopeful.

"You understand what an RCA is?"

"Justin told me. I'd like to hear what everyone has to say."

"I'm happy to have you here, but are you sure you're up to reliving it all?"

Of course she said, "Yes," but did she really understand?

We entered the windowless conference room. Long and narrow, with a huge table that sat at least twenty. Half a dozen seats were occupied so far.

A stout, grandmotherly woman stood at the far end of the room, by a large screen. She nodded and smiled in greeting, then resumed shuffling papers. I chose three seats near the middle and we sat, with Jenn between us. She sat on the edge of her seat, back rigid.

On the screen, a grim timeline of Mr. Greyson's last days shone too brightly.

Ricken limped in and sat directly across from me. Acknowledge him? Ignore him? Being the grown-up sucked. I forced a small smile and tried to make eye contact. I needn't have bothered. Next to him, though, Marcus smiled in greeting.

"We are here today for a root cause analysis of the case of Mr. Alexander Greyson, who passed away yesterday. Let's start with introductions. If each of you will please state your name, department, and your role in his care. I am Marjorie Rollings, a facilitator from the Quality Department." Next was the meeting scribe. Introductions progressed around the table, including the surgical, anesthesia, and critical care teams, as well as OR and ICU nurses and even the scrub tech.

Introductions complete, Marjorie explained the purpose and ground rules. "If you have something to contribute, please raise your hand and refrain from interrupting the speaker. Any questions?"

They started at the beginning. Marjorie asked Marcus to describe Mr. Greyson and the indication for surgery. Justin followed with the anesthetic plan.

"Dr. Downey," Marjorie said, "I believe at that time you discussed rescinding the DNR for the operation."

I described our conversation and my promise to reinstate it after recovery.

Justin took back over. "Induction went smoothly—"

Dr. Ricken scoffed. "Smoothly?"

Marjorie lifted her hands. "I'm sorry, Dr. Ricken, please let Dr. Dearborn finish."

He ignored her. "The student jammed the tube in repeatedly. The man's tonsils were hamburger. Smooth induction my—"

"Dr. Ricken!"

I raised my hand but didn't wait to be called upon, nor did I try to cover my glare. "We don't jam tubes anywhere. Our student carefully inserted the laryngoscope. She had a good view, but the tube went into the esophagus instead of the trachea. It happens. She removed the tube, adjusted the stylet, and then intubated successfully. No jamming involved. I was standing right there and would have stopped her were there any cause for concern."

"Then how do you explain—"

This time I interrupted Ricken. "The tonsils were not bleeding at that time. We suctioned his mouth soon after and there was no blood. Hamburger would have bled." So the last part was unnecessary, too bad.

Marjorie took over. She asked Marcus to briefly review the operative procedure, then she returned to Justin. "During the case, were there any concerns from your standpoint?"

"None."

"And you were present for the entire case?"

Justin's eyes cut to Jenn. "Actually, no. A CRNA relieved me for about fifteen minutes."

In a case that lasted less than two hours, he took a break?

Marjorie looked to her scribe quizzically. "Who was that? I don't think we have anything on the record." The scribe shuffled pages.

Justin said, "I don't know the guy's name."

Jenn raised her hand slowly. Marjorie nodded to her. "His name was Brad Jernigan."

"Oh, come on," Dr. Ricken interrupted again, "the CRNA was there for a few minutes in the middle of the case. What difference does it make? The trauma had to happen at intubation."

Marjorie acknowledged him with a curt nod. She'd obviously given up trying to control his outbursts. They reviewed the wake-up—uneventful—his time in the recovery room—slow, but uneventful—my decision to admit him overnight out of an "abundance of caution" for his weakened state, and, finally, his transfer to the floor with the reactivated DNR order.

Marjorie pointed to the timeline. "At 8:25 p.m., a nursing assistant activated the Code Blue alert when she found him unresponsive. Who responded to the code?"

"I did," answered Dr. Layton, sitting on the far side of Justin. "Our team responded immediately. His nurse was off the floor, but the charge nurse told us he had ALS and had undergone G-Tube placement earlier that day."

"To be clear, did anyone mention he had a Do Not Resuscitate order?" Marjorie asked.

"Absolutely not," said Dr. Layton, his voice clear and loud.

Many heads turned toward the charge nurse, seated in the far corner. I didn't join them. Misery needed only so much company.

Dr. Ricken said, "Did you ask?"

Dr. Layton turned to him, his tone icy. "No, we didn't ask. We were saving a life. We don't ask about DNR status at every code."

Heading off Dr. Ricken, Marjorie asked Joe, "What is the protocol when the patient has a DNR?"

"The protocol is not to call a code. That's the point."

I took silent pleasure in the daggers Dr. Layton stared into Ricken.

Dr. Layton offered information about the hospital policy. "The DNR is recorded in the patient's medical record, including an order for the nurse to secure a sign over the patient's bed. In this case, that sign was found later on the floor."

"So one action item might be a better way to designate DNR patients," offered Marjorie. "Something foolproof."

"A tattoo on their sternum?" Justin suggested. A few people chuckled.

Jenn cautiously raised her hand again. "How about their ID bracelet? That never comes off."

"If they don't have time to ask a question, they're not going to read an ID band," Dr. Ricken said. Did he speak any way but condescendingly?

"Not text, I mean like the color," Jenn said. "Now it's red if they have drug allergies—how about another color to indicate DNR? Or striped."

I gave her a small smile. Good for her, and brave.

Marjorie made a note. "Nice idea—" she glanced at her seating chart—"Jennifer."

They went on to discuss the code, with blood in the airway hampering intubation, his transfer to the ICU, discovery of his DNR status, discussion with his family, and the decision to withdraw life support.

In the end, no one was officially blamed, as promised, and a couple of ideas came out to prevent a repeat performance.

Once the crowd dissipated, I led Jenn to my office a few doors away. "Brad Jernigan gave a break during that case?"

She nodded.

"Was that the time he asked you to leave?"

"He didn't really ask." She followed me into my office. "That puts him in the room with all three deaths, doesn't it? It wasn't just you and Dr. Ricken."

CHAPTER EIGHTEEN

BEFORE LEAVING FOR the day, I met with two of the young women on the rotation, who asked to remediate their session. My chairman offered to observe, which felt like major overkill, and a bit like I was a resident again, but whatever. These kids needed a chance to show what they knew.

Both did a great job, taking turns with the scenarios. They weren't perfect, but without their classmates, they spoke up and knew their stuff. "You need to do work like this no matter who is around. It's always appropriate to speak up if you think something's being missed."

"I know," said the student who had cried, "but Robert intimidates me. He's so domineering."

"There will always be domineering personalities, but they aren't always the smartest in the room. If you think things aren't right, you have to speak up. You can go to someone more senior in the room first, if need be, but the patient is depending on you."

Both women nodded and beamed as I complimented their progress and performance.

James was satisfied and had little to add.

* * *

An unfamiliar dark SUV was parked in front of our house. Aunt Irm rarely entertained and never at night. Shadow greeted me at the door as usual, whining around a ball in his mouth and demanding to have every inch rubbed simultaneously. Past him stood Christian O'Donnell, in jeans and a blue polo shirt. Aunt Irm stepped between us in her *I don't need a recipe, I'm German* apron. She kissed both my cheeks and said, "We have a visitor."

"So I see."

"What a nice man he is, kindchen," she whispered. I barely remembered not to roll my eyes. In a normal voice, Aunt Irm added, "He called this afternoon and said he has news and couldn't reach you, so I invited him for spaghetti."

I nodded and reflexively pulled my phone from my pocket. He'd called during the RCA, when my phone was silenced.

"I'm sorry," he said. "I have the records from my aunt's operation. I was just going to drop them by, in case you had time."

"No, it's fine," I said. "I need to apologize anyway for yesterday morning. I want to figure this out, and I appreciate your help."

Aunt Irm examined me in her uber-motherly way. "Something has happened. Tell us." She led me to a barstool next to Christian and poured me a too-full glass of red wine.

To Aunt Irm, no problem existed that a good glass of wine couldn't fix.

I took a sip, collecting my thoughts.

She stared at me expectantly.

"It's all relative," I said, hoping she'd understand. Compared to losing a father, my day was inconsequential.

Unfortunately, Christian understood before Aunt Irm. "Oh no you don't," Christian said. "I've had my turn. Let's hear it."

Still, I hesitated. "I've just had to interact with a few sociopaths the last couple of days, and I'm not good at dealing with them." I took a larger gulp of wine. It was good.

"Dr. Ricken," Aunt Irm said with distaste.

"Among others."

Without waiting for confirmation, she said, "What did he do now?"

I told them, in broad strokes, without using names, about Mr. Greyson and Ricken's note, and our confrontation, and Jenn's kindness.

"Is this Jenn the student you said does not have senior disease?"

"Senioritis, yes. She's considering switching to anesthesia, or at least she was before all this."

"Is it not the job of someone else to deal with this surgeon's abominable behavior?" Aunt Irm asked.

I gave a sad smile. "I don't know how to deal with that person, either."

She cocked an angry eyebrow.

"Since Ricken isn't part of the faculty, he's not under the chair of surgery. He, I could deal with. Instead, I had to go to the chief of staff, but we don't have the best history, and Ricken got there first."

Aunt Irm knew nothing of my probation. At the time, she'd only just arrived, having lost her brother, then left her friends and her home to take on the care of an invalid. It was much too large a task for an octogenarian. Much too large a task for any one person. I couldn't add to her burden then, or maybe I couldn't bear to see her misplaced esteem shaken.

"You told him Dr. Ricken is killing patients, yes?" Aunt Irm asked.

I shook my head, glanced at Christian, who'd taken the words in stride, and changed the subject. I went to the stove and stirred the sauce. "What did you guys talk about before I arrived?" I dipped a finger into the sauce and stuck it in my mouth. As I looked up, Christian's eyes twinkled. "Oops," I said around my finger. "Sorry.

My hands are clean. I—" Tattletale Shadow leaned against me with a moan. "Yeah, not so clean."

Christian laughed. "No problem. I know a good doctor if I get sick."

I blushed, then realized he must be talking about his brother, and blushed more.

Aunt Irm, having just tasted the sauce with her own, cleaner fingers, declared it perfect, ending my misery.

I poured the boiling pasta into the colander at the sink, steam rising to dampen my face. I returned the pasta to the warm pot, where Aunt Irm added a small amount of her signature spaghetti sauce, "to keep the pasta from clumping."

"About that letter you received," Christian said. "My friend in Jacksonville is happy to draft a response, but needs to talk with you briefly first. I emailed you his contact information."

"Thank you. I'll call him tomorrow."

At Aunt Irm's questioning look, I explained and she nodded, again with the evident distaste. I'd pushed the letter to the back of my overly taxed mind.

Once seated around the small kitchen table, and after first bites and compliments to the chef, the conversation resumed.

"Christian was telling me about growing up here, in such a big family, and finally moving away. I'm sorry, I cannot explain what you do in South Florida."

He grinned. "Mostly acquisitions, one company buying another. Pretty boring compared to saving lives." The admiring glow in his eyes resembled Aunt Irm's. Did they imagine I spent my days administering CPR and brilliantly averting death at every turn? I'd be a crappy anesthesiologist if that were true.

"Let me see those records," I said, eager to shift the conversation again.

"You must catch me up," Aunt Irm said. "From the beginning, please."

"As I told Kate earlier, my aunt Edith died last year under circumstances much like those of my dad. I got her records from New Castle so Kate could see if there are any similarities."

Aunt Irm held her fork in midair. "New Castle, Pennsylvania?"

He nodded.

"I used to live there," Aunt Irm said. "Near the library on Delaware."

"I've never actually been there myself," he said as he pulled a thin packet of papers from the inside pocket of his coat hanging on the chair back. "I have the OR and anesthetic records."

I wiped my mouth and hands with a napkin and took the pages. Scanning them quickly, everything seemed to be in order.

"Is it Dr. Ricken?" asked Aunt Irm.

I found the printout listing the procedure and staff, and my irrational hope was dashed. "No, Ricken is not the surgeon, I don't recognize the anesthesiologist, and the CRNA is Brent Johnson." I dropped the pages to the table. "There's no link."

"Dad's CRNA was Brad something."

"Jernigan," I said.

Aunt Irm said, "Brent, Brad, they are so similar." She picked up the sheets from the table.

Christian grinned. "That they are."

My aunt was grasping at something much smaller than straws, filaments maybe.

"Tell me more about this Brad person," Aunt Irm said. "Was he involved with all three patients?"

"He was, actually, at least part of the time."

When she didn't respond immediately, I glanced up to see her face drain of color as she stared at the papers. "Aunt Irm?"

"It was the same day as Max, at the same hospital." She stood, a bit unsteadily, but shook me off as she strode to her bedroom. Christian and I exchanged a look. She returned with a manila folder, "Max Surgery" written on the tab. She thumbed through the pages and pulled out a record that looked nearly identical to Edith's. "It is the same initials, BJ." She slumped into her chair. "My Max was killed."

The statement was too absurd to argue.

Moments later, she bolted upright, miraculously recovered. "Why have you not mentioned this Brad Jernigan before?"

Did she think I mentioned everyone with whom I worked? "He's a temp, a nurse anesthetist whose only been here a week."

Shadow whined at the back door. Grateful for the break, I took him out. Aunt Irm read too many *krimis*, her German language mysteries. She saw conspiracies everywhere.

Too soon, Shadow bounded up the back step in search of an I-did-my-business-and-came-back treat.

As he inhaled his Milk Bone, Aunt Irm said, "Something is not right about your Brad Jernigan." She sat next to Christian, leaning forward to read his laptop.

"He has no internet presence," Christian said. "I've tried every version of his name I could think of."

"What about Brent Johnson?" Aunt Irm asked.

"I'm afraid that name will be much too common." But Christian typed it in anyway.

"We can compare the signatures of our two BJs," Aunt Irm said, channeling a German Watson.

"We don't physically sign anything anymore," I said. "It's all electronic."

"Perhaps you can make up a form he needs to sign," Aunt Irm said.

"And compare it with what?" I asked.

Her mouth formed a grim line.

"Probably best not to approach him," Christian said. "Just in case."

"Yes," Aunt Irm said. "We cannot tip him in."

"Off, tip him off; tip in is for basketball." The sport had been new to her when the season began; now she was an avid, if not well-informed, fan.

I squeezed the bridge of my nose. "This is ridiculous."

"You're skeptical, I understand that," Christian said, "but even if it's only the three deaths, he's either incompetent or worse."

"Anesthesia incompetence won't kill someone two days later," I said. "Are you sure about the surgeon?" However unprofessional, I still wanted Ricken to be the culprit.

Christian typed some more, then turned his laptop for me to see. The surgeon listed on the records existed, practiced at the New Castle Hospital, and looked nothing like Charles Ricken.

"Too bad."

CHAPTER NINETEEN

THE DOORBELL RANG, and Shadow barked. Not exactly on the ball tonight.

"That must be Jenn," Aunt Irm said, bustling to the door.

"Jenn?" What was happening to my world?

"She called while you were out with Shadow," Christian said, grinning at my befuddled expression. "Your aunt invited her over."

Of course, she did.

"Have you eaten?" Aunt Irm asked before Jenn and her companion had removed their coats. "There is plenty of pasta."

They both declined, and yet Aunt Irm filled them each a plate.

Jenn introduced us to Todd, her orthopedic surgery resident boyfriend.

They politely accepted the food and ate while Aunt Irm quizzed Jenn about her life and future. She was forthcoming about her father's expectations.

"I apologize to your father," Aunt Irm said, "but you would be a wonderful anesthesiologist. My Kate thinks so and so do I."

"Well, that should definitely tip the scales," I whispered to Christian, as he and I poured coffee for everyone.

"She's tough to argue with," he said.

"By the way," I said, returning from the kitchen, "Dr. Wheaton, up in Atlanta, said he'd be happy to have you next rotation. I gave him your contact information."

Her smile widened. "That's great. Thanks." She'd cleaned her plate, even wiping up the sauce with a slice of garlic bread. "That was delicious." Her fork finally rested on the edge of the plate. "I was hungrier than I thought."

"Me too," Todd said. "Thank you."

I took their plates to the kitchen while Christian passed around the coffees. "Now you can tell us what you found, Jenn," Aunt Irm said. Todd pulled a laptop from his backpack and opened it on the table, Jenn close by his side. Christian invited Irm to sit on Todd's other side, while he and I stood over their shoulders. The spreadsheet Todd opened looked much like mine, but more extensive.

"When we realized Brad Jernigan was involved in all three cases," Jenn said, "I decided to see if any other patients died and if Brad Jernigan or Dr. Ricken was involved."

"Or both," Aunt Irm said.

"Todd's a computer whiz, so I asked him to help."

"She's doing the dishes for a week," Todd said.

She punched him playfully. "I always do the dishes."

Young love.

"We pulled all the OR cases since last Monday," Todd said, "including patient name, birth date, surgical and anesthesia teams, and operation. Then we googled each patient, together with the word 'obituary.' It needs more work, but it's a start."

"Do not keep an old woman in suspense," Aunt Irm said.

"Five more people died," Jenn said.

"Five?" Aunt Irm's hand flew to her mouth.

"Most are explainable," Todd added quickly. "One was a multi-trauma that I was in; he barely made it to the OR. Another was a neonatal congenital cardiac surgery, and one was an organ harvest."

"Don't think we can blame Brad or Ricken for those," I said.

"But the other two are similar, and you weren't the anesthesiologist," Jenn said triumphantly.

Todd pointed to the patients in question: a bronchoscopy and tumor excision, and a tracheotomy revision.

"Brad isn't listed as the anesthetist on either," Jenn said. "But he might have given a break."

After a moment of contemplative silence, Aunt Irm said, "All but Mr. Greyson are from last week. What about this week?"

"Aren't you just a ray of sunshine," I answered, but the more I thought about it, I realized she was right. Monday's patients would not yet have an obituary. It was only Wednesday. And those from Tuesday might be dying that very moment.

"Brad Jernigan hasn't been listed on any cases since Monday," Todd said. "And the cases Dr. Ricken did today were different—bigger operations, and they're still inpatients."

I phoned Sam Paulus with a single question: "Did Brad Jernigan work Tuesday or today?"

"He did not," Sam said. "Family emergency. He left after work Monday. That man is proof that one must look a gift horse in the mouth."

It took me a second. At first, I thought he was channeling Aunt Irm somehow. I would follow up later.

"Thanks, Sam." I hung up before he could ask why.

"He left," I said. "Brad Jernigan—he left after work on Monday. Who did he anesthetize that day?"

"Mr. Brighton," Jenn said. "I intubated him with Brad there." Then her eyes rounded and her face paled. "Did he take care of Mr. Sanderson, too?"

I could see her mind working, a step ahead of mine. She was right.

Jenn stood so quickly her chair toppled backward. "We have to go." She strode to the door. "They live in Cypress Hammock."

The popular multi-level-care retirement community was less than a mile away.

"I'll drive," Christian said.

Aunt Irm uncharacteristically declined. "I will stay and clean up." She'd never been able to leave a dish unwashed, but the tremor in her voice betrayed her anxiety. I wanted to reassure her that everything would be okay, but I couldn't.

"You go," she said. "We'll have dessert when you return."

We climbed into Christian's SUV and Jenn gave directions. The Sandersons' home was small but tidy. A streetlight illuminated the postage-stamp-sized front yard and steps up to a porch crowded with two rocking chairs.

"What happened to the flowers?" Jenn said. She rushed ahead, to planters flanking the front door. Some foliage remained, but flowerless stems had been sharply cut.

When Christian's knock failed to elicit a response, he rang the doorbell. Jenn phoned, but the ring went unanswered.

She headed back down the stairs. "The kitchen is in the back."

A metal gate squeaked open and slammed shut. Christian and I followed Todd around the side of the house after Jenn.

Unlike the front, the moonlit backyard appeared neglected. Sparse long grass and weeds mingled with sand. Untended azalea bushes grew wild along the fence line, covered in blooms of an indeterminate color in the gray light. A soft glow came from the kitchen.

Jenn knocked hard on the back door and yelled, "Mrs. Sanderson." No answer. She cupped her hands to a large window to the right of the door. "They're in there," she said, and banged on the glass. "Something's wrong."

I looked. She was right. Despite minimal lighting, I saw two forms on the bed facing the picture window.

Jenn tested the knob, rattling the door in its frame, then pulled a key from under a nearby flowerpot.

"Jenn, we should wait," Todd said, but there was no stopping her. She flung open the door, disappeared inside, and screamed.

We found her standing in the doorway of the master bedroom, hands to her open mouth, her breath coming in gasps. As Todd pulled her back, I peered into the room, immediately assailed by the odor, sickly sweet flowers, urine, feces . . . death.

"Oh God," Christian said.

"Call 911," I said.

On the bed, Mr. and Mrs. Sanderson lay entwined. Her head on his shoulder, arm across his chest, both deathly pale. Flower petals lay strewn across the bed and the bodies. I took small breaths through my mouth as I checked for a pulse I knew I wouldn't find. Both bodies were cold. Next to Mrs. Sanderson lay an open photo album, and on the bedside table, an envelope and a prescription bottle. I touched neither, but bent down to read the label—oxycodone for Mr. Sanderson. The envelope had no name, and it was all I could do not to open it. I heard scratching and looked for the source. A record player. Christian stopped me from touching it, but the sleeve lay nearby, classical music.

"Kate," Christian said. "We can't be in here."

Outside, an older man stood on the porch, official looking in black pants and a white dress shirt peeking out from under a coat.

"He's from the security office. Someone alerted him," Todd said.

Trembling, I shook his hand and introduced myself. "We should have come to you first. Jenn knows the Sandersons."

He offered me a seat at the wrought-iron table, next to a sobbing Jenn. Todd sat on her other side with a consoling arm wrapped around her shoulders. Sirens approached.

"I called a friend on the police force," Christian said, but it only vaguely registered.

A blur of images flashed through my mind: Jenn hugging Mrs. Sanderson, the woman refusing Jenn's involvement in her husband's case, the flowers, the pill bottle. I had to know what the note said.

When Christian touched my shoulder, the surroundings had changed, lights illuminated the patio and house, men and women in uniform milled about. "Kate, this is Lieutenant Garner."

I moved to stand, but he stopped me. "Tell me what happened."

Christian must have already told the story, but I did as he asked. "Mr. Sanderson had outpatient surgery earlier in the week, and Jenn knows the family well. She and her boyfriend came over for dinner and this house is nearby, so we drove over." I went on to tell what we found on our arrival.

"What do you think happened?"

I glanced at Jenn and stood on unexpectedly shaky legs. "Let's take a walk." I led Lieutenant Garner to the far side of the patio; Christian followed. "I think Mr. Sanderson either died or was killed, and his wife committed suicide."

"Do you think she killed him?"

I thought about that. "I don't know." The scene would haunt me for months, maybe forever, the flowers, the photo album. "There was an envelope. Was it a note?"

"Our forensic people are working on it."

"I have to know what it said." I caught Christian's eyes.

"Can you just summarize it?" he asked Garner.

He glanced around at his colleagues and said quietly, "She begs forgiveness for what she did to end her husband's suffering."

She did it. But herself that night, or did she arrange something during the operation? I thought of the trembling, thoughtful woman.

"Are your husband's parents alive?"

"His mother is, but she is incompetent due to dementia."

"Any children?"

"No."

"Has he named a health-care surrogate?"

"Yes, me."

"And did he prepare a Living Will?"

"He did not." We'd talked about it. I even printed one off and filled out most of it for him, but he wouldn't answer the most important questions, about what he wanted or didn't want. "I trust you," he'd said.

"Did he ever discuss with you what he would want regarding life-sustaining therapies?"

"We talked about it when he was getting deployed. But he said he wanted to leave the decision up to me, since the situation is rarely cut-and-dried."

"His brother claims he had a more detailed conversation with him, in which he stated he would never want to be kept alive by machines."

"Does he have any proof of this conversation?" I said. "Adam has ulterior motives."

"What ulterior motives?"

"His mother left Greg in charge of her trust. Apparently, listed me second."

"I'll need to look at that document. Does it list you by name or as Greg's wife?"

"I don't know. Does it matter?"

"Depending on the wording, Greg's death may or may not help Adam." He was silent a moment. "Okay, I'll draft this and send it to you. We can countersue if you want."

"No. No countersuit. I just want Adam to leave us alone."

CHAPTER TWENTY-TWO

BETWEEN CASES ON OB, the staff took a lunch break, which gave me time to focus on the other two suspicious deaths Jenn had found. The first, a Mrs. Armitage, had long-standing throat cancer and was undergoing a procedure to improve her breathing, but not cure her cancer. The second, Brody Reece, was only twenty-one. He'd suffered a traumatic brain injury from a motorcycle accident the year before and underwent tracheotomy revision. He was reported stable before and after the operation.

Fortunately, the surgeon, Rob Cassini, was a friend. We'd been residents at the same time and were both lifers at University. To my surprise, he answered my call.

"Rob, I need to ask you a strange question. It's about two of your patients from last Friday who passed away."

"Ah, yes, poor Mrs. Armitage was no surprise. The bronch was purely palliative, an attempt to get her out of the hospital to die, but I was skeptical all along, and the tumor was just too extensive." He paused briefly. "Brody Reece is another matter. Appalling situation, but he was stable. Nothing wrong with his body, just his head. I was surprised to hear he passed, but I guess there are worse things than death."

I said nothing, phone pressed tightly to my ear.

"He was here for less than a week, apparently hired through the chief of staff's office."

"Jernigan?"

I nodded. James' head seemed to sag on his shoulders.

"Do you know him? Why was his hiring so unusual?"

"I don't know him personally, no, but he came highly recommended." He stared at the table. "Walker asked me a few weeks ago to take on this CRNA as one of the locums we were finally allowed to hire, even though he wasn't from our normal agency. He said it was a favor to a wealthy donor."

"What donor?"

James shrugged. "He had the credentialing packet already approved through the hospital."

"Too good to be true," came to mind. It must have shown on my face.

James squeezed the back of his neck. "We needed the help. I couldn't very well ask for more locums, complain about how long it took to clear them, then turn down one wrapped up with a bow."

"Awfully pretty bow."

"Yeah, hindsight." He sat up straighter, wincing. "He's gone now?"

"Yes, but he could be working somewhere else."

"And you think he's involved in these deaths."

"He's the only common denominator I can find."

"What could he possibly do that kills people two days later?"

"I don't know yet, but it may be even bigger. Last night I talked with Christian O'Donnell. He's looking into his father's death and—"

"Stop right there." James raised a hand, palm out. He closed his eyes. Uh-oh. "Walker says he can prove you were meeting with a dead patient's son. I didn't believe him. Tell me you aren't talking to the son of a patient about his father's death at our hospital." His voice became louder, harsher.

"He asked me to review the record with him."

"Kate, what are you thinking? You know this kind of communication has to go through Risk Management. Everything you say is discoverable."

"It's not like that. Christian doesn't blame me."

"It's not just you, it's the whole institution." His raised voice was new to me and not reassuring. The bruise on my ego darkened still more.

I chose to quit while I was behind. The link to Pennsylvania was tenuous at best, only initials.

"We have to stop him," I said.

"That's challenging when we don't know what he's doing, if anything."

"True, but if we could find out where he's gone . . ."

He blew out a frustrated breath. "I'll check with Walker's office. Maybe they have a forwarding address."

"We also don't have a photo of him. It wasn't in his file, and he'd been deleted from the security database."

James raised one eyebrow, whether surprised by the information, or the fact I'd done the research, I couldn't tell.

"Considering your status with Walker, you need to let me handle it from here. We can't give him any more reason to act on your probation."

I nodded, but under the table, my fingers were crossed—new depths of immaturity. Call me paranoid, but I didn't trust Walker or Ricken. For once, I would be proactive and prove my own innocence. No more waiting for others to take the lead. This was my life and my career. If I wouldn't fight for it, who would?

CHAPTER TWENTY-FOUR

I WAS BACK on Labor and Delivery when Dr. Duffy called. "Robert Barton, the student from your simulation, is disputing your upcoming evaluation."

"How can he dispute something that hasn't been submitted yet?"

"Trying to head it off, I guess. He's claiming bias against him because he rebuffed your advances."

I was speechless. *Advances?* I thought back. Had I done anything that could be misconstrued? No, dammit, this kid was pathological. "Absolutely not. He acted upset and I comforted him. A hand on his shoulder at most. I can't believe this. I was trying to *help* him."

"He claims you held him after class, alone."

Wow. No good deed goes unpunished. "He's the one who insisted we be alone. What's his story anyway? Why did he transfer fourth year?" False accusations elsewhere forced him to leave maybe?

Silence.

"Yeah, I know, student confidentiality. What do you want me to do?"

"The Academic Status Committee is meeting again at three o'clock. We'd like to hear your side of the story."

"Have they interviewed the other students? There were several witnesses during the simulation itself."

"We're trying not to involve them for now. Can you make it at three?"

I promised to try and get coverage for Labor and Delivery, then called Nathan, the simulator engineer, and told him of the meeting, but not about the ridiculous accusation.

"I wonder why they haven't called me as a witness."

"Can I suggest it?"

"Of course, I hate that kid."

"Maybe leave that part out."

* * *

We'd finished the scheduled cases by three, and Sam Paulus offered to cover for me. "Is this about Dr. Ricken?" he asked.

I explained the situation, the whole story this time. "He's basically accusing me of sexual harassment."

"You're having quite the week. When did this happen?"

"On Monday. I should have called in sick."

As I walked to the meeting, I thought about that. A lot had happened since Monday, though the first two deaths had already occurred.

Dr. Duffy welcomed me into the room. I tried to nod to Robert, but he pointedly ignored me. A dozen committee members surrounded the large table, most of whom I recognized. I took the only remaining seat, at the end of the table.

"Dr. Downey, thank you for joining us. I'm Elaine Lasher, Chair of the Academic Status Committee, and this is a special meeting in response to concerns raised by Robert Barton, MS4, who believes he was unfairly treated during and after a teaching session. We would like to hear your version of the events from Monday morning."

against him would still be in the appeals process, so it would be epically stupid for him to have done this."

"What's this student's name?" Garner said.

"I really don't think I'm allowed to say. He hasn't threatened me or anything."

"Until now, maybe," Christian said.

"I'll check with the Dean of Students and get back to you on that," I said.

Garner made a note. "What's the other possibility?"

"I have been looking into the deaths of recent patients at University."

"Mr. Sanderson."

I nodded.

"You think these deaths are criminal?" Garner asked.

"I don't know. It's possible, but I can't prove anything yet, and any suggestion could damage the hospital's reputation."

"Was that someone from work you called?" Garner nodded toward my phone.

"My chairman. He'll update the chief of staff."

"I'll need their contact information," he said, pen poised over his notebook.

Not good. I gave him James' information.

"And the chief of staff?" Garner said.

"Apparently he is a problem," Christian said.

"Only for me," I said.

Garner still sat waiting, pen poised.

"I've told Dr. Walker part of the story, but he's not inclined to believe me and would very likely fire me for talking to you. Can you start with my chairman and keep it out of the press for now?"

"How many patients are we talking about?" Garner asked.

"Several," I said noncommittally.

"More than ten?"

"No." I said it emphatically, then wondered if it were possible. "Was there anything on Mr. Sanderson's tox screen?"

He shook his head. "Not even the prescription narcotics. He didn't have a full autopsy, but there's no evidence of foul play, other than the letter. And no real reason to pursue it, with her death."

I glanced at my watch—after ten. "I need to pick up Aunt Irm and find a hotel that allows pets."

"Thanks for your help," Christian said, leading Garner to the front door. Shadow lifted his head, put it back down.

"I'll be in touch," he said.

Christian returned before I could finish my hotel search. He sat on the coffee table in front of me. "You'll stay with me."

My eyes narrowed; he was getting entirely too bossy.

"I know you're strong, and tough, and you can handle all of this. I know you'd be fine in a hotel that takes pets, but think of Aunt Irm and Shadow. They'll be more comfortable at my parents' house." He wasn't wrong. He also wasn't done. "You scared me tonight. More frightened than I've been in a really long time."

I broke eye contact. This was too intimate.

"I know you love your husband," he continued, "and I respect that. But we're a team on this, and teammates watch each other's back. Please don't make me do that from a dog-friendly hotel."

Appealing to Aunt Irm and Shadow's comfort was entirely uncalled for.

"And Riley can entertain Shadow," he said.

"Riley?"

"My Lab. He loves company."

"What about your mom?"

"It's a big house," he said.

CHAPTER TWENTY-SIX

TWO HOURS AND a surprisingly quick trip to the emergency vet later, Aunt Irm and I followed Christian to his childhood home on the edge of Payne's Prairie, a twenty-thousand-acre state park south of town. "Home" was an understatement—more like estate. The half-mile-long driveway circled before a two-story antebellum-style mansion.

"Wow," was all I could manage.

I parked where instructed, and Christian opened Aunt Irm's door. "Sorry about the house," he said. "I should have warned you. Luke and I call it Tara."

The reference was lost on Aunt Irm. I was too tired to explain.

The front door opened and a yellow Lab bolted outside, barking feverishly. Shadow barked back, but after a few sniffs, they switched to wagging. Riley tried to start a game of chase, but I held Shadow. I couldn't have him reopen his wounds and bleed all over the O'Donnells' mansion.

"Riley, back inside," Christian said. The dog obeyed immediately.

"Show-off," I said.

Christian grabbed our bags from the trunk. The house was even more impressive inside, with a sweeping staircase around a massive chandelier.

"Oh, my," Aunt Irm said.

"I'll give you a tour tomorrow," Christian said.

A Hispanic woman not much younger than Aunt Irm took her arm and led her to the kitchen. "I am Gabriella. Would you like some tea?"

Christian stared after them. "So much for introductions. Gabriella has worked for our family since I was in diapers."

We followed into the enormous kitchen, where Aunt Irm was declining tea and cookies. "Gabriella is going to show me to my room; good night, kindchen." She pulled me into a tight hug, then moved down a hallway off the kitchen.

Christian and I sat in a cozy corner of the kitchen, drinking water. Shadow lay comfortably at my feet gnawing a rawhide, a foot from his new buddy, Riley.

Christian's phone rang. "It's Luke."

While he answered, I texted Jenn: Call me when you get this

My phone rang immediately.

"Jenn, I hope I didn't wake you."

"No, I'm up. Almost done studying for the test tomorrow."

"We'll worry about the exam another time. I want you to go ahead up to your sister's in the morning. You can have a couple of extra days with your niece."

She was silent for a moment.

"I promise, it won't affect your grade."

"Has something happened?"

"I'm afraid so. Someone isn't happy about our digging. I'm not sure whether they know you're involved, but it's not worth the risk. Please go up to Atlanta until this is resolved."

"Are you okay?"

"Yes, we're at Christian's house for a while. Someone broke in and left a message. No real harm done."

I asked her for Todd's cell number. "Dr. Wheaton will be expecting you Monday morning." She agreed and we hung up.

Still on the phone, Christian said, "She's been through a lot tonight. We can talk tomorrow."

I shook my head. "It's okay. I won't be able to sleep anyway."

"Neither can I." Aunt Irm returned from her bedroom.

"Okay, give me a second," Christian said into the phone and disconnected. He pulled a laptop from a briefcase on the floor and set it up at one end of the kitchen table. Immediately, the familiar Skype ring came through, and Luke appeared on the screen. He looked remarkably like his brother, though I couldn't make out the color of his eyes in the glare.

"I'm so glad you guys are okay," Luke said. "You sure you're up for rehashing everything tonight?"

"I am," I said, glancing at my aunt, who nodded agreement.

"Alright. I think we should start from the beginning. Make sure we all have the same information."

"Chronologically? Or in the order we figured things out?" I asked.

We decided on chronological.

And so I started at the earliest related event. "We can't be completely sure, but your aunt and my great-uncle received G-Tubes on the same date at a hospital in New Castle. They had the same surgical team, including a nurse anesthetist named Brent Johnson. They both died the following night."

"Christian told me about your brother, Irm. I'm sorry."

"Thank you, Luke. Continue, Kate."

I couldn't help but grin at her instruction. "At some point, a wealthy donor requested that Brad Jernigan be hired as a temp here at University."

"You've not mentioned that before," Christian said.

"I only learned it today."

"Do you know who the donor was?" Christian asked.

"I don't."

"It has to be Mom," Luke said. Christian nodded. Both had the same grim expression.

"The hire came through the chief of staff's office, rather than the usual channels, and he was presented to my chairman as a done deal. The first time he showed up on the OR schedule was last Thursday. I'm told he was unusually demanding about his case assignments. That first day, he and I cared for a woman with rapidly progressive multiple sclerosis, who underwent G-Tube placement. She died at home Friday night."

I remembered my conversation with her physician. "Oh, and she had an anniversary party that afternoon."

"A family reunion to say good-bye," Aunt Irm said. "I wonder, did she know?"

"Her physician said she insisted on the party."

For a moment, we were silent, reflecting. What would it be like to choose your own time of death? What would you do in those last hours?

Luke recovered first. "What were your other cases that day?"

"She was an add-on. Before that we did a gastric bypass and a gallbladder with a different surgeon; both those patients appear to still be alive. Friday, I was asked to take care of your dad when my chairman sustained an injury."

"And Mom had her premonition," Luke said with distaste.

Christian looked around for eavesdroppers and gave Luke an admonishing look.

"Your dad's physician said the hernia was not an emergency, but your mom had already contacted Dr. Ricken and lined everything up."

Christian and Luke exchanged a look across the miles. I felt like an intruder in their personal pain.

"I'm sorry," I said.

"No, don't leave anything out," Luke said.

"That was Ricken's only case on Friday. After that, I worked with other residents, and Brad's not on the schedule, but he gave a lunch break to a resident caring for a young man in a persistent vegetative state after a motorcycle accident. According to the surgeon, the patient's mother insisted on the trach revision, even though it could have been postponed. He died at home two days later."

"Sorry to interrupt," Luke said. "Did any of these patients have an autopsy?"

"No. No one has been autopsied, and, except for one, they've all been cremated."

Aunt Irm whimpered.

A bang sounded from the computer speaker. *Hand hitting table?* "You were right on that, too, Christian. She overrode his will, not because he changed his mind, but to destroy evidence. I can't believe this."

Christian glanced toward the kitchen door again.

"It was the same with my Max," Aunt Irm said. "We were supposed to be buried together. We agreed years ago, after Martina left him, that we would be buried side by side. I didn't want to be buried in Germany with Heinrich." As she wiped her eyes with a napkin, the simple gold band on Irm's right ring finger winked. I reached for her other hand. "He promised, but Martina said he changed his mind and wanted to be cremated. She said his urn could be buried with me. His urn. Not my Max." A single tear spilled over and down her cheek, but she did not sob. She looked up with resolve. "She destroyed evidence, too."

My head swam.

"Cremation requires Medical Examiner approval," said Luke. "The records must be clean. Go on."

"On Monday, I worked with Ricken yet again. We did three G-Tubes in a row. For the first, I had a resident, but Brad gave him a break, and forced the med student from the room."

"That was our Jenn," Aunt Irm said.

I nodded. "The other two cases, I did with Brad. Two of the patients from that day have since died, though one was unusual. And the third patient was rushed to a different hospital on Tuesday."

"Tell me about the one that was different," Luke said.

I told him about the bleeding tonsil, code, and eventual withdrawal of care.

"Jenn's essay is heartbreaking," Aunt Irm said.

I stared at my aunt. She'd read the essay?

"She dropped it by this afternoon and invited me to read it." She sounded almost defensive, but continued, "The way she described his movements when the end was near . . . Everyone who says death is so peaceful, like falling asleep . . . they never watched. She described just what I saw with my brother. It brought tears to my eyes." They glistened even now. "She didn't mention Mr. Greyson's eyes, but for Max, I'll never forget. Pure terror. Uncle Max was no angel in life, but he did not deserve to see the devil's minions come to retrieve his soul."

I stared at her. "Do you have the essay?"

She pulled it from her purse.

I read about the jerky movements that gradually subsided and puzzle pieces snapped into place, forming a horrific image. "Oh my God, I know what it is . . . but it can't be . . . It can't take that long. How could . . ."

"Kate?" Christian and Luke said together.

"Could you complete a thought, please?" Luke said.

I pulled out my own laptop, logged onto Christian's Wi-Fi, and loaded PubMed, a database of medical journal articles published since 1950. "Luke, I'm searching PubMed for 'delayed-onset muscle relaxant.'" To Aunt Irm, I said, "The twitching you describe is not typical for patients dying a natural death. Usually, as the brain becomes less interested in breathing, the patient just stops. The heart follows soon after and they die quietly."

"But that is not what happened. To Max or Jenn's Mr. Greyson."

"No, what you both describe sounds more like someone who wants to breathe, but can't. Like suffocation."

Aunt Irm made a sound. Shadow seemed to mimic the groan from the floor at my feet. I looked at my aunt. "I'm sorry. Are you okay?"

"I am. Please go on. I want to know what happened to him."

I turned back to the computer. "It sounds like a patient who has been given muscle relaxants." My search failed to find anything of interest, so I tried the more broad, 'delayed-onset drugs' and scanned through the list of articles.

"Muscle relaxants?" Aunt Irm asked. "Like the Soma for Carmel's back?"

"No, not that kind. These are IV drugs we use in anesthesia to paralyze people for surgery."

Luke said, "Holy—"

Christian hit a button, muting his brother.

"But Max did not have an IV after we left the hospital."

"The drug works in minutes when given by IV. If I'm right, it was given some other way, with a delayed onset."

Christian clicked his laptop again.

"Sorry," Luke said. "Could it be oral? Added to his antibiotics or pain meds?"

Aunt Irm said, "He had pain pills, but I did not give him any. He did not seem to be in pain."

"No, I don't think it could be oral," I said. "That would have to go through the pharmacy, and these are big, charged molecules that would be hard to get across the GI tract."

After several more search terms, I leaned back in my chair. "I can't find anything."

"Me either," Luke said. "It's not like there's any market for such a drug. Long-acting muscle relaxants maybe, for ICU patients, but not delayed onset."

"I need a pharmacologist." I found a number in my phone, one I'd not dialed in more than a year, maybe ever. Steven Wood had played basketball with Greg. For a while, he'd checked in every month or so, and insisted I keep his number in case I needed anything, or there was news. There was no news, but at last I needed something he could provide.

"You know what time it is, right?" Christian asked.

"Yeah, just checking that I still have his number. I'll call in the morning."

"The anesthetist in both places has the initials BJ. What else do we know about this guy?" Luke asked.

"Just what's on his CV," I said. "He gave a home address in Miami, but he has no presence on the internet."

"Which is impossible," Christian said. "You'd have to live under a rock not to be on Google."

"Actually," said Luke, "scorpions live under rocks and they're on Google."

"Smart-ass," Christian mumbled. "Has to be an alias."

Computer keys clicked in the background. "Give me his address," Luke said.

I read it to him, then added, "If his CV is to be believed, he was a student at Ohio University ten years ago, then did his CRNA training in Miami."

"The address is bogus," Luke said. "Doesn't exist. What about his paycheck? Where is it sent?"

"Probably an internet bank," Christian said.

"Speaking of money," Luke said. "Christian, you have access to Mom and Dad's financials, right?"

"I do," Christian said. "You're wondering if money changed hands."

"Exactly."

"Any idea what to look for?"

"Wait," I said, "you guys think your mom paid—"

"I know," Aunt Irm interrupted, "the Schierling Society." She paused a beat while we all stared, dumbfounded. "Max and I do our taxes together. We use Dietrich Rolf. His mother was my bridge partner in Pennsylvania. She was not very good. Last year, Dietrich asked me about two donations to this Schierling Society he could not identify. Martina—"

"Martina was Max's wife," I interrupted.

"She was not his wife. She left him for years."

"She came back," I said. "To take care of him when he had the stroke."

"She did no such thing." Aunt Irm pointed to her chest. "I took care of my brother. She did nothing but complain. She came back to take his money."

As far as I knew, he had no money, but why let pesky facts interfere with a good story? I nodded for her to continue.

"She said the donation built a playground in a town in Bavaria they visited on their honeymoon, but this was a lie. Max was stationed near there during the war. He would not have gone back. And why suddenly build a playground fifty years later? I did not believe her."

"May I ask how much money is involved?" Luke asked.

"Two donations of ten thousand dollars each."

"When?" My voice quavered.

"Two weeks before and one week after Max died. I have the tax form at home."

"How do you spell Schierling?" Luke asked. "S-h?"

"S-c-h-i-e-r," Aunt Irm said.

"Got it." There was a brief pause. "Besides the town and some surnames, I'm getting images of a plant."

Aunt Irm gasped. "*Mein Gott*," she said. "I did not think of it. Schierling killed Socrates."

"Hemlock?" Christian and I said in unison.

Only clicking keys over Skype broke the ensuing silence. "She's right," Luke said. "It's German for *hemlock*. Holy . . . smokes."

"There is a Hemlock Society," I said. "They deal with right-to-die issues."

"They do," said Luke. "But only for competent people with terminal illnesses. Don't ask why I know that."

"But this one allows others to make that decision? Is that what we think?" Christian asked.

I massaged my temples. "I don't think anything, except that my head's going to explode." Christian and Aunt Irm looked at me with concern. "Figure of speech; this is a lot to take in."

More clicking. "No hits for Schierling Society. I don't think it's the German branch of the Hemlock Society, though, Kate. Germany's group is called Dignitas."

There was a long, contemplative silence. I worried about Aunt Irm, but it had to be even worse for Luke and Christian. A family member they loved and respected—most likely their mother—may have arranged the death of her sister and their father. How does a child of any age deal with that?

I caught Christian's eye and asked, "Are you okay?"

He gave a small, heart-wrenching smile. "I am for now, thanks. If Mom did it, it was out of love."

"Not Martina," Aunt Irm said. "She did it for money and I will never forgive her."

The call ended soon after. I walked Aunt Irm back to her room and gave her a tight hug. She seemed surprisingly okay, her long-term suspicions finding traction at last.

"You look beat," Christian said as I returned.

I didn't argue.

He led me to the second floor. I stopped at a magnificent portrait hung near the stairs. Unless he had a twin, the family in the ornate mahogany frame was his—a beautiful wife and adorable girl of about one, with a bow in her blond curls and a Pooh Bear in her arms. All three looked blissfully happy, so unlike the typically staid professional portraits.

Christian reached up and nearly touched the blond curls. "My wife and daughter. They were killed by a drunk driver a few months after we sat for this."

My heart seized at the beautiful child. "Christian, I'm so sorry." This must be the Helen and Caroline he'd mentioned. His mother had said God took them too soon. The truth of it made me shudder.

"It's been several years now. Caroline would have been four next month." Despite the elapsed time, his eyes glistened.

Gravity seemed to double. He'd lost his father, his wife, his daughter. The cruelty of the world was unfathomable at times. "When does it get easier?"

The corners of his mouth turned up, but no smile reached his eyes. "Oh, it does. Each year it's a little more bearable." He continued up the stairs and showed me to an elegant room with a four-poster bed and adjoining bath. Shadow followed and curled up on a dog bed set in the corner.

"You're too much. Thank you, Christian."

"Better than a pet-friendly hotel?"

I smiled. "I do worry about your mom, though."

"I'll be down early to run interference." He smiled. "My room is across the hall if you need anything."

All at once, my eyes filled. I couldn't explain it; I also couldn't stop it. He pulled me into a hug, and I dampened his shirt with my tears for several moments, unsuccessfully stifling sobs. At last, I pulled away and wiped my face. "Sorry. Don't know where that came from."

Hands still on my arms, he rubbed. "Let's see, your dog was attacked, your home broken into, and you were threatened. Meanwhile you're tracking a potential serial killer and being thwarted by your own boss. I'd say you're entitled to a few tears."

I thanked him and turned away. His eyes were too kind, too consoling, too . . . I needed space. We said good night and I prepared for bed.

I couldn't bring myself to invite Shadow onto the bed, especially with potentially bloody paws, but I needed warmth tonight, reassurance. I took the comforter onto the floor and curled around Shadow, wishing with all my heart he was Greg.

CHAPTER TWENTY-SEVEN

SIX O'CLOCK CAME quickly, when sleep hadn't. I'd lain awake until three, my mind conjuring images I didn't want to see, of Uncle Max suffocating to death, of Christian's beautiful daughter in a casket, of skeletal Mr. Greyson. Still, work awaited, so I showered, dressed, and tried to keep Shadow quiet on the wood stairs.

For once, Aunt Irm didn't beat me to the kitchen, but Christian did. "Good morning," I said. "I hope you didn't get up for me."

"No, lawyers always rise before the sun." He grinned, definitely kidding. "What would you like for breakfast? I make a mean omelet."

"I can grab something at the hospital."

He gave me a strange look. "You really don't like people taking care of you, do you?"

"It's not that." Or maybe it was.

Shadow whined at the back door.

"Riley's outside," Christian said. "I'll take Shadow out. Grab something you can eat in the car." He opened the pantry door. "Take anything."

Great, now I'd offended him. "Thank you."

I gave Shadow a pat, then waited until Christian closed the door before heading out the front door. In truth I had time, but I needed distance. Distance from his kindness, from his helpfulness, and definitely from his touch. My marriage vows had echoed in my head all night. "In sickness and in health . . . 'Til death do us part."

I changed into scrubs and prepared instant oatmeal from the packages I stored in my office for emergencies. An omelet would have been better.

At morning conference, the topic of the day was my least favorite—amniotic fluid embolism, a rare but nearly always fatal complication of pregnancy and delivery, and the cause of my only obstetric patient death. It occurred to me how depressing conference frequently became, focused on all the complications and potential disasters looming.

Geez, I was downright morose. Nothing like the delivery of a healthy baby to a welcoming couple to clear the gloom. The schedule looked obliging—three elective repeat cesareans in women with no major medical problems.

The first case was delayed as two women on the floor decided to deliver simultaneously, tying up all the obstetricians. In the meantime, I made a call to my friendly neighborhood pharmacologist. "Steven, this is Kate Downey."

"Kate, how are you? How's Greg?"

"I'm fine. Greg's the same, I'm afraid, but I have a question for you."

"Bring it on."

"I need to know how you would alter a drug to give it a delayed onset."

"Like an enteric coated pill?"

"No, something that can be injected."

"You'd be hard-pressed to make anything administered by IV that has a delayed onset, unless it required some very slow metabolic pathway to become activated."

"What if it was injected as a depot somewhere, for delayed release? Like intramuscular injections."

"It would still start to be absorbed right away. You'd need a coating for the drug molecules, with specific breakdown characteristics for the intended time frame. You'd also have to choose a depot location that has a decent and consistent blood supply, to pick up the drug once the coating wore off." He paused, I waited. "My PhD advisor applied for an industry grant for something like that back when I was in school. Why do you want to know?"

My heart skipped a beat, or two. "I'm working on a little theory. Can you tell me more about that project?"

"Not really. He didn't get the grant, but I guess whoever did was unsuccessful, because they approached Dr. Beecher again right before I graduated. He had a grad student for it, but I don't know the status at this point."

"Do you know who got the initial funding?" It was a long shot, but the time frame was about right.

Steven was silent a long time.

"I know these are strange questions. I wouldn't be asking if it weren't important."

"I'll find out," he said, resigned.

I thanked him and disconnected just as an alarm blared overhead. The Code Yellow alarm—shoulder dystocia—a baby was stuck.

I joined the throng running to Labor Room 15 and pushed my way through. The patient was on her hands and knees as they tried desperately to free the baby's shoulders. Minutes dragged on. The pediatric team arrived; I moved to the background and said a silent prayer. The obstetric attending shouted maneuvers, names of long-dead physicians who devised ways to free such babies. The patient and her companion remained surprisingly calm, and at long, long last the baby came free, limp and silent.

The pediatricians began breathing for her, started chest compressions; moments later, she gave a cough and started crying, weakly at first, but growing rapidly stronger.

My first breath in a while came soon after, and I wasn't alone, as staff smiled at one another with relief, but not relaxation, never relaxed. Disaster averted, this time.

My cell rang. Marcus Culpepper, Ricken's PA. I stepped away and answered.

"I'm afraid I've found nothing," he said. "The manufacturers of the tubes and the suture have had no other concerns raised, though, of course, we could just be the first. I gave them my number in case something else comes up."

That news came as no surprise. "Thanks for looking into it."

"Oh, and no way on the autopsy. Mr. Greyson's body is being donated to medical research."

"Yeah, I heard that. Can I ask you a different question?"

"Of course."

"There was a CRNA here last week. His name was Brad Jernigan and he was in a number of those cases with us. Did you know him?"

"Brad Jernigan? No, don't think so."

No point describing him. He had no distinguishing features, at least not behind a surgical mask, and it would sound crazy to mention he might go by aliases with consistent initials. "Did you hear about Mr. Brighton? Our last case from Monday?"

"What about him?"

"He was admitted by ambulance to North Central on Tuesday. I haven't been able to get any information. Maybe you can."

"Weird. I'll definitely follow up."

"Let me know. Thanks, Marcus."

One would think the physician at the other hospital would have contacted the surgeon who cared for his patient just days earlier. Maybe he or she had spoken with Dr. Ricken directly. No doubt that would dissuade them from further contact.

We started our first cesarean of the day. Once the baby was out, my thoughts returned to the murders. A depot somewhere. A place an anesthesia provider could readily inject a drug that wasn't intravenous. Behind the surgical drapes, we had unobserved access to the head and shoulders. Mr. Greyson underwent a CT scan of his head and neck after his tonsil bleed. I pulled up his scans and reviewed the report. No mention of an unusual liquid density anywhere. The only abnormality mentioned was the enlarged tonsils. I examined the images but was quickly out of my depth.

First case done, I took the elevator down to radiology. Dr. Kim Rice sat in the reading room, the only light emanating from dual computer screens on each desk. Having relieved the pain of Kim's labor less than a year ago, I felt a little less guilty asking for a favor.

"Kate, hi, what brings you to our dungeon?"

"I wonder if you could look at a CT with me." I handed Kim a folded slip of paper with Greyson's name and medical record number. "I'm especially interested in his tonsils."

Kim pulled up the scan from the archives and scrolled through the series of images while I asked about her daughter and life as a new parent. "Doing great," and "Loving it," were the answers.

"By the way, I hear you likely helped us dodge a bullet," she said.

"And what bullet would that be?"

"Robert Barton. The fourth year who didn't match. They were trying to force us to make a position for him."

So he went through the residency match and was not selected into a program. It happened to a few students at University every year, usually ones applying to highly competitive specialties, not radiology.

"Rumor has it his dad was trying to buy him a spot and the chair was actually considering it. You averted a faculty revolt. The kid's a sociopath."

Which made me wonder why they didn't get him kicked out and save me the trouble.

I didn't smile. "Do you know who daddy was pressuring to offer him a spot?"

"Who do you think? Walker, of course."

It wouldn't be the first time a less-than-qualified applicant was taken as a favor to someone, usually the spouse of a new faculty member or highly-sought-after resident in another specialty. But bribery? That I'd never heard of.

Kim stopped on an image. "Hmm, it's a tough call." She adjusted the contrast, more white, then more black, then more white. Like photo-editing software for the color-challenged. "The tonsil is definitely abnormal. There are no tissue planes at all." She scrolled through more images higher and lower in the throat.

"What do you think it might be?"

"It's strange. Liquid density," Kim said, adjusting the contrast again.

"Blood?"

"No, blood would be bright." She pointed to a light gray area in the throat. "It's more like edema within the tonsil. But it doesn't extend into the wall of the pharynx like an infection. Very odd."

She opened the report on the other screen. "It wasn't noted in the report, but it's pretty subtle. I probably wouldn't have noticed if you hadn't asked specifically."

I decided to take the leap. "Could it be injected liquid? Have you ever seen an intramuscular injection on CT? Does it look anything like that?"

Her eyes cut to me, then back to the screen. "Hmmm, I suppose it could be consistent with an injection. But why?"

My heart quickened. "I'm not quite there yet, but I appreciate your help."

"Kate, what—"

The door banged behind me as I rushed from the reading room. I'd have to make it up to Kim later. Practically running down the hall and into the stairwell, I texted Christian and Luke: I've got it!

By the second floor, my phone rang.

"Hello," I said, out of breath.

"Are you on a run again?" asked Christian.

"Only up the stairs."

"So what have you got?"

My phone beeped with another call.

"Hang on. Your brother's calling too." I merged the calls as I entered the anesthesia office on Labor and Delivery and closed the door.

I fell into the rolling desk chair. "He's injecting the tonsils. But we'll need a biopsy to prove it." My breathing returned to normal.

"Garner's chief said we need more before he would call the Medical Examiner to intervene with the Greyson family, but how about Mr. Sanderson?"

Of course. I disconnected and called Jenn. She was still packing.

"I know this is difficult for you, but I need permission to run one more test on Mr. Sanderson. Do you know who is making decisions about their bodies?"

"Their son is. What kind of test?"

"I think I've figured out what Brad is doing, but I need proof. I think he may be injecting something into their tonsils."

"That's why Mr. Greyson bled?"

"Right. So I need a biopsy of the area. Do you know their son?"

"I don't, but the funeral is in California."

I called Christian. He would find out where Mr. Sanderson's body was, and how to get permission for the biopsy.

CHAPTER TWENTY-EIGHT

My secretary called. "Dr. Downey?" Mary never called me that. "I'm terribly sorry to interrupt when you are caring for patients." And she was never "terribly sorry." Something was up.

"Mary?"

"There's someone here to see you."

"I'm between cases."

"Oh, okay." She sounded disappointed. "Can we meet you at your office?"

"Sure, of course. What's going on?"

"We'll see you there."

What now?

When I reached the hallway, Mary stood by my office door with a tall man, dark suit, close-cropped brown hair, briefcase. Not a physician. He looked more like an attorney. Mary unlocked the door as I approached, and blocked the man so I could enter first. I looked at her questioningly. She mouthed, "I don't know," but looked scared. She moved to leave, but the man stopped her.

"Please, join us as a witness." He held his briefcase over my small table and caught my eye. "May I?"

I cleared a space. No one sat.

With the solemnity of an undertaker, he pulled a large yellow envelope from his briefcase and held it toward me. "Dr. Kate Downey?"

I nodded and accepted the envelope.

"On behalf of the Florida Board of Medicine, I hereby serve you these documents of official complaint and inquiry. You have five working days to respond in writing."

Mary gasped. "Five days?"

I waved her off.

"In the meantime, myself and another investigator will review records and interview your colleagues. You are instructed not to discuss the accusations with anyone."

Heat rose from my chest into my neck. Thank God it was Mary witnessing this rather than my partners. But they'd all soon know, soon be asked about my competence. Rationally, I had nothing to fear, yet self-doubt welled. I thanked the man, by reflex. What the hell was I thanking him for? He indicated where I should sign, then Mary.

She closed the door almost before he'd fully left and opened her arms wide for a hug. I complied.

"What in the world?" she said. "I was so scared when he demanded to see you in person. What's going on?"

"Well, I guess I'm not supposed to talk about it." I broke the embrace. "But you'll hear anyway. Dr. Ricken accused me of malpractice."

Mary's face came alive. She could be so animated. We'd been friends since I was a medical student, and Mary remained steadfast even as I withdrew after Greg's accident. She refused to be forced away. I considered all the other relationships I'd abandoned, the unanswered calls, ignored emails and texts. Did I deserve the support of my colleagues now?

Mary trembled. "That man is evil. The residents and CRNAs talk about him all the time."

"It's going to be okay. I took good care of these patients. It'll be painful, but I'll be cleared."

"I'm so sorry. This is the last thing you need."

My phone rang. Mary took it from my hand, glanced at the screen, and answered, "Dr. Downey's phone." She looked at me. "I'm sorry, Nancy, she's not available right now, may I take a message?" If possible, Mary's face fell even further. "I'll tell her." She clicked off and handed the phone back, tears in her eyes. "You're to report to the chief of staff's office immediately." She snatched a tissue from the desk.

"Thanks for all your support," I said.

"I'll call Dr. Worrell," she said.

"No. I can handle this on my own." I couldn't keep using my chair as a buffer.

She nodded and closed the door behind her. I stared at Greg's photo a long moment, but couldn't hear his voice through the buzzing in my head. I felt myself shrinking, every vertebra collapsing down on the one below, like gravity had doubled. Suddenly my less-than-fulfilling life since Greg's accident seemed desirable.

On the way to what I now considered the antechamber to hell, I called Labor and Delivery. Everything was stable. I told them not to roll with the next case until they checked with me.

Nancy didn't meet my eye and ushered me immediately into Dr. Walker's office. He looked up at my entrance. "Have a seat, Dr. Downey." I did. "It has come to my attention that you are under investigation by the Board of Medicine."

That news traveled fast. "I have done nothing wrong."

He held up his hand. "Until you are cleared, you will be on a paid leave of absence."

A pit the size of Madagascar opened in my stomach. Leave of absence? "But—"

"This is not up for discussion. These are serious charges. I cannot have one of my staff under such a shadow and in good conscience allow them to continue caring for our patients."

I schooled my features to display a calm I didn't feel. "I understand, but may I say something in my defense?"

He nodded, but looked back down at the papers on his desk.

"The deaths. It was a CRNA." Should I add it was the one he hired?

Walker looked up and raised an eyebrow. "Earlier this week you accused Dr. Ricken. Today it's a CRNA?"

"No. I didn't accuse Dr. Ricken. I merely asked if he had any idea why they were dying."

"That is not what he heard. Regardless, the Board of Medicine will now get to the bottom of it. You will make yourself available to them, but will otherwise stay away from the hospital."

Technically, my office was in the College of Medicine. Better to ask forgiveness than permission, but he anticipated my intent. "Not anywhere on the medical campus, Dr. Downey. Do I make myself clear?"

"I have teaching responsibilities."

"Not anymore."

"I will finish today's cases. I already met the patients."

"No. As of this moment. Your chair will find coverage. If and when you are cleared, you will be reinstated."

If, he'd said. I fought to maintain control. The chief of staff generally supported the faculty, but apparently not in my case. I rose and had the briefest sense I should apologize. Not a chance.

Numb, I stumbled to the chairman's office four floors above and was ushered directly in to see him.

He greeted me at the door. "I don't know what to say. I'm sorry about the forced leave, but it's probably for the best."

"Not under these circumstances, it's not. I can't believe Ricken would—"

"It wasn't him," James said.

My head jerked up. Another physician thought I was incompetent?

"It was Dr. Scott Barton, a surgeon in Pensacola."

"Barton."

"Know him? Or how he knows anything about your cases?"

I chuckled softly to myself. "When it rains it snows," Aunt Irm would say. "Robert Barton is the student who didn't want to remediate the simulation."

James' eyes widened. "I'm surprised it's so easy to start an investigation. That was just yesterday. The Board doesn't have a reputation for being nimble."

"Dr. Walker probably has connections; he really doesn't want me working here."

"Just take some time off and let this get resolved."

"How long?"

"However long it takes. It's going to be okay." His words reassured, but his face looked grim.

For the first time, it occurred to me that maybe it *wouldn't* be okay. Could the events be twisted in such a way that I was implicated? Could these cases, together with my probation, end my career?

That couldn't happen. We had to find Brad Jernigan and prove my innocence, and we had to do it before he killed more people.

CHAPTER TWENTY-NINE

I RETURNED TO Labor and Delivery to turn the board over to my replacement, Dr. White, a new young faculty member who did OB only when on call. How could this be happening? But when I arrived, chaos reigned.

A seizing preeclamptic patient with critical hypertension required a stat cesarean, but Dr. White was in the next elective case. I started the emergency, stabilized the patient, and observed the delivery, a twenty-two weeker—too small, with lungs too immature for life outside the womb. I squeezed the patient's hand, even though she was asleep. We were a sisterhood now. Sisters in the loss of a child.

We didn't put grieving parents next to happy ones in the recovery room. They needed privacy. I found the husband alone in our smallest labor room, the one with an anteroom of unknown purpose. He sat with a tiny bundle cradled in his arms, his shoulders heaving. I'd been there, staring at tiny, perfect features, wishing it were a dream, begging God to change his mind, to let my baby live. I knew firsthand that comfort was unattainable, but still I approached. "Your wife is awake. She'll be here soon. I'm so sorry for your loss."

Looking up, his face tortured, he said, "How am I going to tell her?" He lifted the bundle, then his shoulders crumpled.

I sat beside him, a hand on his back, but offered no platitudes, just sat, one experienced grieving soul consoling a newcomer. When he calmed, I said, "When I lost my baby, I thought I'd never see the sun again. And I didn't for some months. It's still hazy some days, but coming into focus."

He wiped his face and turned slightly toward me.

"When it happened," I said, "someone arranged for professional photos of the baby."

Wide-eyed, he shook his head.

"I know, I refused at first. It seemed so morbid. But now I cherish those photos. They're my only proof that Emily wasn't just a fantastic dream."

He looked away, toward the window.

"May I call the photographer? They're volunteers for just this situation, and they're wonderful."

He wiped his eyes. "Okay." Then with resolution. "Yes, please."

I patted his back and stood. "Is there anyone else I can call for you?"

"Our families are on their way. Thank you."

The door opened as the patient was wheeled in.

I left the room, unable to watch the reunion.

"Dr. Downey?" It came from behind, from the anteroom as I passed through. It was a uniformed security officer, tall, black, and with caterpillar eyebrows, the same one who couldn't help me with the badge photo. He wiped his eyes with a handkerchief.

"Are you okay?" I asked.

"Yes, ma'am. The missus and I, we lost a baby as well. It was nice what you said."

But Arnold the security guard had a reason for being there, and I had a guess what that was. Not yet. "I need to make this call. I'll be with you in a minute."

He waited patiently.

I told the nurse about the photo plan, checked one more time on the couple, and went to the labor board to sign out to Dr. White.

"Thanks for your help," she said.

"I'm glad I could be here." I said it a little too loudly. It wasn't Arnold's fault.

I reviewed all the patients on the labor board with her. It took longer than necessary, Dr. White asking dubious questions, and the nearby obstetricians joining in with comments that could wait. At long last there was nothing more to say. "Alright. Time for me to go. Call if you have any questions."

Dr. White stopped me and pulled me into a hug. "We're all behind you, Kate."

I closed my eyes. This was real. I was being forced from the hospital, my home away from home for more than a decade. I'd spent far more hours in these buildings than outside them.

"You're an amazing doctor and a wonderful person. Don't let them get you down," she said.

I thanked her and opened my eyes to find a swarm of doctors and nurses reaching out to touch my back, my arms. What did they know? Likely most were confused but reflexively sympathetic. It warmed my heart, but would this event put a nucleus of doubt in some minds? Even if exonerated . . . *when* exonerated, might some still question my skills? My decision making?

I wanted to say something, "I'll be back" or "See you soon," but would I? I settled on "Thanks," squared my shoulders, and led Arnold off the ward.

He waited outside the locker room while I changed, then escorted me to my office where I pulled papers from my desk.

"I'm sorry, Dr. Downey, I can't let you take any papers from here."

I turned, incredulous. I had talks to prepare, references to review, research paperwork. It was mostly available online, but I still liked to highlight on paper. "This is unrelated to—"

"I'm sorry, ma'am. I really am." And he looked sorry. He was just following orders. But it took effort for me not to lash out.

I walked to the door and flipped off the light, wondering when I would return. Should I take my photographs? That seemed too final. Just one. Our wedding photo. Not one of the formal altar shots we paid so much for, but a candid by a guest. My brown hair, longer then, done up with white flowers, and Greg, with his military buzz cut, looking all too gorgeous in his dress uniform. We gazed at each other, laughing at something, more of his face visible than mine, and the look in his eyes—love, adoration; in it I saw optimism for a future stolen away.

I wondered if I should resign. I could go to another institution where they supported faculty against false claims. But we would have to move. Jacksonville had the nearest academic medical center but without a medical school. It was near Greg. But our home; he was still there. His clothes hung in the closet.

No. I wouldn't cave, couldn't let Walker win. As I exited the hospital, cold rain interrupted my train of thought—so fitting.

"I'm sorry you had to do this," I said, turning toward Arnold, but he was on the phone.

"He'll have to say that himself . . . I will not . . . She saved that woman's life . . . Dr. Downey?" He held out his phone, his eyes narrowed in anger.

I took the phone. "This is Kate Downey."

"Dr. Downey? This is Nancy in the chief of staff's office."

"It's okay, Nancy. Let Dr. Walker know Arnold has done his job. I am out of the hospital and leaving campus as we speak."

"I know, but—" She was silent for a moment. "Never mind, Dr. Downey, I'm sorry to bother you."

A voice in the background, then the foreground.

"I told you to leave." It was Dr. Walker. "If we get sued over that dead baby, you're on your own."

The line disconnected.

"Wow," I whispered.

Arnold shook his head. "He's way out of line, Dr. Downey. You were kind to that family. I'll tell 'em."

I gave him a small smile, the largest I could muster.

"You take care of yourself now, Dr. Downey." He pulled something from his pocket and slipped it into my hand, furtively it seemed to me. "Camera memory wasn't wiped." I clutched the folded paper as I watched him return through the glass doors into a place I was no longer welcome.

Straightening, I headed to the parking garage, opening the note as soon as I reached the cover of my car. My breath caught when I saw the image, a scan of Brad Jernigan's photo ID. The photo was small, and I didn't recognize him, but the image was clear, and recent. Arnold had come through.

I had the afternoon off. Shadow would be pleased. I would focus on him; he would never leave me to the wolves.

CHAPTER THIRTY

IN MY CAR, away from prying eyes, Greg stared at me from the photo. What would he say now? "Focus on what you can change." Or was that Dad? Maybe both, it was good advice. I couldn't change Walker's decision, and probably it was the right one if I was being fair. I hated being fair. Meanwhile, BJ was out there killing people. Two birds with one stone. Stop BJ and prove my innocence. Pity party, over.

On the way back to Christian's, I stopped by to check on my house and wasn't surprised to find him there. He introduced me to a clean-cut young man from a security company. Not my security company. But then, I'd disabled the alarms for Aunt Irm's sake. She couldn't figure it out and kept setting it off, then couldn't remember the password. The sliding glass door had been replaced, and the house cleaned to spotless. I learned to operate the new system. Simpler than the old one. Perhaps Aunt Irm could handle it.

I thanked him and insisted he substitute my credit card for Christian's. Though I tried to ignore it, Christian's scowl filled my peripheral vision.

"Thank you for getting the house in order," I told Christian. "You really went above and beyond. I'll run by and pick up Aunt Irm in a little while, if that's okay."

"No rush." He glanced at his watch. "What are you doing out so early?"

"I am officially on a leave of absence." A quivering chin belied my fake cheer.

His eyes scanned my face and my facade. Too close. I feigned interest in the new security pad.

"What happened?"

"It seems the Board of Medicine is interested in accusations of malpractice made by one Dr. Scott Barton, the father of the medical student who blames me for his troubles. And the chief of staff does not wish for a physician under investigation to continue to practice at his hospital." That was harder to get out than I'd expected.

"I'm sorry, Kate."

I stepped away from the panel, away from Christian. "You know what? It's for the best. Now I can focus on catching BJ."

"We."

"What?"

"*We* can focus on catching BJ."

"Yes, of course." I gave a thin, grim smile. "Can we get a biopsy of Mr. Sanderson's tonsils?"

"Unfortunately, no. Both he and his wife were already cremated, to facilitate transport to California."

"You are kidding me. It's only been a couple of days." Would the roadblocks never end? "Okay, then Mr. Brighton."

"He's been discharged from the hospital."

"Perfect." I went to the computer in my home office and printed out a hospital release-of-information form. "Now I have an excuse to stop by, so I can review his readmission records."

Then I remembered the photo in my pocket. I placed the image on the scanner, then emailed it to Christian, explaining its provenance.

"That's great," he said as he ignored his ringing phone. "Let's go."

I set the alarm and locked the door. The rain had stopped.

His phone rang again before we reached the car. He groaned, but answered on speaker. "What's up, Mike?" But he didn't sound like he cared.

"Christian, what's taking you so long? Mom needs her prescription."

"I'll get it on the way home."

"She needs it now."

"I have a few more things to do. If she needs it now, you'll have to get it."

"I can't leave her here alone, and I'm not going to load her into the car, either."

"Aren't Gabriella and Irm there?"

"Dammit, Christian, can't you just do this for Mom, for once?"

"I'll take care of it." He clicked off. "Sorry you had to hear that."

"He sounds stressed. I'll run out to the Brighton place, then go by and pick up Aunt Irm. Maybe it'll help if we get out of his way."

"You were threatened, Kate."

"Yes, but now I have a security system to rival Fort Knox. We'll be fine. More than fine, since Aunt Irm will probably set it off accidentally a dozen times in the next few days."

He chuckled. "We can go by the Brightons' tomorrow."

My expression told him otherwise. He'd said it the night before— I didn't like being taken care of. Not anymore. If you depend on someone, there's too much to lose.

"Okay," he said in a tone that said the opposite, "I'll see you at the house in a little while."

We each drove away, me toward the Brighton residence northwest of town, him in the opposite direction.

Steven Wood, my pharmacology friend, called. "The investigator who worked on delayed release drugs was Dr. Elias Dunn at Ohio

University. According to my PI, it ended badly and Dr. Dunn's retired now, down in The Villages."

That was only a hundred miles away.

"Can you get me an introduction? I'd like to ask him a few questions."

"I don't even know the guy."

I waited.

"I suppose I could ask my PI to call. What am I supposed to tell him?"

"That I need to ask him some questions about the work he used to do. He's an expert on delayed-onset drugs, right?"

His loud breath sounded like static. "I guess."

"I'm not on call this weekend if it's possible to go see him tomorrow or Sunday."

"I can ask." He sounded uncertain.

"Thanks, Steven. I promise I'll fill you in when I can."

If not for GPS, I never would have found the Brightons' home down a network of partially paved and dirt roads, into the beautiful countryside of north central Florida.

I passed few vehicles, mostly trucks and SUVs that dwarfed my little Accord and kicked up enough dust to give it a good coating. At the end of a dirt track, a chain-link fence surrounded a small wood home in need of repair. Its peeling paint was once dark blue, faded by years in the relentless Florida sun. A formerly red, late-model truck sat in the side yard.

From inside the home, a dog's bark announced my approach, but no one answered my knock. The dog whined, but the sound weakened as I stood there. Giving up already?

I thought about calling their number, but had no cell signal. I peered through the grimy front windows into a small family room. The television was on, and I thought I could make out a form on the couch, with a head on the armrest. I banged harder. The dog didn't respond. My neck prickled and my heart started thudding again.

The front door wouldn't budge so I jogged around back. The door to the kitchen was half glass. It, too, was locked. An old-fashioned corded phone hung from the wall. I tried not to think about what I was doing, picked up a fist-sized rock from the neglected yard, and smashed it through the back-door's window. Reaching through, I unlocked the doorknob and the dead bolt. More shattered glass. Hopefully the dog would steer clear of the shards, but no dog appeared to greet or attack the intruder.

"Hello?" I yelled. "Anyone home?" I smelled coffee. Not freshly made, but not burned, either. I hurried through the kitchen and smelled something else. The scene at the Sandersons' flashed through my mind, minus the flowers.

Fox News played on the television, the sound muted. I recognized Mr. Brighton upright in the chair, his head lolling to one side. Mrs. Brighton lay slumped on the sofa, as if she'd fallen asleep watching television, wearing bright red lipstick.

I pressed fingers to her neck, no pulse, and cool to the touch. I moved to her husband. Same. I felt light-headed myself. This couldn't be happening. Not again. I ran back to the kitchen and called 911, gave the address, then returned to the family room. The dog lay motionless by the front door. He had a weak pulse. Or did he? My hands tingled. Was I hyperventilating? Having another panic attack? I went back to Mrs. Brighton, then looked at her husband, and wiped a finger across his cherry-red lips. Not lipstick.

My brain felt muddled, but cherry-red lips rang a bell, a loud and dangerous bell. Carbon monoxide. I unlocked the front door and pushed it open, pulling the dog out after me. I went back for Mrs.

Brighton, but stumbled on the threshold. With tremendous effort I fought to pull myself onto hands and knees. "Kate," Greg said in my head, "you cannot save her. Get out."

I obeyed, crawling back. As I rolled down the porch stairs, blackness descended.

CHAPTER THIRTY-ONE

I HEARD MY name, first at a distance, then closer and clearer, and more desperate. A hand held mine. Fingers caressed my forehead, brushing my hair back. Greg. He was here. I squeezed his hand.

"Oh, thank God," he said, his voice muffled. Shouts and movement all around, but it didn't matter. Greg was home. I felt a hot tear drip from the corner of my eye. It was wiped gently away. I'd missed him. Soft lips kissed my forehead. My eyes refused to open. I lifted a heavy arm to pull him close.

"Rest, you need the oxygen." He sounded so far away.

Cool air blew in my face. I smelled plastic and smoke. Another kiss on my forehead, so soft. Greg. I forced my eyes open. Brown eyes gazed into mine. Warm brown eyes full of love, but with gold flecks that shouldn't be there. Not Greg. I pulled away. Why couldn't I think?

"Kate, it's okay. You're safe."

An old house. A dog. Shadow? Red lips. "Carbon monoxide," I said, but couldn't hear myself speak. "The dog needs oxygen."

"He's going to the vet. Don't worry." He squeezed my hand, a hand he shouldn't be holding. He wasn't my husband.

I tried to pull away, but darkness closed in again.

When next I woke, Joe Layton sat next to me in a submarine. No, not a submarine, the dive chamber at the hospital.

"Hey, sleepyhead," he said. "Going to join me?"

I blinked to clear my vision. Greg wasn't here. Greg was gone.

"You couldn't stand to be away, huh?"

I tried to swallow; my mouth was too dry.

"Quite the triumphant return." He held a cup and slipped a straw between my lips. The cold water tasted incredible.

"You're going to be okay. We're at three atmospheres, displacing that carbon monoxide at breakneck speed. How do you feel?"

"Muzzy."

He cocked his head. "Is that muddled and fuzzy?"

I shrugged.

"Neologism is not a known side effect of carbon monoxide poisoning. Maybe I can publish a case report. I'll make you a coauthor."

"How much longer?"

He looked at his watch. "We start ascending in ten minutes. That'll take half an hour. Plenty of time for you to tell me what the hell is going on."

I considered how much to say, but darkness descended again before I could decide.

When I opened my eyes, Joe was maneuvering the stretcher from the dive chamber. He smiled down at me. "That's one way to keep from telling me your secrets."

"Sorry."

He wheeled me down the hall, a nurse guiding the foot of the stretcher toward the intensive care unit.

"Is this really necessary?" I said.

"Let's check your levels again, then we'll talk." He helped me transfer from stretcher to ICU bed.

"Thanks for sitting with me, Joe."

"You're very welcome. I'll be back."

Once the nurse had me attached to monitors, Aunt Irm appeared at my side. She hugged me, tear stains on her cheeks.

"I'm okay," I reassured her.

Christian followed, his forehead full of unfamiliar creases. Too much concern. He grasped my hand in his, warm and caressing. "You sure you're okay?"

"Yes, fine." I pulled my hand away, ostensibly to adjust the nasal cannula. "The Brightons?" I asked.

Christian shook his head. "Lieutenant Garner would like to ask you some questions. Do you feel up to it?"

I nodded and he stepped away. The nurse brought a chair for Aunt Irm, but she continued to hover.

Christian returned with Garner.

"That was too close for comfort," Garner said.

"It took me longer to figure out than it should have," I said.

"The Brightons were already gone. The ME puts time of death at least half an hour before you arrived."

I nodded. "But the dog? He barked."

"Must have been in a different room," Garner said.

"He's at the vet," Christian said.

They should have let the dog into the dive chamber with me. If it were Shadow, and I were conscious, I would have insisted.

"Walk me through it," Garner said.

I told him about my arrival, the barking dog who stopped, my impression that someone was on the couch, breaking into the back window, finding the couple cold and pulseless, recognizing the cherry-red lips, and pushing the dog outside. I left out the part about hearing Greg.

Throughout, Aunt Irm squeezed my hand, the pressure varying with the danger.

"So what happened?" I asked. "It couldn't have been an accident."

"No," Garner said. "The heating system shows evidence of tampering. It appears they were killed with carbon monoxide, then a fire was set to hide the evidence of tampering."

"Arson?" I said.

Garner nodded. "But your call allowed rescue to arrive in time. You didn't smell smoke?"

"No, just stale coffee." I closed my eyes, trying to remember, and trying to get my head around the close call. The house had burned in the moments after I crawled out. Greg saved my life even as his faded. Did he exist on some other plane? Purgatory maybe? A plane I'd briefly entered? The kiss on my forehead. Could I go back there?

"We need the records from North Central," Christian said. Christian. Not Greg. It had been Christian. My irrational dream vaporized.

"Already working on it," Garner said.

Soon after, Christian walked him out, and Dr. Layton returned with my lab results. Aunt Irm hugged him.

"I see you've met," I said.

"Oh yes, your wonderful aunt. She has promised me German pancakes." He turned his bright smile on her, then grew more serious. "Your carbon monoxide levels are coming down. You'll be able to go home in the morning."

My own smile crumpled. "I can wear oxygen at home."

"Not happening. Sorry, Kate. If you were anyone else, tomorrow would be out of the question, too."

I opened my mouth to argue, but when he lowered his chin and shot me his not-in-a-million-years look, I didn't bother. I'd seen that look when the program director tried to reduce the complement of residents scheduled in the ICU. It didn't happen. And I wouldn't be going home.

A passing anesthesia resident glanced at us, then did a double take. In an instant, his face took on emotions ranging from disbelief, to surprise, to pity. Was the pity for the condition of my health or my career?

"Please, Joe," I said in an urgent whisper. "I can't be here." Anesthesia ran the ICU and staffed it with residents I worked with every day.

With a grim smile, he agreed. "I'll get you a private room."

After he left, Aunt Irm said, "Something is going on, kindchen. Something you haven't told me."

"Later," I said. "When we're alone."

Christian returned, followed soon after by the nurse, who said, "If you will give us a minute, I'll get her ready for transport."

Christian and Aunt Irm stepped from the tiny glass-walled space, and the nurse pulled the curtain. She handed me a set of scrubs. "Dr. Layton thought you might prefer these."

I could kiss Joe. "Thank you." The thought of traveling the halls in a hospital gown nearly convinced me to stay put.

She helped me change, disconnecting the monitors and my IV. She left the catheter in, but disconnected it from fluids. I really could go home, but Joe had been so kind, I wouldn't fight him.

A knock on the glass. "Wheelchair's here."

"It's not often our ICU patients leave in a wheelchair. You're an overachiever."

If she only knew. "Thank you for taking care of me and for protecting my privacy."

"You're very welcome. You're registered under Ms. Smith, by the way."

"Creative."

The transporter wouldn't let Christian push the wheelchair. I prayed we wouldn't cross paths with anyone I knew, but after so many years in the hospital, that was an impossibility. Liz, a nurse from Labor and Delivery, joined us in the elevator on the third floor.

"I'm fine," I said in answer to her open-mouthed stare. "Just a little accident." She exited on the sixth floor, while we continued upward. It occurred to me I didn't know our destination. I hated being out of control.

We arrived at the last room on the ninth floor, the one on the end of the hall, like on a cruise ship, the VIP suite with double the space of the standard cabin.

"Welcome, Ms. Smith," the floor nurse greeted me at the door and insisted on helping me into the bed. She attached the nasal cannula to the oxygen source and checked my vital signs, oriented me to the nurse call button and the staff listed on the whiteboard by the door, then left us alone.

"How are you? Are you tired?" Aunt Irm asked.

"No, I feel good."

That might have been the wrong answer, as she immediately launched into cross-examination mode. "Then tell me what is going on."

A small smile creased my lips. "I went to check on Mr. Brighton—"

"I know about that. What about here? Where you work? You are uncomfortable here amongst coworkers and friends?"

Ah, I really should have said I was tired.

"The Board of Medicine is investigating a complaint against me, so the chief of staff put me on leave."

"Who is your chief of staff?" Christian asked, typing on his phone. I told him.

"Tom Walker is a past member of the Board of Medicine. He just rotated off last year."

"He pushed them to do this to you?" Aunt Irm said.

"Why would he do that?" I asked. It gained him nothing to have a faculty member who wasn't generating clinical revenue.

"Good question," Christian said. He looked at me expectantly, as if I had information. "Luke said a leave of absence is overkill for a Board investigation."

"You told Luke?" Of course he did. Why would I think the investigation would remain a shameful secret?

"I'm sorry," he said quickly. "But the whole thing is—" he glanced at Aunt Irm—"crap. You've done nothing wrong."

"I'm no longer sure that's enough." Not against people with power. We worked in a meritocracy only so long as you flew below the power-broker's radar.

"What does this Dr. Walker have against you? He does not treat you fairly."

I gave my aunt a small smile. "Not everything bad that happens to me is someone else's fault. But I love you for thinking it is."

Joe came by to check on me before he left for the day. I thanked him for all he'd done and told him I'd be leaving in the morning. He cocked an eyebrow, then rolled his eyes. "Patients these days. Ten minutes on Google and they think they know best."

I grinned.

"We'll see what your levels look like in the morning."

If I had to borrow Aunt Irm's blood for the test, I was going home.

"Doctor," Aunt Irm said. "I wonder if I might trouble you to show me where to find a decent cup of coffee."

I said, "I can tell you," at the same time Christian said, "I'll get it."

But Joe offered his arm to escort her. "I'm headed that way. Anyone else?" Christian and I both declined. Joe winked at me as I shook my head. Crazy aunt.

Once they left, Christian said, "So, are you going to finish the story about Walker?"

I groaned. "Do I have to?" I hated to even think about the situation, much less say it out loud. Besides Walker and my chair, only the people directly involved knew what I'd done.

"Yes. I'm beginning to think it might be relevant."

Not likely, but suddenly I wanted to share my shame. "Last year, I made a medication error. The case was an organ harvest. Coordination in those cases is everything; kidneys can keep for days, but livers, hearts, and lungs have to be transplanted right away. So the teams at the receiving hospitals have to be ready—patient in-house, anesthesia and surgical teams alerted."

"I'm sorry, but why does an organ harvest need anesthesia? Isn't the donor already dead?"

"Brain dead, yes, but they still have to have a heartbeat or the organs aren't useful. Our job is to keep the heart beating and the organs perfused until the last possible second. It can be challenging, and we were losing him before the recipient team was ready to take the heart. In my effort to stabilize him, I gave the wrong dose of epinephrine. It's double diluted, but I grabbed the wrong syringe and gave ten times more than I intended."

The scene still haunted me, his pulse suddenly racing, much too fast. The blood pressure over three hundred, much too high. The receiving cardiac surgeon yelling, swearing at me, demanding my name, threatening my job. His dark eyes piercing through my heart, my confidence.

"Go on," Christian said. Aunt Irm and Joe returned, so I sped through the rest of the story.

"The heart couldn't be transplanted. After the case, the chief of staff informed me the intended recipient died, and the receiving surgeon refused to work with our hospital unless definitive measures were taken to ensure we wouldn't mess up again. He said he could have fired me, but instead put me on probation. All my anesthetic records are subject to review, and I can be terminated without due process for one year."

I finally met Christian's eyes—they were troubled. Two horizontal furrows ran between them. "I'm not sure that's legal."

"My chair didn't think so either. He offered to fight it, but I chose not to. I'd screwed up in a huge way and cost someone his life. It was a small price to pay."

"That's bullshit," Joe said. "You didn't kill anyone. The recipient got a heart the next day. Walker was pissed because the man made a huge donation to be split between the donor and recipient hospitals."

I stared at Joe.

"The donor was my patient," Joe said. "I told the coordinator he wasn't a good candidate, but they came up anyway."

"The recipient lived?"

Joe nodded. "You probably saved his life. That heart wouldn't have lasted a year."

He couldn't know that, but Aunt Irm squeezed my arm with pride in her eyes, and a weight lifted from my conscience.

"If it had been any other harvest, nothing would have happened. I can't believe he made up this probation shit."

In a way, Joe's ignorance was comforting. I'd assumed everyone knew I was on probation and presumed the worst. Because of it, James Worrell decided not to have me present my error to the department at our weekly patient safety conference. He feared if my colleagues learned it resulted in probation, they would be reticent to admit their own errors.

"Walker is an ass," Joe said. "Totally focused on becoming CFO when Richards retires next year." His phone rang. He glanced at it. "I have to take this. I'll see you in the morning."

"Thanks, Joe."

"That doctor is a nice man," Aunt Irm said when the door had closed. She proceeded to fill us in on his life since childhood in Lebanon. As she droned on, her voice began to fade. I tried to focus, but the room dimmed. It had been a really long day.

CHAPTER THIRTY-TWO

I WOKE IN semi-darkness. It took a moment to remember where I was, and why. I heard regular, deep breathing to my left. Aunt Irm must have stayed the night. I closed my eyes. Noise is a constant in a hospital, but my room at the end of the hall was somewhat quieter, far from the bustling nurses station. When I rolled to my right side, something pulled my arm. My IV had been reconnected. In the dim light, fluid dripped steadily from the bag into the chamber.

I started to drift off, then my eyes flew open. The IV was dripping free, without a pump to control the rate. We did that only in the operating room under continuous observation. I pressed my nurse call button and clamped the tubing. "I need my nurse in here, now," I said to the clerk who answered the intercom.

Aunt Irm sat up. "What is it? What's happened?"

"Did you see anyone come in here? When was this IV reattached?"

"It was not when I went to sleep. I do not recall . . . wait, yes, a nurse came in. He was very quiet and careful."

"He?"

She blinked several times. "Yes, but it was dark."

"How can I help you, Ms. Smith?" My nurse was an older woman, black, competent.

"Is this who came in?" I asked my aunt.

"No, it was a man."

"Did Dr. Layton order my fluids restarted?"

"Not that I'm aware of." The nurse turned to the computer. With a tap on the keyboard, the light from its monitor illuminated the area. The bag was saline, without a label of additives.

Aunt Irm handed me her phone. I didn't need to ask who she'd called.

"I'm on my way," Christian said. "What happened?"

"Maybe nothing. I'm probably overreacting."

"Aunt Irm said someone started your IV."

"There is no order here," the nurse said.

I pulled the phone away. "Thanks. Can you get a clamp for the bag? I need to save it."

She nodded uncertainly and pulled out her own phone.

"I knew I shouldn't have left," Christian said over the phone. "I'll be there soon."

I handed the phone back to Aunt Irm, feeling dazed. Caused by something in the IV? Aftereffects of the carbon monoxide? Or was I going crazy?

The charge nurse came in first, and I repeated my concerns. Lieutenant Garner beat Christian to my bedside, as did Dr. Layton. "They didn't need to get you up," I said to Joe.

He did a quick neuro exam, listened to my heart and lungs, checked my vital signs. "Any symptoms?"

"No."

"Could it have been a mistake?" Garner asked. "Wrong room?"

"Not a chance," Joe said. "That setup violates every protocol, no label, no pump, and there's no male nurse on this ward tonight. Now tell me what's going on."

I glanced uncomfortably at the nurses.

"I'll take it from here," Joe said as he ushered them toward the door.

He'd been so wonderful, staying with me in the chamber, coming in late at night. He deserved an answer. "I'm looking into the deaths of several patients, and someone isn't happy about it."

His eyes flicked to Christian. "Dr. O'Donnell?"

I nodded. "And Mr. Greyson from the ICU, and several others. Someone broke into my house as a threat a few days ago."

"The carbon monoxide?"

"Mr. Brighton was another target. My guess is his wife changed her mind and saved him, only to be killed along with him."

"Changed her mind?"

"We think these are mercy killings for hire."

"Relieving families of caring for tiresome dotards," Aunt Irm added with disgust.

"You're shitting me," Joe said. He paced. The room shrank as he strode back and forth. The rest of us remained silent. "How?" he asked.

"We haven't quite worked that out yet, but I think it involves a delayed-onset non-depolarizing muscle relaxant."

Garner examined the IV bag. He held it, in a clear plastic evidence bag, near the only bright light in the room.

Joe gestured toward it and raised his eyebrows at me.

"Yeah, he may have tampered with it, though it wouldn't be delayed onset given IV."

"May I?" he asked, and reached for the bag. He held it upright. "Nearly full. Good thing you woke when you did."

A whimper escaped Aunt Irm. I squeezed her hand. "I'm fine."

"We'll get it tested," Garner said.

"I need to get out of here," I said, feeling suddenly confined and vulnerable.

"You're not going anywhere until we know what's in this IV," Joe said, handing it back to Garner.

I hung my head. He was right. I again surveyed my body—headache, but that had been there, nothing else.

"I'd like to stay," Christian said. "If it's okay with you ladies."

Aunt Irm said, "Oh, thank you. I will feel much better with you here."

God help me, so would I.

CHAPTER THIRTY-THREE

WITH AN OFFICER stationed outside the door, Aunt Irm on the second bed, and Christian on the couch, I slept surprisingly well. The poor nurse had a heck of time getting through the gauntlet to check my vitals. By the time Joe wrote the order the next morning, I was in a wheelchair headed down the hall, Officer Melrose in tow.

Aunt Irm drove me in her car. Mine had made it as far as the hospital, driven by some officer or other. We would pick it up another day.

Unable to convince us to stay with him, Christian promised to bring Shadow home right away.

I showered and dressed in real people clothes, then obeyed Aunt Irm's order to sit on the couch while she made soup.

She also insisted on answering the door and was nearly bowled over by an out-of-control Shadow. He circled her, then ran to me, leaping onto the couch and flopping across my lap, rolling and wagging and licking. Heaven for both of us. I checked his paws. They appeared healed. Dogs were amazing.

"Did you see Garner's email? He said he sent you the records from North Central." When I moved to get up, Christian said, "Where's your laptop? Although you don't really have a lap at the moment."

"I'll make do." I kissed Shadow's head and accepted the laptop from Christian. He sat in the nearby recliner, with Luke on the phone. Irm brought a colander of green beans to her seat and continued snapping off the ends as she listened in. Lieutenant Garner had emailed a PDF of Mr. Brighton's records. From what I could glean, his wife stated he seemed weak and needed to be admitted. Initial notes discounted her concerns and even tried to send him home, but she refused. I tried to picture mousy Mrs. Brighton demanding anything. But then, she'd most likely hired Brad to kill her husband, then changed her mind and saved him. Mousy on the outside only.

She and her husband sat in the ER waiting room until Mr. Brighton became too weak to sit upright. The staff brought him back into a room and, soon after, intubated him and put him on a ventilator. He underwent a brain scan, which was negative for stroke, and tests for various drugs and poisons, which came back negative as well. Even the opioids he'd received during the operation were gone from his system.

Hours later, according to the notes, he simply woke up, back at his neurologic baseline. They kept him another night, but finally discharged him with a presumptive diagnosis of a transient ischemic attack, a mini-stroke that resolves quickly.

His reprieve from death was also transient, I thought. Killed just hours later in his own home.

"Try this on," Christian said. "BJ found out about the admission to North Central and couldn't leave a survivor."

"Or someone who violated his contract," Luke added.

"So he killed them both," Christian said.

"And planned to char the bodies in case there was any evidence left," Luke said.

"That's sick," I said.

"You have a better explanation?" Luke asked.

I wanted to suggest an accident, but didn't bother. It was far from a better explanation. The heating system had been tampered with. Not an accident.

We caught Luke up on the other information, then disconnected. Aunt Irm took her beans back to the kitchen.

"Listen, I don't mean to be presumptuous, but I'm happy to crash on your couch until this is all over."

I shook my head, but before I could say a definitive no, he continued, "I'd feel better knowing you're both safe . . . all three of you." He patted Shadow and avoided making eye contact. As if unseen reluctance turned it to acceptance.

"We're fine, really. Sleep in your own bed."

He looked around, uncomfortably. "It was our pleasure to have you at the house."

"Your mom doesn't need guests right now," I said. "And we have round-the-clock guards, thanks to you." A police car was parked outside.

His half-hearted smile made my own heart ache.

"Have you heard anything about the Brightons' dog?" I asked.

"Still on oxygen when I called an hour ago, but they expect him to recover, and one of the grandkids wants to adopt him."

"Thank you." An awkward silence followed, the first I could remember between us.

I pulled back as he reached a hand toward me, but it was only to pat Shadow's head. "What's going on? Why so much resistance?" There was such pain in his eyes. He'd lost so much, and now I was adding to it.

Aunt Irm banged pans in the kitchen, pretending not to eavesdrop.

I pressed back against the couch and looked at him. "At the Brightons', I thought you were Greg." *I nearly kissed you.* "You've been so kind, and I've . . ." Should I tell him I'd come to depend on him? To care about him too much? No. "I don't want to mislead you. I love my husband."

"I get it, Kate. Don't worry about me. You and Aunt Irm are like family."

I searched for the lie in his beautiful eyes but found none. "Okay."

He stood to leave, uncertain and uncomfortable.

"Thank you, Christian," I said.

Aunt Irm walked him to the door. "Say goodbye to your mother for me."

When she returned, I asked, "You met his mother?"

"I did. She's a lovely woman."

"So you don't think she killed her husband after all?"

"I don't know, but if she did, it was not to free herself like Martina did with Max."

Aunt Irm returned to the kitchen while I checked my email. Steven Wood had come through. Dr. Elias Dunn would meet me in the morning at his home in The Villages, before his ten-a.m. tee time. Except Dr. Layton ordered me not to drive, and Aunt Irm had plans with Carmel.

Before I could overthink it, I texted Christian.

He replied almost immediately: Happy to chauffeur.

CHAPTER THIRTY-FOUR

CHRISTIAN ARRIVED AT seven thirty the next morning for the hour and a half trip south to The Villages. My fears of awkward conversation were unfounded as we immediately fell into amiable banter, about our alma mater's prodigious athletic history, about his career and mine, about growing up on a farm and in a university town.

It seemed too soon that the GPS announced our exit and helped navigate the endless winding roads of the retirement community to Dr. Dunn's home, directly on the golf course. His golf cart, loaded with clubs, sat in a miniature garage adjacent to the full-size two-car garage. I half-expected to see another, even smaller, structure, extending off the end, for the poodle, maybe.

We walked the short sidewalk to the raised front patio, similar to the Sandersons' home, except this one had manicured bushes and flowers blooming from boxes on the railing. Dr. Dunn answered my knock. Mid-sixties I guessed, with thinning gray hair and a thickening body, in light blue golf pants with a pink polo shirt. He offered his right hand, pale to the wrist, and covered my hand with the tan left one.

He led us through to the patio overlooking a fairway, where his wife stood, pouring lemonade.

"I didn't mean for you to go to so much trouble," I said.

"It's no trouble," Mrs. Dunn said.

I took a sip of the lemonade, then a gulp. Delicious. Then took one of the homemade oatmeal cookies on offer.

We wasted little time on pleasantries. "I understand you have questions about timed-release medications," Dr. Dunn said.

"Yes. I'm interested in how someone could give a single injection, but have the drug's onset delayed about thirty-six hours."

"Interesting. Nothing for the first thirty-six hours?"

"Right."

"That seems an odd requirement."

I had nothing to say to that, so I waited.

"Much depends on characteristics of the drug, of course—metabolism, etcetera, but also how long it must remain active, therapeutic window, and so on."

"For now, assume it needs to release all the drug into the bloodstream after the time frame. That's it."

His eyebrows came together and I feared he would request more details.

"I'm told you had a graduate student working on something similar?" I said.

"Much more complex, actually, but the initial onset was immediate. We received a grant to administer a depot of drug that maintained therapeutic levels over an extended period of time. Our approach was to encapsulate the drug in a number of coatings with differing delay characteristics, so a single injection could suffice for a week, replacing daily or even twice-daily injections."

"What kind of drugs were you trying to administer?"

"I can't name the companies, but they were in fertility and blood coagulation management. Not that it matters anymore. We failed to complete the work." Eyes downcast, his gravelly voice had gained additional weight.

Mrs. Dunn patted his knee. "It's the only grant Elias didn't complete on time."

"I didn't complete it at all."

"Can you tell us what happened?" I asked.

"My student made progress with the coatings, but then the depot site became a problem. The blood flow to intramuscular sites varied too much. If the experimental animal exercised, drug levels bounced all over. His last update reported preliminary experiments with other injection sites. Then he disappeared."

I waited for him to continue; his wife didn't.

"It's a sad story, really," she said.

Dr. Dunn made a sound, not one of agreement.

She ignored him. "Elias took Brian as an MD/PhD student."

"Brian?" I said.

"Yes, Brian Jacobs."

BJ. Gooseflesh rose on my arms. Christian pressed his knee into mine.

"Such a pleasant young man. I used to have all Elias' students over for dinner at the beginning of each semester, and he's the only one who ever volunteered to help clean up."

"He might have started out that way," Dr. Dunn said.

"Poor Brian had a lot on his plate," his wife countered. "His mother had Alzheimer's disease, and he helped take care of her. Elias was able to take him on early, so he could do his lab work first and have more time to help with his mom, before the MD courses."

Dr. Dunn grunted. "Biggest mistake of my career."

"It was the right thing to do, at the time, but when Brian's dad died unexpectedly, he became his mom's primary caregiver and things became more difficult."

Seemingly annoyed at his wife's diplomacy, Dr. Dunn said, "It was ridiculous. He would come in late afternoon, looking like hell, then work all night."

"He had someone sleep at the house with her," his wife added.

"He should have taken a leave of absence or made other arrangements. Our children wouldn't neglect their responsibilities like that."

Mrs. Dunn rolled her eyes. "You're right, they wouldn't."

To us, she said, "Brian was too proud to accept help, at least from me. He missed the last two dinners. Soon after, I saw in the paper that his mom died. I took over a casserole, but the house was empty. He'd already moved away."

"No forwarding address," Dr. Dunn grumbled. "He took the research notebooks, which belong to my lab." His wife patted his hand.

"It was a long time ago," she said.

"Not to me, it wasn't." Anger flared in his eyes. "The funding agency pulled out, of course. But I returned every last dollar of that grant." He banged an index finger on the small table with each word.

"Could I possibly read his last reports?" I asked.

Head cocked in clear wariness, he said, "Those are work product of the funding companies. Confidential."

"Even though the project is over?" I asked.

"Forever."

I needed to see that report. "I'll sign a nondisclosure agreement. I'm not looking to steal the research ideas."

"Why *are* you interested?" he asked.

Options raced through my head: trying to save lives, solve a mystery, catch a killer. I settled on, "I'm concerned Brian may be in some trouble, and it may be related to that work."

The couple's expressions were a study in contrast. Maternal concern versus paternal disappointment. Mrs. Dunn said, "That poor young man has had enough sadness in his life." Dr. Dunn stared at me, then Christian, for several long moments. We held his gaze. His wife broke the stalemate. "Oh, let them read it, Elias. What harm can it do?"

He stood and went inside. Leaving us, or retrieving a file, I couldn't tell.

"Would you happen to have a picture of him, of Brian?" Christian asked Mrs. Dunn.

Then it was her turn to stare, but only briefly. She stood. "I'll go look. We have some old departmental photos in the den."

Dr. Dunn returned with a folder. "I can't give you a copy, but you can read it here."

"Thank you, sir." I opened the folder to a single-page summary.

"His reports got shorter and shorter. That's the last one."

I skimmed rapidly, afraid he'd change his mind. Christian leaned toward me, our heads nearly touching. The report reiterated what Dr. Dunn had said, that blood flow to muscle was too variable, as was skin with its temperature dependence. It listed possible sites with more consistent blood flow, including cardiac muscle, the diaphragm, bone, nasal mucosa, and lymphatic tissue, none of which seemed commercially viable to me.

I handed the folder to Christian. "I'm sorry to have brought up bad memories. You had a remarkable career." Probably too obvious, but a change of subject was in order.

"Brian Jacobs was my one blemish. A brilliant kid, but I should have seen him breaking down. In hindsight, I noticed his report quality declining, less attention to detail, probably some spurious data. If I had caught it in time . . ."

"Regrets are not useful," I whispered. Christian heard and gave me a look.

Mrs. Dunn returned with an old three-ring-binder-style photo album opened to a departmental photo from at least ten years earlier. Of the dozen people arranged in two rows, I recognized Dr.

Dunn in the center back, with more hair and less of everything else. Mrs. Dunn pointed to a small bearded man at the left end of the front row, set off a bit from the group. I studied the image. A bit below average height, maybe, though he slouched. His face was in shadow and covered by a thick mustache and beard. No way to compare the photo with the Brad Jernigan I'd met in the OR or his ID badge.

"May I take a picture of this?" Christian said, gesturing to the photo.

Both Dunns shrugged.

I checked my watch. "We need to let you get to your tee time. Thank you for your help."

"Let me package up some cookies for the road," Mrs. Dunn said, bustling into the house with the still-full plate.

Dr. Dunn stood, glanced after his wife, and said in a conspiratorial voice, "If Brian's in trouble, don't try too hard to help him."

I smiled. "I promise."

CHAPTER THIRTY-FIVE

I SPENT MOST of the drive searching the internet on my phone and identified a house in Cleveland owned by Brian Jacobs. At last things were coming together. I searched for flights to Ohio. "There's one this afternoon at three with seats available."

"Check Tuesday. I have to be in Miami tomorrow for a client meeting."

"I think I can fly to Cleveland myself."

I could tell he wanted to argue, but thought better of it.

Christian had emailed the departmental photo of Brian Jacobs to me. I opened it and zoomed on the hairy face. The thick moustache and beard obscured his mouth and chin, but the eyes . . . maybe. "Wow, tough to tell if this is the same guy as in the ID photo. It's tiny, and furry."

"Yeah, not the best, but I have a friend who does age progression work. I sent him the ID photo and that one. He's going to take a look at it."

"You have a lot of friends in useful places."

"That I do." He smiled. "Fraternities aren't all about partying."

I raised a skeptical brow.

"Okay, maybe they are, but once we get it out of our systems, we can become contributing members of the community."

* * *

Aunt Irm insisted on traveling to Ohio with me while Christian took Shadow to his mother's home to play with Riley overnight.

"I promise we'll go for a long run when I get back," I told Shadow, rubbing his ears.

Aunt Irm drove to the airport while I updated her on our morning visit to Dr. Dunn. Nothing concrete, but I became more convinced of BJ's guilt as I reviewed the story. "The house is still in his name. An older woman answered the phone, so we'll start there."

"You talked to her?"

"Not really. I told her I had the wrong number and hung up."

Aunt Irm frowned at behavior she considered juvenile.

"I didn't expect anyone to answer."

"I hope you have more to say when we arrive at her home."

"Good point."

The flight arrived on time, despite snow flurries. We took a car service to Brian Jacobs' address in Cleveland's Old Brooklyn area. The small Tudor-style home was red brick with white window casings and a single dormer window. More than an inch of snow coated the short sidewalk. I gripped Aunt Irm's arm as we made slow, careful progress to the front door. Both of us shivered in our inadequate coats. My breath clouded before me as I pressed the doorbell. The peephole darkened. "Who is it?" an older woman called out in a singsong voice.

"Sorry to bother you. We're looking for Brian Jacobs," I said.

The dead bolt clicked and the door swung open revealing a woman who couldn't be related to a serial killer. Her mostly gray hair hung softly around a face with kind gray eyes.

"Brian doesn't live here right now. I'm sorry. But please, come in out of the snow." It occurred to me Aunt Irm's presence likely prompted the invitation.

Grateful, I stomped the snow from my shoes on the mat and entered the wonderfully warm home. A fire burned in a stone fireplace warming a seating area of two small sofas separated by a coffee table. "Your home is lovely."

"Oh, thank you, dear, but it's not really mine. It's Brian's, though he's never here. I'm Eleanor, Brian's aunt on his mother's side."

I offered my hand. "Kate, and this is my great-aunt Irm."

"I was just making a cup of cocoa; would you like some?"

Irm said, "That is wonderful, let me help you." As she followed down a narrow hallway, Irm raised her chin toward the photos on the mantel. More frames decorated nearly every flat surface in the small room. Prying into this woman's private life felt wrong, something the old me would never do. Good thing she was on holiday. Playing at amateur sleuth in a crime novel, I studied the photos. With no idea what to look for, I hoped some clue would jump out or maybe glow like in an old episode of *Psych*.

The array of subjects initially confused me, until I realized it was two different families, Eleanor's, with her husband and children, and her sister's with her husband and two sons, one of whom was BJ. I stared into the eyes of the child that would become a killer, trying to spot malevolence behind the clear blue, but the shy smiles in the mundane images gave away nothing.

More recent photos occupied a round corner table, including a framed image of BJ's older brother in a military uniform, American flag to his right. It sat atop a flag case with a bronze label: CORPORAL FIRST-CLASS BENJAMIN JACOBS 1980–2008. The brother was dead. I ran a fingertip over the engraved name.

Nearby was a photo that had to be BJ, at high school graduation, flanked by his parents, who had aged considerably from the photos on the mantel. By the time BJ graduated college, his parents' decline was unmistakable—dad in a wheelchair, mom with the absent stare and slack face of dementia. I snapped a picture of BJ's face in a graduation cap.

Too late, Irm's voice broke through and Eleanor found me examining the family display. "I'm sorry for your loss," I said. Same phrase twice in a week, and no less lame.

She touched the corner of the frame. "Ah, Benji," she said, a genuine fondness in her voice.

"Such a wonderful boy. He and my son were best friends growing up. You would have thought they were all brothers, the three of them." She selected a photo from the mantel, three shirtless boys, skinny arms draped around bony shoulders, with the carefree smiles of youth.

"They were fortunate to grow up together," Aunt Irm said, handing me a mug. I warmed my hands on the hot surface. A reminder why I could never again winter outside Florida.

Eleanor's wistful smile tugged at my heart.

"They were. Unfortunately, we moved away when the older boys were fifteen. I wonder if things might have been different had we stayed."

Aunt Irm and I exchanged a glance.

"Sorry, you didn't come here for that. How can I help you?"

She motioned us to sit on the sofas. Aunt Irm and I on one, Eleanor on the other. "I was hoping you could tell us how to find Brian," I said. "The cell number I have is no longer working."

"Oh goodness, how old is the number? He changes it so often."

I wanted to ask why, but thought better of it.

She answered anyway. "It keeps him one step ahead of the spam callers, he says."

"How do you contact him?" I asked.

"He calls to check on me regularly. I can ask him to call you."

"Thank you," Aunt Irm said. "But we need to see him right away. Do you know where he is?"

Her eyes turned wary. "May I ask what is so urgent?"

She'd pushed too hard.

"It's for some signatures," I said. "I can overnight the papers to him, if you have an address."

I took a sip of cocoa to hide my face. The lie might be believable, maybe.

Eleanor's face relaxed, as did my shoulders. "I don't know where he is. He travels all over for work, but he checks in at least once a week, so I can have him call you."

Crap. This visit wasn't such a good idea after all. But since we were here . . .

"I'm sorry I didn't get to know Brian better—he's obviously a very generous man."

"Oh, he is. He's been such a blessing to our family. When he decided to come home for medical school, I wondered if he might be better off avoiding the drama and attending somewhere else. Benji was back and helped me take care of their parents, but he wasn't well. On Brian's very first day of medical school, Benji . . ." she cleared her throat ". . . did it." She whispered the words, hiding them from view, but looked toward the small memorial. He killed himself. Brian's brother committed suicide. Wow.

"I couldn't handle them on my own," she continued, "so Brian switched around his school schedule so he could help out. It meant he couldn't start on rotations with his class, but he was willing to sacrifice for us.

"He was always the smartest of the three boys. After her husband died, Adelaide would go out to look for him. I couldn't keep up with her all day. Brian, God bless him, got permission to stay home all day and work at night. With all the locks switched to the inside, and the sleeping pills her doctor prescribed, I could handle her at night, but I started worrying about Brian's mental health. They say suicide runs in families."

She paused. I broke the silence. "My friend's father suffered from dementia as well. He recently passed."

Eleanor's expression returned to the present. "I'm sorry. I hope he passed peacefully, like Adelaide. She died in her sleep. Just didn't wake up one morning. It was for the best."

"May I ask, did she have surgery in the days leading up to her passing?"

"Surgery? No, her body was healthy as a horse." She shook her head sadly. "Between the two of us, we made one healthy person."

"I'm sorry," I said. "How did Brian take his mother's death?"

"He was sad, of course, but determined. He donated her brain to medical research. A woman doctor came to the house several times to run tests, and Adelaide had a brain scan every few months. Brian says the work that doctor is doing will cure Alzheimer's disease, and Adelaide helped." She looked off. "Hmm, they must have taken Adelaide's brain from the back, because she looked lovely at the viewing."

"She wasn't cremated?"

"Heavens no," she said. "We're Catholic."

CHAPTER THIRTY-SIX

I GAVE ELEANOR my number, but would be shocked if BJ called me. Finding the "researcher who would cure Alzheimer's" was more challenging than I expected. With funding in the hundreds of millions of dollars annually, Alzheimer's research was a popular career among neuroscientists.

Even at the hospital where BJ worked under Dr. Dunn, there were several possibilities. We checked into a hotel room with two queen beds near the medical center, ordered room service, and I skimmed faculty web pages, PubMed, LinkedIn, and Google while Aunt Irm updated Christian via speakerphone. The closest I could find were two faculty members with publications in the area of correlating specific behaviors in Alzheimer's with MRI findings. Though older papers had both authors' names, more recently they had published independently.

Aunt Irm looked over my shoulder as I showed her photos of the two researchers, both women.

"Should we ask Eleanor?" Aunt Irm asked.

"The person who visited the house was likely a grad student, rather than the primary investigator."

I sent the links to Christian. He said, "Who are you going to visit first? The senior professor or her protégé?"

Sandra Deacon, PhD, Professor of Neuroscience, had been at the university for more than twenty-five years, while Assistant Professor Gloria Zhu, PhD, had barely ten years' experience.

Dr. Deacon's CV listed three current grants, two NIH and one Alzheimer's Association. Her former post-doc listed no grants, but her online CV could have been out of date. "We'll just see who we can find, I guess."

Aunt Irm and I slept soundly, ate breakfast in the hotel restaurant, and took the hotel shuttle to the medical center, which turned out to be the easy part.

Inside, we stopped for directions three times before locating the lab the researchers shared on the third floor of a separate research building behind the main medical center.

The reception desk was empty. "Hello?" I said, leaning through a door into the lab proper. Black workbenches covered with expensive-looking equipment lined every wall, as well as a large island in the center. A door on the far side led onward. "Hello?" I said again, louder.

A door to our left opened, labeled "GRAD STUDENTS." From it emerged the quintessential grad student, a young man with a ponytail, wearing jeans and an Ohio State sweatshirt. "Can I help you?"

"I hope so. I'm Dr. Downey, here to see Dr. Deacon. Do you know where we might find her?"

"Uh, sure, she was in the lab earlier." Grad students aren't practiced gatekeepers. He led the way around the first space and through the far door. The second lab led to a third. The place was enormous. "Dr. Deacon, someone's here to see you."

A woman, at least ten years my senior, stared into a microscope, one hand operating the scope, the other jotting notes in a notebook. "Who is it?" she asked.

"Dr. Downey," I said before the grad student could answer. "From Florida. I've come to ask you about your research."

She sat up at this and eyed Aunt Irm and me with obvious doubt. "I don't recall an appointment."

"No, we were in town and your name came up. We have to fly back this evening, but hoped to borrow a moment of your time."

She huffed out a breath, sat back from the scope, but continued to clench her pencil, ready to start back any second.

"It's about Adelaide Jacobs," I said.

Her face showed nothing. "Who is that?"

"An Alzheimer's patient whose brain was donated to this lab." *Maybe.*

She held up her hands. "I had nothing to do with that. Check the signatures. Mine is not on the paperwork." She turned toward her scope.

"Was it Dr. Zhu's project?"

"It was not mine," she said, ending the brief conversation.

The grad student motioned us toward another door. "Dr. Zhu's office is over here."

"Sorry about that," I said.

He shrugged. "She and Dr. Zhu have a difference of opinion on that project." He knocked on a door labeled GLORIA ZHU, PH.D. An unintelligible response came from inside. He cracked the door open. "Someone's here to see you."

To my surprise, Aunt Irm pushed the door open and we slipped in.

"Roger, I—" Clearly annoyed at the interruption, Dr. Zhu stopped when we stood before her. Straight black hair shone around her face like a helmet. Distinctly Asian features combined with no accent suggested second-generation American.

"We're sorry to interrupt, Dr. Zhu," I said. "But we need to ask you some questions about Brian Jacobs."

Her eyes widened. Even in my limited ability to read expressions, that had to mean something.

"You collected his mother's brain after her death."

Now her eyes narrowed. "I have all the documentation for the donation."

"It's not about that. I need to get in touch with Brian."

"His aunt thought you might know how to reach him," Aunt Irm said. Dang, she was good.

"I have an email where I send progress reports, but that's it. He never replies."

"May I have that address?" I asked.

She moved to a nearby computer.

"So he continues to fund your work?" I guessed.

Again, with the eyes, shifting this time. "Not directly, but through his charity."

"The Schierling Society?" I asked.

"Schierling? No. Adelaide's Hope, named after his mother." Her computer scrolling paused. "Let me send him an email to contact you instead."

I provided my chairman's email and office phone number, thanked her, and left.

Returning through the maze of corridors, Aunt Irm said, "Was his mother the first victim?"

"I don't think so. He didn't have her cremated, and she didn't have surgery. Besides, he wasn't a CRNA yet. He went to school in Miami." I stopped walking. "You know who else trained in Miami? Ricken."

"Is not Christian in Miami right now? This he needs to know."

CHAPTER THIRTY-SEVEN

IT WAS NEARLY ten when we landed. My third day in a row without work. The longest I'd gone since Greg's injury nearly a year before. I routinely volunteered to work holidays so colleagues with families had time together. It was the least I could do after all the support offered me following Greg's accident and my miscarriage.

As soon as we landed, I switched on my phone. I had a missed call from Mark Wheaton, the anesthesiologist Jenn was working with in Atlanta, but it was too late to call him back. And several text messages: two from Jenn, one from Christian, and several from colleagues. I read them in the order received.

The first several were from colleagues interviewed by the Board of Medicine. All were supportive, often including colorful words for the investigators.

Reassuring to read, I continued to scroll.

Joe Layton wrote: Your IV contained pancuronium. BE SAFE.

I shuddered but chose not to tell Aunt Irm. The drug would have paralyzed all my muscles, just as it did all his other victims.

Christian wrote: Call me. Info on Ricken.

Aunt Irm nudged me, our turn to deplane. The airport in Newberry is mercifully small and we were in the car, talking with Christian over the car's Bluetooth, moments later.

"I gave Mike your flight information. He'll bring Shadow home in an hour."

"He doesn't have to do that. I can pick him up or meet your brother halfway."

"It's no problem. Are you ready to hear about good Dr. Ricken?"

"Tell us," Aunt Irm said loudly, head tilted toward the microphone over my head.

"He's well known down here. Lieutenant Garner put me in touch with a Detective Brown, who provided some interesting history.

"Ricken got into some trouble with gambling during college here at the University of Miami. Took a few years off and had a couple of minor drug arrests, but no convictions."

"No convictions?"

"None. Brown implied Ricken's father pulled some strings. Anyway, he left for medical school somewhere in the Caribbean, then came back to Miami for surgery residency. His dad died soon after."

"Big inheritance? Tell me daddy didn't let his son operate on him," I said.

"Ha. No, it was cancer, but he left Charles' money in a trust administered by the oldest son, Malcolm III."

"Smart man. That can't have made Charles happy."

"Probably not, but as luck would have it—"

"The older brother died."

"You're spoiling my story."

"Sorry."

"So his brother dies a couple of months later."

"No!"

Christian growled, really growled, low in his throat.

"Let him talk, kindchen," Aunt Irm said. "You drive."

"Thank you, Aunt Irm," Christian said.

I suppressed a laugh while he continued.

"Guess how he died."

"Is this rhetorical?" I asked.

"He died at home a couple of days after minor surgery."

Aunt Irm inhaled sharply.

"His wife refused an autopsy, his third wife I might add, and many years his junior. She stood to gain quite a lot of money from his death, which made her a person of interest, so they went ahead with the autopsy, but found nothing. He died of respiratory arrest."

"Don't they all," I said.

"Was BJ involved?" Aunt Irm asked. "Did he do the anesthesia?"

I pulled into the garage. "He did his CRNA training down there about the same time."

"I sent you scans of the anesthetic record, but it's illegible. Gives chicken scratch a whole new meaning."

"Our Kate will read it," Aunt Irm said.

"No pressure there," I said.

I switched the phone from car Bluetooth to speaker and we went straight to the computer to view the scan. Christian was right—blown up it resembled the claw prints of a mammoth chicken.

"This is BJ," Aunt Irm said, pointing to a messy signature block near the top. "The third line in the middle section."

Adjusting the zoom, I could imagine the 'J,' less so the 'B.' How much was wishful thinking? Christian agreed with me. Inconclusive.

"Is there no document listing the staff? Usually the nurse fills out a form."

"This is all they've provided so far. How about you guys?"

We moved to the kitchen and, while Aunt Irm made coffee, I caught Christian up on Brian's aunt, the suicide of his brother, loss of his parents, his generosity in caring for his mother, providing for his aunt, and funding Alzheimer's research. "But the foundation is called Adelaide's Hope, not Schierling."

"Adelaide's Hope." Christian's inflection sounded like he was writing the words as he spoke. "I'll look into it."

The doorbell rang. I checked the peephole. "Gotta go. Your brother's here with Shadow." I ended the call as I opened the door, prepared for Shadow's exuberant greeting, and still I nearly lost my balance. "Thanks for bringing him back. I'm sorry you made the trip. I could have picked him up."

"It's no problem," Mike O'Donnell said, stepping inside with Shadow's bowl and a rawhide bone.

"I hope he wasn't any trouble." I knelt, petting his head as his whole body waggled with his tail.

"None at all." He nodded past me to Aunt Irm. "I wonder if I could speak with you for a moment."

"Oh." I stood, suddenly wary. "Sure." I led him into the family room, surprised Aunt Irm had returned to the kitchen without offering coffee. "Can I get you anything?"

"No, this will only take a minute."

He didn't move to sit, so neither did I.

"It's about Christian," he said.

My whole body stiffened. Was I becoming a mama bear like my aunt? "I'm not comfortable talking about him in his absence."

"I love my brother, and I will protect him."

"From what?"

His look implied a who . . . me. "You know about his wife?"

I held his hostile gaze and nodded.

"What did he tell you?"

"They were killed by a drunk driver."

He shook his head, disappointed by an adolescent's excuse. "He still hasn't come to terms with it."

"He lost his wife and child," I said, poorly disguising my growing anger. "Of course he hasn't come to terms with it."

"He hasn't come to terms with his role in their deaths."

A sucker punch to the diaphragm would have shocked me less.

His face turned a condescending version of apologetic. "Christian was out that night, doing something he shouldn't have been doing."

The first thing to cross my mind was an affair, but that was impossible. Though my certainty defied logic.

"He was drunk, again. The bartender phoned Helen to pick him up."

"That doesn't make it his fault. Lots of people get drunk at bars."

"Married men? Whose wives are on bedrest after a miscarriage?"

I swallowed.

"She had taken pain medicine. She wasn't supposed to drive." His bitterness held a touch of desperation. "But rather than care for his wife, my little brother went out, forcing her to not only get up late at night and against doctor's orders, but to bundle her sleeping baby into the car in the middle of a storm."

I looked away, unsure what to think, but certain I wanted to hear no more.

"She wouldn't have been on the road that night if it weren't for Christian. If it weren't for him, they'd be alive."

Poor Christian. I could hear the "if onlys" across the years.

"We nearly lost him. He became inconsolable, self-destructive, so obsessed with the case that he lost his job. He not only sued the other driver, but he researched the guy's whereabouts before the accident and sued every bar he'd visited. He tried to sue the guy's friends for allowing him to drive. A half-dozen suits. He lost the house, his car, and then when he won a couple of the lawsuits, he donated all the money to Mothers against Drunk Driving."

That, I could see.

"It took years, but we finally got him back. Now it's starting again, this time with our father's death. We can't lose Christian to another obsession. Mom won't survive it. So please, let my father rest in peace."

I could only stare. Mike was trying to protect his brother. BJ had to be stopped, but Christian didn't have to be part of it.

Aunt Irm approached with uncharacteristic noise. "Mr. O'Donnell, thank you for watching Shadow. It was kind of you to bring him home." She moved past him to open the front door.

Stunned by her behavior, I barely got out a "good night" as he departed. Aunt Irm locked the door firmly behind him.

"What was that about?" I asked.

"I do not trust him."

She read my confusion.

"Perhaps the mother did not hire BJ," she said. "Perhaps it was the eldest son."

Something I hadn't considered. I wondered if Christian or Luke had.

"So you didn't want me to share our suspicions with him."

Aunt Irm gave a knowing nod.

I hugged her. Such a smart woman. Suspicious, but smart.

We said good night.

My phone buzzed a text as I brushed my teeth—from Christian. He would return by late afternoon.

I fought the warmth that thought evoked.

Another unread text followed, from Jenn, hours earlier: He's here.

CHAPTER THIRTY-EIGHT

BJ IN ATLANTA? At the same hospital as Jenn? What were the odds? I considered driving up immediately, but my rational side, however muted, prevailed. The text could have been misdirected—Jenn informing her attending that a patient had arrived at the operating suite. She would have called if it were really BJ. Maybe.

It was too late to call with her sister's baby in the house, and my text went unanswered.

I wanted to talk to someone. I wanted to talk to Greg. Christian was a viable, if too comfortable, substitute, but his brother's words echoed. Was Christian at risk in some way? Aunt Irm would immediately conclude Jenn referred to BJ and insist on calling . . . who? The police? Hospital security? We had proof of nothing. I would call Mark Wheaton in the morning.

Sleep came in short bursts filled with frustration dreams: difficulty making a phone call or finding transportation, or recognizing a key item of missing clothing mid-chase. The pre-seven a.m. call came as a relief, though I hadn't expected it to be Mark Wheaton.

He dispensed with a greeting. "Kate, what's up with this student you sent me?"

I sat up; Shadow groaned in protest. "Can you be more specific?"

"Jennifer Mason. First day here and she's caught stealing narcotics."

"What?" Surely, I'd misheard.

"Yes, she was caught leaving the hospital with two vials of fentanyl in her pocket last night."

"That has to be a mistake." I pictured her, boundless energy, terrific attitude, conscientiousness personified. Back in residency, Greg's brother had energy, and a good attitude, and seemed conscientious. He worked late without complaint, gave breaks, and found ways to be helpful. In the end, he'd been diverting drugs, taking a little from each patient, each break, then more, until he overdosed. Greg found him in the call room and saved his life but, in Adam's twisted mind, ruined his career.

Had I misread the signs in Jenn, too? I didn't want to believe it.

"Mark, I really don't think she's using. Maybe it was an accident. Can I talk to her?"

"That's up to the police."

"The police? She needs evaluation, not prosecution." Generally speaking, recovery networks handled clinician drug diversion rather than the legal system, at least the first offense.

"She was caught leaving the hospital with a controlled substance for God's sake."

I told myself his anger was understandable, that he didn't know Jenn like I did, that his conclusion was not completely unreasonable bordering on insane, in his position. But still I struggled to control my own anger.

"I didn't call the police," he conceded. "They met her at the door. I only found out when they called to confirm her status with our department."

"At the door?"

"Yeah, I don't have the details yet."

"Where is she now?"

"Northside station." He recited a number.

"Thank you. I promise you she's clean. This has to be a misunderstanding."

"I hope you're right, but you know we can be fooled." He knew Adam.

We were about to end the call when I remembered Jenn's text. "Mark, wait, do you have a locums CRNA who started within the last week? Five-eight guy, average build."

"You have a name?"

"His initials are BJ."

Silence.

"I know it sounds crazy, but can you check?"

"Yeah," he said grudgingly. "I'll call you back."

Calls and texts to Jenn went unanswered. No surprise, she wouldn't have her phone. Also, no surprise, the police station switchboard refused to provide any information, or allow me to speak to her. Again, I considered the trip, just a six-hour drive, but if they wouldn't tell me anything on the phone, they weren't likely to invite me in for a visit.

I tried to call Jenn's boyfriend, Todd, but it went straight to voice-mail. Before I could leave a message, my phone signaled a text from him: On rounds, will call soon.

Last, I called Dr. Duffy, Dean of Students. He concurred it had to be a mistake and asked to be kept updated.

Feeling unsettled, I dressed for a long overdue run with Shadow while Aunt Irm bustled in the kitchen. Aunt Irm. I had to tell her. Ugh.

"I'm sure it's some sort of misunderstanding," I said, trying to sound unconcerned, "but Jenn was arrested yesterday for taking narcotics out of the hospital in Atlanta."

Her hand flew to her chest. "For what?"

"Jenn had vials of fentanyl in her pocket."

Aunt Irm tilted her head to the right, reminding me of Shadow faced with unfamiliar sounds.

"It's like super-morphine. Somehow two vials made it into her pocket and she left the hospital with it. The police arrested her as she left."

"Who alerted them?"

"Mark didn't know, but Jenn sent me a text yesterday. All it said was, 'He's here.'"

"BJ," Aunt Irm gasped the initials. "She has found him. He does not want to be recognized. After he planted the drugs on poor Jenn, he set her up. He is a bad, bad man."

I sat down heavily at the table. It made more sense than an accident.

Shadow grabbed his leash from the hook by the door and brought it to me. Smart dog. Not a very patient dog, but smart.

"He planted the drugs to protect himself," Aunt Irm said. "To get her out of the way."

"Once she tests negative, she'll be released, though; so it doesn't help much."

"But they think she stole," she said.

"Yeah, but the hospital won't want the bad press, so it's unlikely they would take it any further."

"Still, she is discredited."

Worth considering. If Jenn made an accusation, it would be that of a potential drug abuser. Not a terribly strong argument, but possible.

My phone rang. "Todd, hi, what's going on with Jenn?"

Aunt Irm pressed her ear next to mine. I pressed the speaker button instead. "Aunt Irm's here, too."

"She's been transferred to Canton Treatment Center," Todd said.

"Have you spoken with her?" I asked.

"Not yet, but her sister said she's okay and denying everything. She has no idea where the vials came from."

"Okay," I said, not that I'd expected anything different.

"So when she tests negative they'll release her, right?" he said.

"I would think so."

Aunt Irm heard the hesitancy in my voice. Possession of the vials raised another possibility, but she was no more a seller than a user.

"Tell her to stay away from BJ," Aunt Irm said.

"What? Who's BJ? You mean Brad Jernigan?"

"Yes," I said. "It appears he uses other aliases with the same initials."

"He set her up," Aunt Irm said.

"We don't know that," I said, glaring at her. "Jenn sent me a text yesterday that said, 'He's here.' I don't know for sure what it means, or even if I was the intended recipient."

"It is too much for a coincidence," Aunt Irm said.

"She's right," Todd said.

Aunt Irm's look was the German equivalent of sticking out her tongue. "He planted the drugs and alerted the authorities to catch her."

My phone beeped an incoming call. "Todd, I'll call you right back, Mark Wheaton's calling."

I clicked over and took the phone off speaker, not willing to risk Aunt Irm's commentary.

"We have a Blake Johnson who started Saturday," he said.

My pulse bounded in my neck. "Description?"

"I haven't met him. What is this all about?"

"We had a locums here up until last Tuesday. I know this sounds crazy, but we're pretty sure he was killing people." A little more blunt than I'd planned, but whatever.

Mark sucked in a breath.

"It appears he does something in the OR that causes them to die at home a day or so later. Have you had any deaths?"

"We're in Atlanta, of course we've had deaths."

I explained in more detail. "These might be mercy killings. People with limited quality of life, undergoing minor, elective, outpatient procedures under general anesthesia. You need to look at all the cases he's been involved with, including ones where he only gave a break."

"Then what? Call the patients and see if they're still alive?"

"Yes, and if they are, you should bring them in for monitoring until they're more than forty-eight hours post-op."

He was silent a long moment. "You're not kidding."

"No. I wish I were." I gave him another moment to absorb. "And if we're right, he may have set Jenn up. I think she recognized him."

"I'll have to take this to my chief of staff."

"Good luck with that." Which reminded me, I wondered how my chair's chat with Dr. Walker had gone. Walker hired BJ. Would he take responsibility? Somehow that seemed unlikely.

"Hang on," he said. A muffled exchange, as if he had a hand over the phone, then to me he said, "He's gone. Called this morning to say he had an out-of-town emergency."

"That's exactly what he did here."

Mark promised to investigate further, and I called Todd back, placing the phone on speaker for Irm's benefit. She returned to my side. "Mark says they did have a locums named Blake Johnson. He arrived Saturday and called this morning to say he wasn't returning."

"He set Jenn up, then ran away. Bastard," Todd said.

Aunt Irm had the opposite response. "Thank heaven, our Jenn is safe."

"I'd really like to talk to her," I said.

"Me, too," Todd said. "I'll let her know."

"How about her parents?"

"They just left for western Canada. Her sister is waiting to tell them."

Good idea, I thought, then I wondered how her dad would react. If his premature planning of her career was any indication, not well. We disconnected and I tied my shoes.

"That poor child, in a lockup with a bunch of addicts." Irm returned to the kitchen.

"You make it sound like prison. It's a decent place."

"How do you know this?"

"I know someone who completed their program a few years back. Once he finally admitted his problem, he said the place was okay."

"But he needed their services. Jenn is a prisoner."

I pictured a therapy session where Jenn obstinately denied having a problem. How frustrating that would be for both her and the counselor, unable to get her past Step One. The image of the exasperated clinician and a stone-faced Jenn made me smile.

Shadow's whine turned into a bark. I felt the same way.

CHAPTER THIRTY-NINE

SHADOW NEEDED EXERCISE, and I needed to think. Running cleared my mind, no focused thoughts, just random wandering, a sanity check. In life "before," Greg ran with me, matching his stride to mine, but not our musings. We ran silently, worlds apart, but together. I missed that.

Shadow led the way, but ran twice as far in his weaving search for the best smells.

Fifteen minutes later, at the perimeter sidewalk of Green Bug Park, Shadow pulled hard on the leash. I resisted, until I saw his target and knew Shadow's neck and my shoulder would never survive. The moment I unhooked his leash, Shadow sprinted the hundred yards to where his brother, Kodiak, sat obediently, tail wagging, a smile on his furry face. Randi, my best friend since undergrad, recognized the maniacal torpedo and waved, then released Kodiak with a gesture so the dogs could play. Show-off.

"I gave Shadow that same signal back on the sidewalk," I said.

"Of course you did."

We embraced.

"How are you?" I asked.

A hand went to her abdomen, outlining a small bump. A jealous pang pinched in the same, empty spot.

"Are you pregnant?" Robbie was not yet one, or I didn't think so. Had I missed a birthday?

"Just four months, but I'm already showing this time."

I hugged her again. "Congratulations."

"So that whole 'nursing makes you infertile' thing? It's crap."

"I see that. How are Craig and Robbie?"

"Craig's fine, and Robbie's cute as a bug, but a Velcro baby. He's going to have some adjusting to do."

"Well, judging from your dog parenting, I expect it will go fine."

She laughed. "Kodiak is way more predictable than Robbie."

After a pause to call the dogs closer, Shadow obeying only to follow his brother, Randi said, "How about you?"

"Fine. Everything's fine." Our lives, formerly parallel, no longer shared the same plane, or even the same three-dimensional space. Randi lived in a Beaver Cleaver world with an attorney husband, a beautiful baby, and a career she loved. Rather than keeping house in a dress and pearls, she taught middle school math, likely sans dress and pearls. Our puppy playdates were supposed to morph into baby playdates, then best buddies at school. We'd even joked about becoming in-laws someday. But that was "before."

"Have you talked to Adam lately?" Randi asked. The bridge of her nose creased, like the words inflicted pain. Hearing them definitely did.

"He and I are..." How to phrase it? He's trying to force me to kill my husband? "... at odds right now—about Greg." I looked past Randi to the park, where kids would soon be climbing, sliding, swinging. Without a care in the world.

"Sorry for the ambush. I called and Aunt Irm said you were out for a run. I took a guess where."

"Ambush? Is something wrong?"

"Craig got a call yesterday afternoon from another attorney. It's about Adam."

Randi's husband had been Adam's attorney during his many scrapes in years past. Was he still?

"Craig feels conflicted about sharing this, but he wanted to warn you."

My breath caught.

"Adam sold your mother-in-law's house."

I exhaled. "Oh, that. He wants to, but he needs my signature. I haven't had time to look at it yet." In fact, it had completely slipped my mind.

"No, he *sold* it."

"Oh, hmm, that's fine." I didn't care if he got around the signature problem. One less thing for me to worry about.

"He impersonated Greg, Kate. Adam pretended he was Greg and signed the papers."

A band constricted around my chest. "That's impossible."

"They look a lot alike. Same build, hair—all he'd need is colored contacts."

True. "But how could they not know about Greg?"

She shrugged. "I don't have any more details, but Craig's worried he could impersonate Greg in other ways."

"Other ways?"

"Your mortgage, credit cards, bank accounts—he could do a lot of damage."

Possibilities flashed through my mind, none pausing long enough for analysis. Would Adam really stoop that low? "I'll have to go through everything."

"Craig's happy to help. Just say the word and he can fix the mortgage. He can't do anything about your mother-in-law's house sale, but can refer you to someone else if you want to fight it."

"I'm not worried about that." I paused a beat, shocked, horrified even. "He really impersonated his own brain-dead brother? That's sick."

"Yeah, but not really a surprise, is it?"

"Kinda, yeah." I knew he was unreliable, manipulative, and self-absorbed, but impersonating my husband? That was above and beyond.

We were silent for several moments.

"I'm sorry I haven't returned your calls," I said. "It is great to see you."

Side by side, we wandered to the walkway, dogs following, leading, crossing our path. I watched the rutted gray concrete pass underfoot. "Adam's demanding I withdraw care for Greg."

Randi said nothing. She'd always been a good listener.

"He sent a certified letter from an attorney. Not Craig." The burning tingle began in my nose and spread to the back of my throat, tears fighting to surface. I refused them. "If there were a switch to turn off and he'd pass quickly and without pain, I might consider it. But there isn't. We'd have to starve him to death." Randi stopped walking. Tears streamed down her cheeks, which made me lose the fight against my own. She pulled me into another embrace, right there in the middle of the path. Several joggers gave us a wide berth, probably annoyed.

She broke the embrace. "I'm so sorry, Kate." After a long pause she added, "Do you have time for coffee?"

"I'd love to, but Aunt Irm made breakfast, and there are some things I have to take care of this morning. Rain check?"

"Sure," she said, wiping her cheeks.

"Thank Craig for the heads-up. I really appreciate it."

"I'm going to call you next week," Randi said. "We miss you." She signaled Kodiak, and he materialized at her side, sitting erect so she could attach his leash.

Shadow followed, nosing Kodiak, trying to start another wrestling match. Trouble dog.

"Look at your brother," I said to him; then to Randi, "How long would it take you to work your dog-whispering magic on Shadow?"

She raised a skeptical eyebrow. "I teach advanced and honors only, sorry."

"Hey." I covered Shadow's ears. "What happened to everyone is special?"

"Oh, he's special, all right." She leaned down to him. "You take care of your momma."

I clipped the lead back on, said goodbye to Randi and Kodiak, and started across the park to the trail on the far side. It had been resurfaced, now a tar black instead of the rutted gray concrete.

I stopped at a bench to tighten a loose shoelace, retied both shoes, then straightened, and hesitated. The spring leaves glowed fresh, wet green in the morning light. An almost unnatural shade, like an inexpertly colorized movie. It reminded me of an evening, on this very spot, not so many years ago. The evening Greg proposed.

He appeared there, on one knee, with such love in his eyes. I would give anything . . . But he would never recognize me, never caress my hand, never kiss my forehead in that way of his. He hadn't felt our baby move, but the look in his eyes during the ultrasound before his last deployment . . .

I rose from the bench and sprinted back toward home—my vision clouded by more than sweat. Shadow kept up, staying right at my side, no weaving or slowing.

CHAPTER FORTY

AFTER I SHOWERED and dressed, my stomach growled. Aunt Irm was on the phone, my phone. "Here she is, Christian." She pressed the speaker button and placed the phone on the table, gesturing me to sit.

"Good morning," I said.

"I hear there's news."

I glanced at my aunt as she placed an omelet in front of me, and the bottle of ketchup. I nodded my thanks. What to tell Christian? His brother's words gave me pause, "obsessed."

"Kate?"

"Your brother says you are becoming obsessed and is afraid of losing you," Aunt Irm said.

I stared at her, open-mouthed. She stared back, without remorse.

"Mike?" he asked.

"When he brought Shadow by last night," I said.

"He told you I became obsessed after Helen and Caroline died." He paused. "It's true, but this is different. You see that, right? Someone hired BJ to kill my father and he's still killing people. We have to stop him."

Aunt Irm nodded. Sometimes I envied her black-and-white view of the world.

"This is not guilt masquerading as obsession," he said.

Christian was right—this was different. "I believe you," I said, and I did, maybe not as completely as Aunt Irm, but I did.

"Tell me what's going on," he said.

I filled him in on Jenn, Aunt Irm adding the rest of the conspiracy theory. "But he left, so we're no closer to catching him," I finished.

"What about the patients he cared for yesterday?" Christian said.

"Mark Wheaton is working on that."

"I'll be back at three. Okay if I come by?"

My disloyal stomach fluttered.

"Of course, Christian, I'll make pierogis," Aunt Irm said.

*   *   *

Randi's words echoing in my ears, I called the credit union where Greg and I had all our accounts, including our mortgage. They had a notice from his physician on file and assured me they would not accept any transactions from him or from someone pretending to be him.

I tried to log in to the medical record system, but my hospital account had been blocked. I called James. "How did it go with Walker?"

"We've had better conversations."

I waited for more.

"He says you're covering for yourself, passing the blame to someone who can't defend himself."

"But I wasn't even involved in one of the cases."

"I'm just telling you what he said. The deaths ended when you were put on leave."

My face heated as I swallowed back an intense wave of nausea. "They ended when Brad left unexpectedly."

"He has a letter from Brad Jernigan stating that he left because you were committing malpractice and he didn't want to be a part of it."

Now, I was speechless. This wasn't happening.

"He demanded that I terminate you. I refused. He threatened to terminate me."

"No," I said.

"It's not right, Kate. I consulted the dean, and he agreed to give you due process."

I let out a breath, my head swimming from holding it too long. "Thank you." After a beat I said, "The CRNA went to Atlanta." I told him about Jenn. "Remember Mark Wheaton? He's looking into victims up there; in case you get a call from his chief of staff."

"He's more likely to call Walker. I'd love to hear that conversation."

"I wonder how he'll blame me for deaths up there."

He chuckled. "You holding up okay?"

"A little stir crazy. I have a grant due in a few weeks—"

"And you can't get to your files. I'll talk to IT, maybe we can find a workaround."

"I don't want you to get in any more trouble on my account."

"Don't worry about me. I'm sorry about your student, but I'm glad this guy is gone and you're both safe. I'm inclined to skip IT and force you to relax."

"That's not funny."

We disconnected, but before I could update Aunt Irm, my phone rang again. Jenn. I put it on speaker. "Jenn, are you okay?"

"Yes, I'm fine. Angry, but fine. You think Brad did this to me?"

"Aunt Irm here. Yes, he set you up."

"It makes sense. I left my jacket on a hook by the anesthesia office, so anyone could have put the vials in my pocket."

"And you're sure it's him you saw?" I asked.

"Pretty sure. I recognized his voice, and he used the same initials again, Blake Johnson."

"Yes, Dr. Wheaton told me. He called out this morning, BJ did."

"BJ, I like it. He left? I'm sorry."

"Why should you be sorry?" Aunt Irm said. "He is dangerous."

"If I hadn't said anything, he might not have run."

"You talked to him?" I asked.

After a noticeable hesitation, she said, "I told him he looked familiar and asked if he'd been at University recently."

I winced.

"I'm sorry," she said quickly.

"It's okay, Jenn. When are you coming back?"

"I'm not. Dr. Wheaton said since the charges were dropped and all the tests came back negative, I could keep working. I'm headed to the hospital now."

"Do you think that is wise?" asked Aunt Irm. "Shouldn't you take some time off? You have been through so much."

"I'm fine, Aunt Irm. Thanks for worrying about me, but I want to work."

"What if he has not left?" Aunt Irm asked.

"I'll be careful."

"I do not like this," Aunt Irm said after we'd hung up.

* * *

Over Shadow's boisterous greeting of Christian, I barely heard my phone ring. It was a grim Mark Wheaton. "We have a dead child."

I stepped out the back door. A child. The chill that swept through me was more than the weather.

"A twelve-year-old girl with profound developmental delay. She had an MRI Saturday morning to evaluate increased seizure activity. Her seizure meds were sub-therapeutic, but her helicopter mom insisted on the MRI anyway."

"On a Saturday?"

"Our health-care dollars at work. Of course, the MRI showed nothing."

"Did they put her to sleep for the scan?"

"Yes."

"Was she intubated?"

"Hang on." Computer keys clicked. "Yes, intubated."

"That's unusual, isn't it?" I asked. "Don't you normally do MRIs with just sedation or maybe an LMA?" The laryngeal mask airway helped a heavily sedated patient breathe on their own, but slid in easily without need for a metal laryngoscope. If BJ was injecting tonsils, he couldn't do it with an LMA.

"Normally. Maybe she had gastric reflux or something."

"Did she?"

More clicking and some mumbling. "No gastric reflux or heartburn. So yes, it's unusual to go all the way to intubation for an MRI, but not unheard of."

"So what happened after the procedure?"

"She was discharged home with her mother two hours after the scan with no complications. Apparently, she was found unresponsive by her father Monday morning. He called 911, and she was brought to the ER but never regained a pulse."

"What was the cause of death?"

"It says 'respiratory arrest,' but I don't think anyone really knows. The mom says she was fine the night before."

"Was there an autopsy?"

"The family declined. This kid was severely mentally retarded." As if that was justification.

"Sounds really familiar, Mark. So who provided the anesthesia?"

"The attending's been here for years, but the CRNA was your guy, Blake Johnson."

Gooseflesh rose on my arms.

"What about other cases?"

"I'm not even supposed to be talking to you. My chief of staff said he'd take care of it and told me to keep quiet."

"Tell him to call my chair rather than our chief of staff."

"I'm not telling him anything. He about bit my head off."

"Sorry about that."

"Yeah, not your fault."

"Thanks for taking Jenn back."

"I almost didn't." He was silent a long moment.

"But . . ." I prompted.

"But she seems terrific; this obviously wasn't her fault, and she made a compelling argument for return."

I could only imagine.

"We'll get her in some good cases."

I thanked him and disconnected but didn't go back inside right away. I stared into our small fenced yard, at the play of shadows on the garden so carefully tended by Aunt Irm. At long last, I went back through the sliding glass door. Christian and Aunt Irm looked at me expectantly. I joined them at the table. "Looks like he killed a child."

"No," Aunt Irm said. "BJ kills elderly folks, not children."

"She was severely handicapped."

"You think her parents . . . ?" Christian's eyes were round, pained.

I shrugged. "Her dad called EMS, so maybe not."

"Like Mrs. Brighton," he said.

Like Mrs. Brighton. "Oh my God, like Mrs. Brighton."

I called Mark Wheaton back to get the name of the child's family. He was surprisingly forthcoming.

Meanwhile, Christian called Lieutenant Garner. It helped to have powerful friends.

"Garner, we might have a problem. I'm here with Kate Downey and her aunt. It appears our suspect reappeared north of Atlanta."

"Brad Jernigan?"

"We think another of his clients changed their mind, like Mrs. Brighton," I said. "Or the parents weren't on the same page. Regardless, their handicapped child still died—"

"Child?" He sounded more disgusted than shocked.

"They called EMS, but it was too late. Maybe someone should check on them? Warn them?"

"Warn them that the person they hired to kill their child takes offense when they change their mind? They'd be safe in prison."

"I'll go up," I said. "It would be better coming from me. I want to check on Jenn anyway."

"No," Garner said. "I'm sorry, I was out of line. You should definitely not go up there. Let me see what I can do."

Reluctantly, I gave him the name and he promised to keep us informed.

Christian said, "Garner's little brother was severely handicapped." My anger softened. "He's a professional. He'll handle this right."

Over an early dinner, Aunt Irm asked, "Christian, what did you learn in South Florida?"

"Oh, I completely forgot. Brian Jacobs was the anesthetist for the operation on Ricken's big brother, Malcolm. He was a student CRNA at the same hospital. And guess who else was there at the same time."

"Dr. Ricken," Aunt Irm said.

"Right, his last year of residency." He took a sip of red wine. "Adelaide's Hope appears to be a legitimate nonprofit foundation. It doesn't seek public donations, but is well funded by anonymous donors."

"In ten-thousand-dollar increments?" I asked.

Christian smiled.

"Why doesn't the Schierling Society just fund it directly?"

He shrugged. "It does seem unnecessarily complicated. Paranoia?"

"Did you find Malcolm Ricken's widow?" Aunt Irm asked.

"Remarried and moved away. She hasn't returned my calls, and I don't expect I'll hear from her."

"I wonder if she and Ricken planned this together," I said. "I guess it doesn't really matter."

We fell silent. I was reminded of times when a major hurricane bore down on Florida. How everything had a pall over it. Nothing in particular had changed, but everything was about to.

CHAPTER FORTY-ONE

MARK WHEATON CALLED from Atlanta as Christian and I cleaned up after dinner. "Hi M—"

"Kate, we can't find Jennifer."

"What do you mean?"

Aunt Irm's head popped up, Christian's too.

"She's not answering her cell. She went to eat around four and no one's seen her since."

"Let me check with her boyfriend. I'll call you right back."

I called Todd. Thank heaven he answered.

"Have you talked to Jenn?"

"Not recently. She left me a message around four thirty, why?"

"Where was she?"

"What do you mean? She was at the hospital."

"Do you know where in the hospital?"

"She was about to do a preop. What's going on?"

"I don't know. I'm going to add Dr. Wheaton to this call."

"Mark, I have Jenn's boyfriend, Todd, on the line. He received a message from her around four thirty. She was on her way to do a preop."

"She said it was in radiology," Todd added. "But she looked lost."

"I'm sorry?" said Mark. "She *looked lost*?"

"It was a video message. She turned around a couple of times, looking for signs."

"In radiology? Hang on." I heard voices in the background; could have been from either phone. "We have no patients in radiology for procedures this afternoon."

"She said someone called while she was eating lunch," Todd said, sounding wary.

"I don't know who that could have been. It wasn't anyone here now."

A chill flashed through me. "Oh God," I whispered.

Hearing only my side of the conversation, Aunt Irm stood still, clenching and unclenching her apron, creating uncharacteristic wrinkles. Christian put an arm around her.

"Radiology?" asked Mark again.

"Yes," Todd said.

"Do you know where exactly she was?" asked Mark.

"She said the basement, I think."

"Radiology's on the ground floor. There's nothing in the basement."

"I still have the video," Todd said. "Maybe you'll recognize where it was shot."

Mark provided his email address as I walked, unseeing, to my home office, followed closely by Irm and Christian. "Jenn's missing," I said to them as I opened my email, unable to meet Aunt Irm's eyes.

I put the phone on speaker and clicked on the video. It was a shaky image of Jenn, smiling, talking, laughing. Though her face filled most of the screen, glimpses of her surroundings could be seen.

"That's not radiology," Mark said. "It is the basement. There wouldn't be any patients down there."

"Send someone down there to look for her," I said. I should have driven up there last night. *Dammit.*

The video ended on a frame of Jenn's lips pursed in a kiss.

"I'll call you back," Mark said.

"Todd, why don't you come over?" I said. "We can wait for news together."

"I still have work to do."

"I'll call your attending. You shouldn't be involved in patient care right now. I'll see you at my house in thirty minutes."

It took closer to an hour, but he arrived, dressed in scrubs and looking haunted. Irm sat him at the table with a plate. "Her parents are still in the air. They cut their trip to Canada short when she was arrested. Her sister is freaking out; she hasn't heard from her since this morning." He rubbed his face. "She should have just come home."

A knife twisted in my gut. I should have insisted. I should have asked Mark not to accept her back.

When the home phone rang, Aunt Irm jumped. Anything important would come through my cell. Only solicitors and Irm's friends called the landline. Moments later, she ended the call. "Carmel has the prayer chain going."

"Thanks." I walked over and gave her a long hug.

Todd brought his dish into the kitchen, untouched. "I'm sorry." He put the plate in the sink. "I can't eat. I need to do something. I need to be there."

Another thing we agreed on. My cell rang.

"Mark, did you find her?" All eyes were on me.

After a long pause, he said, "I'm afraid we did."

"What does that mean?" Concern deepened on all faces. "I'm going to put you on speaker—her boyfriend is here."

"I wish you wouldn't—"

"Sorry." I put the phone on the table.

"We found her in a storage closet."

Aunt Irm paled and rocked back on her heels. Christian grabbed her and helped her sit.

"She had self-administered a large vial of fentanyl."

Todd's face turned ashen.

"I'm sorry," Mark continued.

"You're sorry?" asked Todd. "Sorry about what? What do you mean? Is she okay?"

I leaned close and put an arm around Todd. No one could be okay hours after a large vial of IV fentanyl. Certainly not someone naïve to the drug. She would have lost consciousness and stopped breathing within minutes. I cleared my throat. "We'll be there as soon as we can."

Todd looked at me, tears streaming down his face. "What does he mean?"

Aunt Irm dropped her head in her hands. "Beautiful Jenn?"

I caught Christian's eye and nodded to Todd. He put a hand on the shoulder of the sobbing young man. I took my phone off speaker and moved into the office. "Tell me exactly what you found, Mark."

"I shouldn't have let her come back."

"Mark, stop. I am certain this is not what it looks like. Jenn was not using drugs."

"She was on the floor propped against the wall. The needle and syringe were still in her arm. A twenty-cc vial of fentanyl was next to her on the floor. It was an overdose, Kate, plain and simple. And it's my fault for making an exception and letting her come back."

"It's not your fault. And it's not plain and simple. I'm sorry I got you into this, but there has to be another explanation. Were there any other marks on her?"

"I really didn't look. The police are there now."

"Tell them about my suspicions. Tell them I think there's more to it. Make sure they do a thorough investigation."

"I'll tell them. You'll take care of notifying the family?"

"Yes, but I'm serious, Mark. Otherwise they might assume the obvious and miss something."

"I get it." But he didn't sound convinced.

"I'll be there in the morning."

BJ did this, I had no doubt. I wanted him, wanted to find this man who had killed my patients, ruined my career, and now killed Jenn. I strode from the office with a sense of purpose, and stopped short. Todd sobbed on the phone. Aunt Irm stood at the sink with her back to the room, her shoulders shaking.

Christian spoke quietly into his own phone, then disconnected. "We'll be there a little after six."

"We?" I looked into his eyes.

He took the last step toward me and pulled me into his arms. I resisted. "You don't have to be strong all the time," he whispered. I hesitated only a second, then wrapped my arms around him and rested my head on his broad chest. It did feel good. Not the comforting hug of Aunt Irm, but this protective, reassuring, I'll-take-care-of-it embrace.

Todd ended his call, and Christian and I separated.

"We're on the five a.m. flight," Christian said to him.

"Thanks. I'll pay you back."

Christian waved him off.

"I just can't believe . . ." His shuddering words brought tears to my eyes.

Aunt Irm took over, led him to the couch, and they sobbed together.

I began to shake, not a tremble, but a shake, like the ground beneath me was quaking. This was my fault, for involving Jenn in a murder investigation. What was I thinking? The guy was killing people, and now he'd killed a wonderful young woman whose life was only just beginning.

I felt Christian's arm around me as my legs turned to jelly. A chair materialized behind me. One hand on my shoulder, Christian updated Lieutenant Garner.

Then there was a long silence, everyone in their own thoughts, mine full of self-loathing and if-onlys.

Later, Todd and Christian left to pack. Aunt Irm and I sat together in stunned silence. Shadow curled next to me on the couch, his head in my lap, seeming to sense our tragic loss.

CHAPTER FORTY-TWO

KELLY, JENN'S SISTER, met us at the airport. Her parents were to arrive within the hour. Todd remained with the family while Christian rented a car. In less than an hour, we were at Canton General Hospital, seated at a large round conference table with Mark Wheaton and hospital-issue coffees all around. Always the same bitter flavor. I drank it only as a caffeine vehicle after my sleepless night.

Mark said, "Unfortunately, I have nothing new to report." He glanced at his watch. "But we have a meeting with the chief of staff in ten minutes."

"Where is Jenn's body?" I asked, trying to block out the image.

"Downstairs in the morgue—her sister identified her last night. The autopsy is going on now."

"I need to talk to the pathologist."

"I've already told him about your suspicions. He'll be thorough."

I opened my laptop and pulled up the video message from Todd. "Can you take us down here? Where it happened?"

"I can, but the area is cordoned off. It would be better to wait for the police. They'll be here with the pathologist once the autopsy is done."

Christian leaned close and replayed the video, then again.

"Look at her, Mark," I said. "Does she look like someone who's about to shoot up? Her drug tests were negative. She wasn't a user."

Mark said nothing and only glanced at the screen. The coffee sat uneasily on my empty stomach.

"Look at this," Christian said, pointing at my laptop screen. "Mark?"

He followed Christian's finger. The video was running. I'd seen it dozens of times by now. "Right . . . there!" He hit pause. "Damn, I can't catch the right frame. There's someone behind her."

I took over the keyboard, noted the time stamp of interest, 0:55, and opened the file in a video editing app. I skipped to 0:50 and turned the keyboard back over to Christian.

He bumped my knee under the table. "I should have asked earlier." He clicked through the video frame by frame. "There." Jenn's face filled most of the screen, but over her right shoulder was another face. It was a man, slightly taller than Jenn, looking right at her, menacingly, I thought, but then my objectivity might be questioned.

"It has to be him," I whispered.

Christian zoomed in on the face and emailed a screen shot. "Let's see what George can do with this. Maybe he can enhance it somehow."

Mark leaned back in his seat. "Who's George?"

"Christian's digital photo guru," I said. "Mark, have you found any other unexplained deaths?"

He raised an eyebrow at me. "You're kidding, right? I've been a little busy."

"Do you use Epic here?" Several medical record systems existed, but Epic had the largest market share.

"Yes." He sounded wary.

I emailed him a blank copy of Todd's spreadsheet and explained how to download the information from the OR database. He clicked along but didn't offer me his computer. "Hit Run," I said. "It'll take a few minutes." We passed those in silence, alerted by a ding from his computer.

"How many rows?" I asked. These were patients that had outpatient surgery under general anesthesia between Saturday and Monday.

"Thirty-two."

I explained how to filter the "Dead" column.

Mark's eyes rounded. Christian and I exchanged a look. "There are two, including the kid we knew about."

"Click on the obituary of the other person," I said.

"Oh crap, we're going to be late." Mark closed his laptop and stood. "Christian, you can stay here. If you want breakfast, the cafeteria is down one floor."

He hustled me to the elevator and pressed the button for the top floor. "I have to warn you, he's pissed, and not known for his diplomacy even when he's not."

"You would think diplomacy would be part of the job description," I said. "But that makes two out of two."

The massive office was paneled in light wood with large windows overlooking the front of the hospital. Everything seemed overdone. To the left, an enormous executive chair sat behind a wood desk the size of a tennis court. Diplomas and awards, in frames worthy of an art museum, were arrayed above a low bookshelf on a side wall. In front of the desk were two incongruously severe-looking hard-backed chairs.

Mark introduced me to Dr. Norton, a massive man befitting his office. I would have offered my hand, but the good doctor remained behind his desk, a barrier of distance. Familiar. He gestured to the plebe chairs and sat his generous backside into his own seat. No wonder the chair was so large.

"I'm sorry to meet you under such circumstances, sir." I sat on the edge of the seat, back straight. "How much do you already know?"

"What I know, Dr. Downey, is that your chief of staff vouched for a locums CRNA who you now claim may have committed murder in my hospital." His voice was low and gruff. "Do you have any idea what news of this could do to my hospital?" His beefy face reddened; sweat beaded on his forehead.

Does no one think about the victims? "Yes, sir, I am only too aware. I can't speak for Dr. Walker, but we only discovered the deaths in the last few days. I came here to try to prevent more."

"He's gone. Right, Dr. Wheaton?"

"Yes, sir." Mark nodded. "Yesterday."

"But some of his victims may not be dead yet." I explained the delayed onset of the injections. "We believe this man, we call him BJ, is performing a service for hire, which complicates calling the family."

Dr. Norton's eyes grew wide. "The child?" The reaction somewhat redeemed him in my eyes.

Mark took over. "She was severely mentally disabled. Maybe her parents were exhausted, or broke, or thought she was suffering."

With more confidence, I continued. "You need to bring in the remaining patients who fit the profile—debilitating illness, dementia, who underwent minor procedures, even if BJ wasn't scheduled to care for them."

Dr. Norton slumped in his chair but picked up his pen and started writing.

"Also," I said, "I need a tonsil biopsy of one of his victims."

Dr. Norton's head popped up from his notes.

"That's where we think he's injecting the drug for delayed release. We need proof."

He shook his head. "You didn't get it at University?"

"No. By the time we identified victims, they were cremated."

Dr. Norton grunted. "The little girl?" he asked Mark.

"Too late," he said.

Resigned now, Dr. Norton said only, "Okay. I'll take it from here." He didn't stand to escort us to the door. I could only hope he'd follow through.

Christian had brought bagels and cream cheese back from the cafeteria. "How did it go?" he asked.

"As well as could be expected," I said. "Better than Walker, that's for sure."

Christian's phone rang. "George, you're on speaker, what do you think?"

"Dude, were your ears burning? You sent me that picture like two seconds after I finished running the progression on the other ones. Were you testing us or something? 'Cuz if you were, we got an A+."

"I'm sorry, George, can you say that again, this time in grown-up speak? I'm here with a couple of doctors."

"Ah, gotcha." He adjusted his voice to sound pretentious, with a faintly British accent. Christian rolled his eyes. "The photo you just sent is an almost perfect match to the ID photo, and appears to be one Brian Jacobs, advanced ten years in age from the graduation photo you sent earlier." His voice returned to normal. "The group photo was crap, but it's probably the same guy. We were a bit less generous on the hair, but it's the same guy. You'll see. I'll send it now."

Christian opened the file as soon as it arrived in his inbox. I leaned in, supporting myself on the back of his chair. Mark rose to stand behind us. They were all the same person.

We were silent for a long moment. Mark returned to his seat and resumed working on the patient list. Christian emailed the photos to Luke. I stared uselessly into space, wishing for a different outcome.

Mark let out a low whistle. "The other patient who died after surgery on Saturday had Huntington's Chorea."

In response to Christian's questioning look, I said, "It's like a horrific combination of Alzheimer's and ALS." The description was as good as any and was consistent with our mercy killing hypothesis.

CHAPTER FORTY-THREE

Twenty minutes later, Jenn's father arrived with Todd. Dr. Mason was smaller than I'd imagined from Jenn's stories and looked much older, though yesterday he may have been ten years younger.

"Dr. Mason, I'm Kate Downey. I can't tell you how sorry I am about Jenn." I stepped forward, unsure whether a hug or handshake was the appropriate level of contact. The answer was neither. He looked deliberately past me to Christian and Mark.

"Who are you?" He stood ramrod straight, but with wet, tired eyes. I looked at Todd, crumpled, pale, and disheveled. He shrugged.

"Christian O'Donnell. I'm sorry for your loss, sir."

Dr. Mason merely shifted his penetrating stare to Mark.

"Mark Wheaton. I was your daughter's supervising faculty here." Having seen the man's reaction to me, both waited for him to make the first move toward a handshake. He didn't.

I embraced Todd briefly. "How are you holding up?" He shrugged again, staring at the floor. I whispered, "Did you tell the Masons about our suspicions? About Brad?"

He nodded but didn't meet my eyes.

The awkwardness was interrupted by the pathologist and two uniformed police officers introduced as Oscar and Juan. The more senior officer, Oscar, asked permission to record the proceedings as we all took seats around the table. Juan pulled out a spiral-bound notebook and pencil.

"There were no injuries other than the needle insertion site," the pathologist said. He looked at me. "Based on your concerns, I took samples from under her fingernails. I found a small amount of tissue, which has been sent for analysis. The tox screen is pending and includes tests for common drugs of addiction."

"Include chloral hydrate," I said. The medication was readily available in a hospital and frequently used to sedate children for brief procedures. "And other inhaled anesthetics. He had access to all of them."

"Done. If he used a commercial anesthetic, we will know."

"He, who?" asked Oscar.

My phone rang, I silenced it without looking at the screen.

With a projector attached to my laptop, Christian showed the frame from the video chat. "This man behind Jenn while she's talking on the phone." He showed the zoomed image. "We believe he may have had a role in her death."

There, larger than life, was Jenn's face, so vital, a wide smile on her face, eyes sparkling. Now she was a corpse in the morgue. I squeezed my eyes tightly shut and reminded myself to focus. We would catch Brad. We had to.

"They believe he killed her," Mark clarified.

I looked at him sharply, then at Dr. Mason and Todd. Christian replaced the image with the one from BJ's ID.

The pathologist pulled a plastic bag from his briefcase and poured the meager contents on the desk: a stethoscope, a badge with Jenn's photo, Listerine breath strips, and a small amount of cash. "There was no cell phone at the scene."

"No cell phone? She had just finished talking with Todd." I gestured to the screen. "If it's not there . . ." I didn't finish the thought, but in my mind, it proved murder. Someone had taken her phone. BJ. "Can we trace it?"

"Already tried; it's turned off," said Oscar.

"She had a white coat," Mark said and he made a call.

At Oscar's request, I started at the beginning and relayed the whole story. Dr. Mason had a right to know, so did Mark. No more secrets. "It began with a death that was inappropriately blamed on Jenn." I looked at Dr. Mason. He stared stonily straight ahead. "When a patient she knew, and two others of mine, died the same week, it troubled both of us. She called me last Wednesday, having done her own preliminary investigation. All told there were six similar, unexplained deaths that week."

"Six deaths?" asked a wide-eyed Oscar.

"Yes. I tried to look into them, but didn't get very far."

"Why in hell didn't you call the police?" demanded Dr. Mason. His glare burned into my guilt-ridden conscience.

I kept my voice level. "It wasn't as clear cut as it sounds now. It came together slowly. I followed the chain of command, but was told not to alert authorities outside of the hospital at that time." Though willing him to understand, a grieving father would not be so accommodating.

"Go on, Dr. Downey," said Oscar.

"The common denominators were a surgeon at University—"

"His name?" asked Juan, pencil poised over his notebook.

I looked uncomfortably at Christian.

He nodded encouragement.

"Charles Ricken," I said. "Not all the deaths involved him, but they did all involve this man." I pointed toward the image on the screen. "He's a temp who was at University for just that one week. He works under pseudonyms. We now think his real name is Brian Jacobs. He worked on drug design years ago, and I believe he came up with an injectable muscle relaxant that kills 24-48 hours later and is not detected by standard tests."

Dr. Mason's eyes enlarged fractionally.

A knock at the door forced a pause. Mark answered it and returned with a white coat, which he placed on the table next to the personal effects brought by the pathologist.

"On Monday, Jenn texted me with the words, 'He's here.'" I looked again at Dr. Mason or at least at his profile. "I believe he put the vials of fentanyl in her pocket."

"Which caused the stint in rehab?" asked Oscar.

"Yes," I said.

"And why would he do that?" continued Oscar.

"I think he was buying time and protecting himself," I said. "She confronted him, and he needed space. He quit the department early, claiming an out-of-town emergency." My voice trailed off. If only I'd considered the possibility he'd stayed. Aunt Irm considered it.

"There were also at least two patient deaths here since he arrived," Christian took over.

I forced my shoulders to relax. Christian had a knack for stepping in when I needed a breather.

"We don't know about the deaths here," Mark interrupted, giving me a warning look. "We just learned about them and need to investigate further. All of this remains conjecture for now."

"You're worried about your hospital." Dr. Mason stared at Mark with the eyes of a pit bull, starved and crazed. "My daughter lies dead in your morgue and you're more worried about your hospital's reputation than catching this monster?"

Mark stared at his hands. Todd tried to console Jenn's father, but the tirade wasn't over. He turned on me.

"And you. Involving my daughter in a murder investigation. She was a student. She worshiped you!" His voice cracked. "What kind of mentor encourages a student to put her life in danger?"

I felt Christian bristle and reached for his hand under the table, squeezing it once. I could handle this.

But it was Todd who came to my defense. "It wasn't like that. Jenn was trying to clear her own name, too."

"It's okay," I said quietly. "He's right. I should have stopped her."

"She wouldn't have listened to you," Todd said.

"I had hoped her leaving town would remove her from the situation. I never dreamed he would end up at the same hospital." I paused, briefly. "But I should have stopped her from returning yesterday."

"He said he'd left town," Mark said.

For several long moments, no one spoke. Christian squeezed my hand. I'd forgotten it was still with his and pulled away slowly.

Dr. Mason finally broke the silence. "So where is this bastard?" He glared at the police officers in turn. "What are you doing to find him?"

"Based on what you've told us, this is an interstate matter. We need to contact the FBI. I can't speak for them, but standard protocol would be to send out this photo and the aliases, and wait for a hit."

"Hospitals," I said, my voice unexpectedly gravelly. "Anesthesia departments specifically."

Juan smirked at me. "Yes, we'll check anesthesia departments for new anesthetists." Obvious, maybe, but I wasn't taking any chances. He looked back at Dr. Mason. "And if the fingernail scrapings give us any usable DNA, we'll search the database for a match."

Dr. Mason turned to the pathologist. This time his eyes held a father's grief, rather than rage. "She wasn't, um . . ."

"No, sir. She was not sexually assaulted."

He looked back at his hands, shoulders slightly less tense. "I want to see her," he said.

"Dr. Mason, you know—" Oscar said.

"It's okay," the pathologist interrupted.

"And I want to see where it happened," said Dr. Mason. His resolute voice brooked no argument.

"It's a crime scene, sir," Oscar said.

"We won't touch anything. I want to see where my daughter died." He stood.

"We need to wait here for the FBI," argued Oscar.

Mark stood, too. "I'll take them."

"Not without an officer, you won't," said Juan, standing.

As Mark led the way from the conference room, I hung back and slipped my hand into the pockets of Jenn's white coat. She was always writing notes. I was desperate for anything. From the chest pocket, I withdrew a folded slip of paper, put it into my own pocket, and hurried after the group to descend the same stairwell Jenn had likely taken.

When we reached the basement, I recognized the sparse background from the video, off-white walls interrupted by infrequent wood doors. The only signage consisted of tiny dark green rectangles by each door with the room number in white relief. Mark stopped at a doorway spanned by yellow police tape, with a baby-faced officer standing next to it, donned latex gloves and opened the door. Some of the black fingerprint dusting powder adhered to his glove. A week ago, I wouldn't have recognized the stuff.

We took turns leaning in the doorway to view the scene. I went last. The room was small, less than six feet on a side, with a large sink to the left, and to the right an open area, presumably for a wheeled cleaning cart. "He must have scoped out the area to know this closet wasn't in use," Christian whispered from close behind me.

I shivered looking at the stark floor. Had Jenn known what was happening? Did she look at that bare wall knowing it was the last thing she'd see?

Mark then led the way to the morgue. "I'll wait out here," Christian said as I followed Dr. Mason and Todd inside. The pathologist directed us to a steel table with a body covered in a clean white sheet. I positioned myself close to Dr. Mason, his face now frighteningly pale.

The pathologist folded the sheet down at neck level, revealing Jenn's beautiful, but colorless, face. Dr. Mason and Todd touched her, sobbing.

I pulled my eyes from the heartbreaking scene and watched the pathologist leave the room, giving the men a modicum of privacy. I stepped back as well. Near the door, syringes and needles were arrayed on top of a supply cart, and an idea struck me. If I considered long enough, I would certainly recognize it as terrible, so I didn't consider, and slipped the items into my pockets.

*   *   *

A selection of sandwiches had appeared during our absence from the conference room. I wasn't hungry but took one as an excuse to also place food in front of Todd. Neither of us ate. Around two o'clock, two dark-suited FBI agents joined us. The stereotypical dress reinforced my growing sense this was all a dream. A really bad dream. I'd give anything to wake up.

I repeated the story with little interruption.

"Do you have a motive?" asked one of the agents, the only one who seemed to talk.

Had this guy been listening? "She suspected him of killing people. He was protecting himself."

"Not for the student's attack, a motive for the alleged patient murders?"

He'd said *alleged*. Had I left something out? In my exhaustion, I looked pleadingly at Christian and he took over.

"We believe he's hired by individuals to end the suffering of a family member with an incurable condition and poor quality of life."

"That's giving him too much credit," I said, then realized he was referring more to the motive of the hiring party, like his mom. "Sorry."

Christian continued. "It appears he funnels the money paid by these families into an Alzheimer's charity. His mother suffered with the disease for many years, causing him to drop out of school."

"Is there a money trail we can follow?" asked the agent.

"We have identified an organization, the 'Schierling Society—'" he spelled it for the FBI scribe—"where family members send ten-thousand dollars before and after the deaths. Though we can't prove it yet, it appears the money is then transferred to Adelaide's Hope, a charity that funds Alzheimer's research."

"And how did you become involved in all this, Mr. O'Donnell?"

Christian blinked once but did not break eye contact. "My father was one of the victims."

CHAPTER FORTY-FOUR

IT WAS DARK by the time we finished. Dr. Mason and Todd left first, Todd offering an apologetic wave. Christian and I talked with Mark. "I really am sorry you got involved in all this. If I'd had any idea he and Jenn would cross paths here . . ."

"You couldn't have known," Mark said. "And who knows, it might have saved other patients' lives. Lives that may not be worth living, but who's counting."

His blunt assessment should have shocked me, but I was too tired, and driven, and I needed one more thing from him. "Mark, I know this comes completely from left field—" I tried to sound nonchalant, and it was a long shot—"but Jenn mentioned you guys use disposable laryngoscopes. Could I take one? It doesn't have to be clean."

He looked from me to Christian, clearly taken by surprise.

"We're thinking about getting them and I'd like to see one for myself."

"Uh, sure, I guess."

Moments later, plastic laryngoscope in hand, I walked with Christian through the dark parking lot to the rental car.

"Hungry?" he asked.

"Starved."

I pulled out the note I'd found in Jenn's pocket. It was a list of names, and I searched Google for each one. "I'm betting these are the names of patients BJ cared for. Now we just have to find out if anyone died and isn't cremated yet."

"Oh, is that all?" He pulled onto a major thoroughfare. "Steak okay?"

"Perfect."

The second name was it. Rose McGurn, an elderly widow, had died Tuesday night. The viewing was scheduled the following afternoon at Forest Meadows Funeral Home, followed by cremation and interment.

Christian stopped at a chain steakhouse, and I realized I'd eaten little all day. My stomach growled at the smell of rare steak. After ordering, we both checked our phones.

"We look like college kids on a date," he said.

I grinned but kept scrolling. Several texts from Aunt Irm. I replied but didn't call.

There were multiple missed calls but only one voicemail, from Glenda at Greg's nursing home. "Dr. Downey, Kate, I hate to leave this as a message, but we haven't been able to reach you, and Irm said you were traveling. Anyway, Dr. Kyber is the hospitalist today, and she needs to talk to you about Greg. Here she is." My face flushed and my heart began to race. I felt Christian's eyes on me but stared ahead at the basket of fresh rolls just delivered.

"Dr. Downey, this is Dr. Kyber. I'm taking care of your husband today." Her voice was low and husky. I pictured Kathleen Turner in a white coat. "He seems to be developing pneumonia. He spiked a fever and has consolidation in his right lower lobe. We cultured his sputum and started broad-spectrum antibiotics, but his breathing was labored and his oxygen saturation falling so I made the decision to cannulate his trach and put him on a ventilator." I rubbed my forehead with my free hand. "He's stabilized now." She apologized for the message, and tried to reassure me this was only a temporary setback.

"Sorry," I said. "I have to make a quick call."

I dialed the hospital and spoke to Greg's nurse. She confirmed that he was stable, but the fever had not yet broken.

"You okay?" Christian asked when I put the phone down.

"Yeah. Fine. Greg had a small setback, but they're taking care of it."

*   *   *

Forest Meadows Funeral Home was a low, single-story, gray stucco building with black shuttered windows and a wide portico in front. A hearse was parked in a small lot to the left of the building and a few cars on the opposite side. Approaching the door, I wiped at my rumpled khakis and teal sweater. "I don't exactly look the part of a mourner."

Christian held my elbow. "You look fine. We're celebrating life, not mourning death, remember?"

I eyed him. He'd been through this little more than a week ago for his father. "You okay with this?"

"We do what we have to do." Opening the door, he nudged me through ahead of him. From the small foyer, doors led off in three directions. A somber man in an equally somber black suit greeted us with an even more somber expression. The theme continued with the elevator music. On a placard to the left was a photo of an elderly African American gentleman: REST IN PEACE, BUDDY JACKSON.

The director looked uncertain. "Are you here for Mr. Jackson's memorial?"

I hesitated. This was so wrong. "No, sir, we're not. We're here about Mrs. McGurn. We can't make the viewing tomorrow and were anxious to pay our respects."

"I'm sorry, we can't open a casket—"

"No, no, we don't need it open." Christian steered the man slightly away from me and said quietly, "She just wants to be in her presence. I'm sorry to ask, but it's really important to her." He reached for his wallet. "I'd be happy to make a donation."

Should I look more solemn, or dazed, or what? What does someone who thinks they can commune with a corpse look like?

The director waved off Christian's money and led us into a room to the right, where a mahogany casket sat on a dais at the far end. A placard stood in front with a dated photo of a young woman—seventies by the hairstyle—and her name, Rose McGurn, stenciled below. I moved to the casket and placed my hand on the polished wood.

I'm so sorry, Mrs. McGurn, that I didn't get here sooner. That you had to die that way.

"At least it's finally over." The phrase popped into my mind. Maybe the "long illness" listed in the obituary caused pain she was grateful to leave behind. I tuned in to the conversation near the door. "Do you have any larger rooms?" Christian said. "I have a client..." The voices faded. Where was he going with that? Didn't matter.

Heart racing, I glanced around to confirm I was alone. God, was I really going to do this? I pushed up on the smaller portion of the casket's lid. It lifted without a sound. She lay there, white and still, her makeup not yet applied. I swallowed. At the head of the casket, I stepped up onto the dais and glanced at the closed door, my heart threatening to explode. Adjusting Mrs. McGurn's head, I maneuvered the laryngoscope into her mouth and lifted. Though the jaw was stiff, I had a good view of the tonsils. Left hand holding the laryngoscope, I placed the needle in the tonsil and pulled back forcefully on the plunger. A small splatter of red and white streaked the side of the syringe. I repeated the procedure several times on each tonsil, and could only hope I hit an area BJ had injected, and where residual drug remained. Sweat trickled down my back as Christian's voice grew louder.

I repositioned the head to neutral, closed the casket, leapt from the dais, and was returning the supplies to my bag when the door opened. I forced myself to move slowly back down the aisle, wiping my eyes for effect, and keeping my head down to hide my flushed cheeks. "Thank you," I said.

Christian thanked the director and accepted his business card, then opened the door for me.

"Get what you needed?" he asked as we strolled back to the car, just in case he was watching.

"I hope so." I buckled my seat belt and felt the bounding pulse in my neck begin to lessen. "I would be a terrible criminal. My heart rate is ridiculous."

"*Would be?*"

He grinned, but he was right. I was a criminal. Not a very accomplished one, but a criminal all the same.

"Kind of thrilling and terrifying at the same time, huh?"

I eyed him suspiciously. "Sounds like words of experience."

"I had my misguided youth like all guys."

"Hmmm, sounds like a story."

"Yes, but one for another time. Now it's time for sleep."

I debated finding dry ice for the samples, but the pathologist wouldn't be looking for cell structure, only presence of the drug. Cellular integrity didn't matter. Besides, it was a biopsy from a corpse. Weren't the cells already damaged?

Christian programmed his GPS and headed back toward the airport. He pulled into a Marriott, answering my questioning look with, "I booked it last night." He checked us into adjoining rooms.

When we reached my door, I said, "Thank you, Christian. I don't know what I would have done without you."

His eyes sparkled and held mine. If this were a different place, a different time, a different life . . . I stood frozen. He took a step back without breaking eye contact. "You are most definitely welcome, Dr. Downey. We make a good team." He smiled a crooked smile.

With force of effort, I looked away. "Next time, I'm the decoy and you can commit the felony."

Christian chuckled. "Not a chance."

CHAPTER FORTY-FIVE

WE MADE IT on the first flight home. I stared out the window as the lights of Atlanta's skyline shrank from view. If only I could turn back time. BJ had set Jenn up to get her out of the way. I should have insisted she stay out of the way.

"It's not your fault," Christian said. "Jenn was an adult. She chose to stay."

"I shouldn't have given her that choice. I know how dangerous he is. He kills people for money. She was too young and focused on her career to think clearly. That was my job." Tears threatened again.

Christian reached for my hand. "Regret is not useful," he said softly.

My heart skipped a beat. That was Greg's line, but a common enough phrase. "Words to live by?"

"After Helen and Caroline died, it became a bit of a mantra. If only I had refused to attend her sister's engagement party."

"It was an engagement party?"

He raised an eyebrow. "Why do you ask?"

"Your brother implied you were out somewhere you shouldn't be."

Christian twisted his body toward me, a challenge in a tiny seat in coach. "What did he tell you?"

If I were less sleep-deprived, I might have softened his brother's words. I didn't. "That you got drunk at a bar and your wife had to come get you."

Christian's smile was sad.

"It was a long time ago," I said.

"It was yesterday to me. And he's right. I shouldn't have been there, but Helen insisted. She'd had a miscarriage and was supposed to rest, but feared reprisals from her bridezilla sister. I wanted to stay home with her and Caroline, but I could refuse her nothing when she cried." Wistful now, he seemed to watch the scene unfold. "I had a cold and couldn't stop coughing. Caroline was always bringing home something. My mother-in-law insisted I take cold medicine. That plus one glass of champagne did me in. I fell asleep between dinner and dessert. I would have called a cab . . ."

I let the silence linger, then said, "Why did Mike make it sound so different?"

Christian's face cleared. "I don't know. We've never been close." He shrugged.

I leaned against the cool window and realized I hadn't called Aunt Irm. Aunt Irm. I jerked upright.

"Aunt Irm. What if BJ goes after her?" I should have called from the airport.

"There's a police car parked outside your house, remember? Not to underestimate Shadow as a watchdog." His smile broke the tension.

We landed fifty minutes after takeoff. I ignored a series of text alerts when I activated my phone and called Aunt Irm. I apologized for not calling sooner and told her to expect us in half an hour. She was cooking breakfast for the officer parked across the street and would save some for us.

Christian smiled. "Let's not tell Garner that part."

There were two texts from Todd: Dr. Mason wants to apologize and I want to help find this bastard. What can I do?

I had no answer to that one.

Most of the voicemail messages were from Aunt Irm, with increasing anxiety. I'd been a crappy niece.

Another message came from my chair.

"I have a meeting in the chair's office at noon," I told Christian. The last, tearful one came from my secretary. I passed it along as well. "There's a memorial for Jenn at one."

"Where?" Christian asked.

"By the fountain behind the medical center. Can you bring Aunt Irm? She'll want to be there."

"Of course."

A memorial for a dead medical student, a young woman with a promising career and everything ahead of her.

Christian caught my eyes. "It's going to be okay." I didn't look away immediately. Instead, I allowed the warmth in his eyes to instill a calmness in me I'd not felt since this whole disaster began.

"Thank you." I squeezed his hand, then returned to my phone to text Todd. Someone must have told him about the memorial, but just in case . . .

He texted back: At the Atlanta airport now.

Aunt Irm greeted us with tight but somber hugs. Shadow was less somber. Christian crossed to talk with the officer while Aunt Irm led me inside. "That man murdered Max and Christian's dad, and now our Jenn." Her red-rimmed eyes looked more fierce than sad. "I cannot forgive him."

"No, neither can I." Though the significance of the statement for me paled in comparison to that of a devout Catholic.

Christian closed the door behind him as I helped Aunt Irm fill plates. "Uh-oh," he said, unwrapping the newspaper. On the top fold of the front page, two-inch bold letters screamed, "Atlanta Murder Suspect Linked to Local Hospital."

"Oh boy," I said. "That was fast." And probably explained the meeting in the chair's office.

Aunt Irm offered Christian coffee. He looked up from the paper and kissed her lightly on both cheeks. "I'm sorry we left you in the dark for so long yesterday."

She nodded, her eyes glistening again. Shadow whined, his patience exhausted. Christian leaned down to pet him.

I marveled at the comfort level between Christian and two of the most important people in my life, even if Shadow wasn't a people. I turned back to the paper.

"Someone in our meeting yesterday spoke up," I said. "Dr. Mason maybe?"

"Jenn's father? Good for him," Aunt Irm said. "If your Dr. Walker had acted right away, none of this would have happened. Our Jenn would still be alive."

I sat to skim the article, breakfast forgotten. "Atlanta police are investigating the death of a University medical student as a homicide. The chief suspect is an anesthetist recently employed by a local hospital." The article went on to say the anesthetist "may be implicated in the deaths of several patients." Uh-oh. It didn't specify the university, or name any victims, but implied a link between Jenn and the suspect that may have led to the attack. All in all, the accuracy proved it had been informed by our conversation in Atlanta. Neither Christian nor I was named, small mercy.

My cell phone rang. It was my chairman.

"We need to talk," James said without preamble.

"Noon, right?"

"No, now. We have an appointment with the chief of staff in an hour. I want to speak with you first."

"On my way." I rose from the table and apologized to Aunt Irm for not helping clean up.

"I've got it," Christian said. "Your chairman?"

I nodded, and before I could think better of it, said, "I wish you could come with me." His presence had made the day before bearable.

His smile was small, but in his eyes was understanding. I hugged Aunt Irm. "I'll see you this afternoon." I patted Shadow and walked to the car, dazed.

James and Walker would be in damage control mode. What did they want from me? Ordinarily, I would feel confident James "had my six" as my Air Force pilot brother used to say. Now I wasn't so sure.

CHAPTER FORTY-SIX

I CALLED STEVEN Wood, the pharmacologist, from the car, and thanked him for setting up the meeting with Dr. Dunn. "Now I need another favor. I think someone, possibly his former grad student, is injecting patients' tonsils with a delayed-onset muscle relaxant, which kills them a day or two later."

He was silent so long I wondered if the call had dropped. "Holy shit," he said finally. "So that explains the mysterious questions last week."

"Yes, sorry. At the time I wasn't sure what we were dealing with. Still don't, not entirely. Would you be able to assay a biopsy sample to see what kind of medication might be present?"

"I can, but it would help to know what drug I'm looking for. The assays differ depending on the class, and even the specific agent."

"I wish I could tell you. It could even be a completely new drug."

"I doubt that. Which muscle relaxant would make the most sense?"

"One of the steroidal class, I think. I would guess pancuronium, but that's purely a guess. It's long-acting and readily available." I didn't add that he'd used it on me.

"Sounds like a good place to start. How do I get the sample?"

"I'll be there in ten minutes."

Steven accepted the sample with something akin to reverence. "I won't ask how you got this."

"Thank you. How long will it take?"

"A couple hours, minimum. I'll call you."

"Better text. I'll be in a meeting."

In his office, James asked for an update. His calm was infused with contrasting emotions: anger, fear, regret?

"I assume you read the paper," I said.

"I did. Tell me more about this student."

I stared at the table without seeing it. "I mentioned Jenn the other day. She's the student Ricken accused of causing the tonsillar bleed in Mr. Greyson. I told her it wasn't her fault, but she was devastated. She sat at the bedside and held his hand while they withdrew care so he wouldn't die alone."

The scene was still fresh in my memory.

"Soon after, an elderly man she'd befriended also died. She knew about my suspicions and investigated on her own, identifying several other victims. As you know, some were not Ricken's patients, but all were cared for by BJ."

He looked quizzical.

"Brad Jernigan."

"The CRNA."

"Right. He uses pseudonyms with the same initials, BJ. It was extraordinarily bad luck that he ended up at Canton General, where she was rotating." I provided more details of Jenn's confrontation, discovery of more deaths, the planting of fentanyl, and her suspicious overdose. I made it through dry-eyed.

James was silent for a moment. "I'm sorry, Kate. I should have tried harder to convince Walker."

I said nothing.

"And you? Are you in danger?"

The kindness in his voice came as a surprise, though it wouldn't have a week ago. "There's an officer watching the house, so I think we're okay for now."

"I see why you wanted the police involved. I very much regret stalling."

"Hindsight." But his admission was mollifying, a little.

He glanced at his watch. "So how did all this get into the paper?"

"I can't be sure who talked, but yesterday, in Atlanta, we were interviewed by both the police and the FBI."

"Who is *we*?"

"Me, Christian O'Donnell—"

"That would be President O'Donnell's son." James squeezed his temples.

"Right, as well as Jenn's boyfriend, Todd, who's an ortho resident here, and her dad. Mark Wheaton was present, too—he was supervising Jenn's rotation."

James jotted some notes.

"By the way," I said, "there were at least two deaths up there, probably more. Did you talk to anyone?"

Now it was his turn to look down. "The head of the group was out of town. The acting head never called me back."

"I met with the chief of staff and told him how to identify potential victims before the drug took effect, but I don't know what happened after that."

"It would be tough to explain to a patient or their family."

"Especially since we think a family member hired BJ to commit the murder in the first place."

His eyebrows shot up, but he recovered quickly. "Before we meet with Walker, how do you think that discussion made it into the local press?"

"I really don't know." His stare was too intent. "You think I leaked it?"

He raised an eyebrow.

"Oh come on, James. Why on earth would I do that?"

"You were upset I didn't do more last week. Angry with Ricken and with Walker."

I made an effort to control my breathing. "Yes, I was—am, in fact. But the press?"

James held up a hand. "I believe you, but I had to ask. And you know Walker will, too."

"If I were going to the press, you know Ricken's name would have been included."

"Don't go there, Kate."

I said nothing.

"I'm serious. You really cannot mention Ricken to Walker."

"Why?"

"Just leave it be."

Was Ricken's hiring also shady? He wasn't part of the Department of Surgery, so it had been through the chief of staff's office.

James' secretary interrupted. "It's time." She ushered us into the hallway, handing James his suit jacket and cane.

"A suit?" Had I underdressed? I owned a suit, somewhere, but black dress pants and a black-and-white blouse would have to do. No jewelry, no coat.

"You look fine." Which was nice to hear since I hadn't actually asked.

We walked slowly, James leaning on his cane to limit weight on his fractured hip.

"Is she always so helpful at keeping you on schedule? And dressed?"

James forced a small grin. "I suspect she received a call or two from the chief of staff's office."

"Kind of a big deal, huh?"

He met my eyes. "The biggest in my tenure."

"What do you think Walker wants from me?"

"Tough to say. Just stick to the facts. No conjecture."

No conjecture? It was all conjecture.

CHAPTER FORTY-SEVEN

THE CHIEF OF staff's secretary greeted us with unusual formality and ushered us into a private conference room full of dark suits and darker faces. My somber attire for Jenn's memorial actually brightened the room. They resembled the FBI agents the day before. Black and white. Is that how they saw the world? How they were trying to see this case? My actions fit solidly between the extremes. Crap.

Many of the faces were familiar, if only from the news, but still there were others. Dr. Walker made brief introductions, a veritable who's who of both hospital and university, along with legal teams from both. Really big deal.

I took a seat next to James and directly across from Dr. Walker. He instructed me to tell the entire story, beginning to end. Against my better judgment, and under James' watchful eye, I glossed over my suspicion of Ricken, but couldn't leave him out altogether. His accusation of Jenn was key to explaining her tenacity.

I was interrupted frequently.

"Why didn't you mention your concerns to anyone?"

I avoided looking at James. "I did, but I had no proof. By then, Brad Jernigan was gone."

"She told me," James said. All eyes turned to him. "I instructed her to keep it quiet and passed the information on to this office."

He nodded toward Dr. Walker. "With no evidence, the CRNA gone, and no complaints filed, to take it further seemed all risk and no gain."

Dr. Walker nodded, satisfied, and glared back at me. "Go on."

With great effort, I resisted the urge to argue, to remind the jury Brad was a murderer who would do it again, that we had a responsibility to future victims. Instead, I continued with my account, including the Brightons' deaths, my tampered IV, and finishing with Jenn's murder and the investigation in Atlanta. I thought my voice remained remarkably steady, considering.

"All right," Dr. Walker said, "those are the facts as you see them."

"What do you think is going on?" the dean asked me. "You've had lots of time to mull this over."

Walker's face reddened, but he didn't argue.

I shot James a look. The dean was asking for conjecture. James shrugged, then nodded.

"I suspect that, using the knowledge he gained during his PhD work, BJ developed a mechanism for delayed release of a muscle relaxant, a drug that paralyzes all muscles and suffocates the victim. He injects this into the tonsils during surgery, causing the victim's death the following day. The Schierling Society is his front to provide basically a mercy-killing service for people with a sick and . . ." I considered the right term, ". . . burdensome family member. But these victims die a terrifying death. For twenty thousand dollars, BJ helps the family arrange a minor outpatient operation, at a time and location where he is working as a locums. In at least one of the cases here, the wife scheduled the surgery herself, bypassing her husband's primary physician."

"You call him BJ?" someone asked.

"His real name is Brian Jacobs. He uses aliases with the same initials."

Murmurs around the table, then, "But you can't schedule surgery for no reason," said a young man from the hospital attorney section of the table. He looked out of place with a deeply tanned face framed by curly blond hair. Clearly skeptical throughout the proceedings, he'd rolled his eyes, shook his head, and harrumphed at regular intervals.

"No," I said. "There was always a reason, some more contrived than others."

"Such as?"

"An MRI for increased seizure frequency despite evidence the victim was not receiving her seizure meds, a trach revision or hernia that could wait, but mostly feeding tubes without the usual workup to prove a swallowing disorder."

"And how does that happen? Why would a surgeon just agree to operate?"

Walker interjected here. "We live in a system where patients can demand elective operations. It's not inconceivable."

But I knew the answer. "I believe Brad had an accomplice."

"Be careful, Dr. Downey," Walker said. "Libel is a serious charge."

"I was asked for my conjecture. This is part of it."

"What accomplice?" asked another attorney. "Someone on our staff?"

James winced beside me.

"I have no proof, but if you look at the cases performed here, the majority were performed by a single surgeon."

The chair of the Surgery Department appeared more upset than angry. "Why didn't you bring this to my attention, Kate?"

"He's not in your department." I kept my eyes down, not out of shame, but to hide the pleasure I took in that statement.

The room exploded. "Ricken?" "Charles Ricken?"

"Is he the new hire you fast-tracked?"

Fast-tracked? Ricken? Did Walker push his hiring without the normal vetting process? That would explain a lot.

Dr. Walker's face glistened; an artery pulsed in his left temple. "I'm sorry, gentlemen, and ladies." He nodded to one of the few women in the room. "Dr. Downey and Dr. Ricken have a history that compromises her objectivity in this matter."

My eyes widened. I started to retort, but James put a calming hand on my arm and shook his head.

"The fact is, Dr. Downey is currently on a forced leave of absence because of concerns about her competence raised by Dr. Ricken. In addition, this nurse she is accusing, Brad Jernigan, sent a letter to the same effect after his departure. The Board of Medicine has begun a formal inquiry. It is disappointing, but not unexpected, that she might retaliate in this way."

Anger flooded my senses; I could not let this go without a response. I shook off James' hand. "This is not retaliation. He did lodge a complaint, after I asked him about multiple patient deaths in a week's time, but there were other deaths, too, patients neither he nor I took care of, and now some in Atlanta as well."

Dr. Walker shouted over me. "You've had your say." The room quieted, including me. With unmistakable malice, he said, "I want to know how this story reached the local papers so quickly."

"Several people were present during our discussion with the Atlanta police and FBI," I said. "Jenn was a popular student here and her father is a well-known physician. Someone put it together. It may have been a classmate who talked to her boyfriend, or one of the police officers." I wouldn't throw Jenn's grieving father or Todd under the bus.

"We kept this quiet for fear of lawsuits?" The assistant chief of staff directed the question to the table in general. "If the families were paying to have their loved one euthanized through this society, they weren't going to sue for wrongful death anyway, right? It would be too risky."

Dr. Walker rolled his eyes. That *assistant* may have reached the top of his career ladder prematurely. Several attendees jumped on his comment. "Likely only one family member made the arrangement, others can still sue." "What makes you think people can't sue anyway—win, win?" "The family of any patient who died here could try to make a claim."

The assistant paled and shrank in his seat.

Over the twenty minutes of rehashing and clarifying, we resolved nothing, though what could be resolved? They would work on a press release.

My phone vibrated. I'd ignored several calls already. Now, while the bigwigs immersed themselves in vocabulary and spin, I glanced at the display. There were two calls from Steven, and now a couple of texts: You were right, pandemonium, and something else I've not yet identified; then: Sorry, pancuronium, autocorrect sucks.

I nudged James and showed him the screen. "From a biopsy of one of the victims' tonsils," I whispered. "She was injected with pancuronium."

James stared at the screen.

"This is our proof."

"I thought you couldn't get an autopsy," he said, barely above a whisper. "Which victim?"

"I'd rather not say."

He nodded his uncomfortable approval. "Okay. Might complicate things legally, but I'll tell Walker."

I glanced at the chief of staff. "Isn't there someone else you could tell? He's not exactly impartial on this case."

James grunted.

I received another text, this time from Christian: Where are you?

I checked the time and rose from my chair.

"I'm sorry," I said to a surprised Dr. Walker. "It's time for Jennifer Mason's memorial." Without a backward glance, I straightened and walked out on the people who would determine my fate, not just at University, but my entire career.

CHAPTER FORTY-EIGHT

I OFTEN ATE lunch in the small plaza where the service was to be held. Wedged between two wings of the medical school, and two of a research building, the tiered plaza sported brick terraces, drake elms for shade, and a lovely fountain at the bottom level. Not elaborate or artistic, a simple jet shot up twenty feet, but the crashing water contrasted nicely with the hospital din inside. Normally a scattering of people sat along the brick terraces leading from the glass doors down to the fountain, eating, reading, chatting, enjoying the filtered sunlight.

Today, the fountain was off, and the four terraces packed with mourners, mostly students, but also many faculty and staff. There were so many people, I gave up entering from the back, and instead, took the stairwell, to approach from the front. I'd be in view of the entire crowd, but I couldn't possibly fight my way down from the top, much less find Christian and Aunt Irm. I texted him: I'm here, where are you two?

Front row.

Why am I not surprised?

I stood, inconspicuously I hoped, near the corner, scanning for Christian and my aunt. I found Todd first, in a chair behind a makeshift podium. He was flanked by two middle-aged couples. I recognized Dr. Mason and guessed the other couple must be Todd's parents.

My phone vibrated: Look straight to your left.

As Dean of Students, Dr. Duffy, began speaking, I spotted Christian and Irm on the far side of the podium. Too far. I slipped into the nearby crowd. We would catch up after.

Dr. Duffy's words were kind. Jenn was even more accomplished than I knew. She led one of the medical mission trips, volunteered weekly at the free clinic, and was a pianist and tennis player.

A classmate spoke next. When she was unable to get through her prepared remarks, Todd rose, put his arm around her, and took over reading her notes. When she returned to her seat, still wiping tears, he remained at the podium. Pulling a single sheet of paper from his suit coat, he began his eulogy. His voice was strong and steady as he started with qualities well worn in eulogies, but, I thought, never more true. Like Jenn's penchant for finding the good in people, from professors to the most difficult patients, and in every situation. Her attitude had forced him to rethink his own approach, he said, "and I'm a better doctor for it." Then he made it more personal. "One day last spring we were driving north of town. She suddenly yelled for me to pull off the road in the middle of nowhere. Knowing Jenn, it could have been for an injured turtle, or even a grasshopper." Laughter, and not the forced kind. "Jenn grabbed my hand and pulled me out into a field of wildflowers. She insisted we lie on our backs and take a selfie." He shook his head. "I thought she was crazy, until I saw the photo. It's on our wall, big as life." He choked and cleared his throat. He concluded with, "If Jenn were here, she would want me to say how grateful she is to her parents, professors, and fellow students, for their role in her education both in and out of the classroom. She considered the opportunity to become a physician a blessing and a privilege. A perspective we would all do well to share."

He paused, fighting to retain his composure. "Jenn was everything a great doctor should be and an even more amazing person. I would have been proud to call her my wife." A sob escaped his throat as he stepped from the podium. There wasn't a dry eye in the crowd.

Dr. Mason, next to speak, shook his head and handed Dr. Duffy a piece of paper. It was the Hopi Prayer. He read it with a reverence that did nothing to dry the eyes of those gathered: "Do not stand at my grave and weep. I am not there. I do not sleep. I am a thousand winds that blow . . ."

CHAPTER FORTY-NINE

THROUGH MY OWN tears, I glanced at my phone. Its incessant vibrations had been a distraction throughout the service. Someone was persistent—Adam. I texted him: Can't talk now.

The reply came immediately: Greg needs emergency surgery. Need your consent right away.

I gasped and slipped away as Dr. Duffy gave closing remarks. I wanted to speak to the Masons and, more importantly, to Todd, but Greg needed me. Once at a respectful distance, I called Adam. "What's going on?"

"Ah, you *can* talk."

I ignored him. "What's going on with Greg?"

"His trach is leaking. They have to revise it."

"I need to speak with his doctor."

"Texting the number now."

I dialed as I jogged to my car.

"Dr. Warren," a male voice answered.

"This is Kate Downey, Greg's wife."

"I'm glad Adam was able to reach you. I'm covering today, and your husband is having a problem with his trach. When the respiratory therapist suctioned him this afternoon, there was a large amount of blood."

Blood?

"I understand you're a physician?"

"Yes."

"His oxygen saturation is falling. We can't get it above ninety percent despite high pressures. He's developed a large leak around his trach and we need to revise it."

"A mature trach doesn't suddenly start bleeding."

"There isn't much blood coming out now, but the leak is enough that he's developing subcutaneous emphysema and we can't delay. Do I have your consent?"

I closed my eyes. "Of course." Air leaking into the skin of his neck was most definitely an emergency. No question.

"I'll need you to repeat your consent to the nurse."

"Dr. Downey?" A new, familiar voice. "This is Glenda. You're okay with Dr. Warren fixing Greg's trach?"

"Yes, Glenda, thanks. What happened?"

"I don't know. I came back from lunch and everyone was here."

"How does he look?"

"He needs the surgery. Say a prayer."

God, please watch over Greg. I pulled out of the garage, continuing to pray, first for Greg, then for Jenn and her family and Todd. By the end of the prayer I felt a vengeful desire to corner Brad.

Before I reached the interstate, Aunt Irm called.

"I'm sorry," I said. "It's Greg. He—"

"I know, kindchen. We're on our way."

"To Jacksonville?"

"We'll meet you there."

"But—"

Aunt Irm had already hung up. *We.* Christian to the rescue again. It wasn't right for them to drive all the way to Jacksonville, but I wasn't looking forward to dealing with Adam on my own. I'd not yet spoken to him about the sale of the house, about his imperson-ation of Greg. Did he even realize I knew?

The ninety-minute drive felt twice that long. Ominous black clouds cluttered the horizon, but I made it before the skies opened. I hoped it would hold off until Christian and Irm arrived.

As I approached the waiting room desk, Adam intercepted me. "I just asked. He's not out of surgery yet." In a lower voice, he said, "But you could have let nature take its course. You didn't have to give consent to operate."

"Then why did you call?"

He shrugged.

"Maybe you haven't given up hope after all." But even as I said it, I didn't believe it.

I sat stiffly in one of the plastic molded chairs secured along the wall. All around me, people sat, pensive, waiting for news. Some on laptops, others with newspapers, or watching ESPN highlights on the silent television mounted high on the opposite wall, but none concentrated. The room radiated anxiety like an impending storm, the rumble of thunder, wind whipping in all directions. I wanted to move, to run into the OR suite and find my husband. My leg shook up and down. A nervous habit. I hoped I wasn't shaking the entire row of chairs, but I couldn't stop.

Adam brought coffee. I accepted, but didn't drink.

What could have happened to Greg?

I checked my phone—no messages—and texted Aunt Irm: Still in surgery.

After half an hour of silence, I rose.

Adam jumped up. "I'll check for an update," he said.

I wandered to the glass doors. The rain had begun, large drops pelting the window, the shrubbery outside flailing in the wind. Christian and Aunt Irm should have arrived. I texted again.

Adam returned a moment later. "He's out of surgery and stable. They're taking him to an ICU bed. She said they'll call when we can see him."

"Dr. Downey?" inquired a tall, middle-aged man in scrubs, face mask dangling on his chest, gray hair framing his temples below a surgical cap.

"I'm Kate Downey."

"Dr. Warren." He shook my hand. "Your husband is out of surgery. Please, come with me."

I didn't know whether Adam would follow and didn't care. He stayed where he was.

We entered a small consultation room and sat in cushioned chairs angled toward each other.

"Your husband's trachea was severely damaged."

"Damaged? How could it get damaged?"

"I don't know. Never seen anything like it. But I can tell you this, it was not from over-aggressive respiratory therapy."

My mouth was suddenly too dry to swallow, to speak. Greg couldn't move. Someone else had to damage his trach.

CHAPTER FIFTY

My phone vibrated again. In a daze, I glanced briefly at the name, Jennifer Mason, and returned my attention to the words Dr. Warren was saying. They made no sense.

Jenn? I went back to my phone and clicked the message.

Jenn: I told you to stop.

The room dimmed, as did all sound.

"Are you okay?" Dr. Warren asked. He gripped my arm.

I stood unsteadily as my phone vibrated again.

Jenn: Room EB-110.

"Where's EB-110?"

"I have no idea. Why don't you have a seat, and I'll get you some water?" He opened the door.

I ran from the room, stumbling toward the nearby desk clerk. "Where is room EB-110?" My pulse pounded in my head.

Though startled by my appearance and interruption of the queue, my expression persuaded the clerk to answer directly. "East wing, basement."

"Dr. Downey?" I heard concern in the surgeon's voice, but ignored him. BJ was here. I would finally confront him. He'd hurt so many. No more.

I looked for Adam as I ran to the bank of elevators. He wasn't there. As I stepped into the elevator, I had a moment of clarity. I was going to confront a murderer alone? My hand shot between the closing doors, and I ran back to the desk, again bypassing the line. "Call security!"

My phone buzzed again.

Jenn: Come alone. Your friends are waiting.

Friends? I sprinted back to the elevators. The clerk called after me, but I slipped into the car just before the doors slid closed.

A sign pointed me to the left out of the elevator. EB-102, EB-104, EB-106.

Friends? Aunt Irm, Christian, Adam? It had to be BJ.

Ahead, yellow construction tape stretched across the hall. I ducked under it, dodged the wood railing propped against un-painted wall board, skirted crates of equipment. A sign on EB-110 read SIMULATION CENTER. Like the one at University, their new simulation center would be relegated to a bottom floor.

Breaths came hard and fast. From sprinting, from fear, from the insanity of what I was about to do.

I called out for help, but heard no answer.

No choice.

I pushed open the heavy door into pitch blackness. Was this the right place? A deep voice, amplified over a loudspeaker, said, "Come in, Dr. Downey."

It had to be him. "Where are you?" My eyes ached with the effort to penetrate the darkness. The light spilling through the door I held open reached only an arm's length. Beyond that, nothing. Blackness. I heard nothing over my labored breathing. Or did I? A monitor beeped from somewhere ahead. And something else. Muffled grunts. From where?

A bright light flashed on, illuminating a circle in the center of the room. "Oh God." I ran to Greg. The door slammed closed behind me.

What the hell? Fresh bandages surrounded Greg's trach. A ventilator fired rhythmically; the monitor above continued its reassuring beep.

"What's going on? Why is he here? He should be in the ICU."

"I also had a loved one whose mind was gone." The voice was too loud, vibrating in my ears, in my head, blocking coherent thought.

"Precious resources were wasted on my mother for years. Money, time, so much time . . . my time and my money. The sacrifices I made for her. But it wasn't her." Did his voice break? Distortion from the speaker hid inflection, but still I heard rage, pain, arrogance. "Resources are now being wasted on your husband. But not your resources. The military could be treating post-traumatic stress disorder, providing artificial limbs, but instead they're funding a vegetable garden."

I flashed on the memorial for his brother in Ohio. His suicide must have been related to PTSD.

I became aware of moaning, not from Greg, but I couldn't localize the sound.

"There are not unlimited resources, Dr. Downey. Someone must choose who lives . . ."

A spotlight came on twenty feet to the left.

"And who dies."

Aunt Irm! Silver duct tape covered her mouth, but the terror in her eyes was unmistakable. I ran to her side and peeled off the tape, but she didn't speak, only moaned faintly as her limbs jerked weakly, clanging handcuffs against the stretcher rail. I traced the IV in her arm to a pole in the shadows. Pulling the empty bag forward, I read "pancuronium."

He was paralyzing her, just like the others, only this time, he provided a label. "You bastard!" I yelled into the darkness.

I caressed her head. "It's okay, Aunt Irm. I'm here."

I glanced at my phone. No signal.

"Choose, Dr. Downey. You can save only one. The infirm, the elderly . . . or the young."

A third set of lights revealed another gurney at the opposite end of the large room. Approaching panic, I knew what I would find. Stumbling over boxes and equipment in the darkness, I ran to Christian and pulled the tape from his mouth. Moving much less than Aunt Irm, he must have been subdued first. Though his eyes were closed, he was awake.

I whirled, looking for the source of the voice, but all was in darkness except the three stretchers. I tried my phone again, no way to call for help.

Christian's lips were blue in the bright white light. I tilted up his chin, opened his mouth, pinched his nose, and sealed my lips around his. I'd taught mouth-to-mouth resuscitation on manikins, but this was my first live performance. After three breaths, I yanked on the stretcher, hoping to move it closer to Aunt Irm, but it was secured to the wall and Christian secured to the gurney, just like Aunt Irm.

I gave him a few more breaths, then, on my way back to Aunt Irm, I tried to yell out the door, but it was locked from the outside. I did manage to find a light switch, illuminating the whole room. The control room remained in darkness; its door also locked. Was BJ still there? I couldn't worry about it.

I gave Aunt Irm several breaths, but her ample neck tissue made mouth-to-mouth difficult. The pancuronium would keep her paralyzed for more than an hour.

As I returned to Christian, I scanned the stored equipment as I passed. After giving him a few more breaths, I wrenched open a box labeled, AIRWAY. In it, I found an old face mask. Several more trips, and three more boxes, revealed a breathing bag, laryngoscope, and breathing tube.

I ran to Aunt Irm, apologized for what I was about to do, then opened her mouth wide, inserted the laryngoscope, and lifted— darkness. Crap. The battery was dead. But the trachea had to be there. I inserted the tube as gently as I could, hoping it would end up in the windpipe and not the esophagus.

I gave her several breaths with the breathing bag. Without monitors or a stethoscope, I could only pray I'd placed the tube correctly. Aunt Irm's chest rose with each breath, and mist appeared in the tube. All reassuring, but not proof. I needed a monitor.

Back to Christian, I connected the breathing bag to the face mask and gave him several breaths. Much easier and less tiring than mouth-to-mouth, and the oxygen in room air was higher than that in my exhaled gas, especially with all the running.

Nonetheless, this couldn't continue. Tears filled my eyes. I knew what I had to do. There was no other way.

I ran to Greg, kissed him on the lips, then disconnected his ventilator and struggled to roll the heavy machine to Aunt Irm, alarms squawking.

I, not Brad, was killing my husband. I was saving a life in the process, but . . . I forced such thoughts from my mind and adjusted the ventilator for Aunt Irm's smaller lungs.

Back with Christian, I squeezed the breathing bag, holding the mask tightly to his face. The ventilator alarm quieted, replaced by Greg's pulse oximeter alarm. He needed oxygen. Tears streamed down my face. How could I let him die?

I left Christian, attached the breathing bag to Greg's trach, and squeezed, but his chest barely rose. I tried again. His lungs had grown stiff with the pneumonia. He needed the higher pressures supplied by the ventilator, but Aunt Irm needed it more. If I had to let him die, I wasn't going to listen as it happened. I switched off the monitor and returned to Christian.

Time passed; I lost track. I moved Greg's oxygen monitor to Aunt Irm, reassuring me that she was getting enough oxygen. With her oxygen supply turned down to minimal levels, I tried to calculate how long the tank would last. The math was beyond me at the moment. My hand cramped on the breathing bag, but resting was not an option. I spoke reassuringly to both of them through my tears.

A knock sounded at the door. I yelled. To my relief, a face appeared in the partially open doorway, followed by a woman's body in the uniform of a security officer. The clerk had come through.

"Call for help!" I yelled. "We need the Code Blue team down here, now, and anesthesia!"

A door slammed, from the control room. BJ was getting away. I described him to the closest security officer, and she sent two others to give chase, then called for more assistance.

When the code team arrived, I explained the situation. "Give them some sedation and check with anesthesia about reversing the muscle relaxant." A senior resident took over masking Christian. I tentatively approached Greg and grasped his already cold hand. Rage replaced desperation and I ran from the room.

CHAPTER FIFTY-ONE

BJ HAD ELUDED security so far. I had to find him, to stop him before he moved on. First, I located the OR suite. The front desk was unoccupied so late in the day. Despite my street clothes, I barreled through the double doors. The first OR was in disarray; a case must have just ended, which meant the anesthesia cart had likely not yet been locked. In the top drawer was the succinylcholine powder, a highly concentrated, rapid-acting muscle relaxant. I dissolved it in a 10cc saline syringe, capped the needle, and slipped it in my back pocket. As I ran back into the hallway, my phone rang. "Where are you, Kate?" Adam asked. "Is Greg okay?"

Breathing hard, I said, "I can't talk now. I have to find someone."

"Wait. Let me help you. Where are you?"

His help was unwelcome, but two of us stood a better chance of finding Brad. "Meet me at the OR front desk."

A clerk had appeared. "What are you doing back there?" she asked, clearly upset to see me emerging from the OR suites. I ignored the question as Adam appeared.

"Follow me," I said.

Around the corner, a room marked CONSULTATION was empty. Three chairs lined the windowless walls, leaving a small amount of floor space near the door. Cheaply framed pictures of wet green foliage adorned two walls.

Adam stood with his back to the door. I moved farther into the room but couldn't sit. "So what's going on?" he asked.

I pulled up Brad's photo on my phone. "We have to find this guy. His name is Brad—or Brent—or Brian. He's a murderer. He just tried to kill Greg, my aunt, and a friend."

Adam's eyes widened slightly. "*Tried?*"

"Yes, tri—" and then it clicked. "Oh, my God." I lunged for the door, but Adam's position was no accident. Anger and betrayal flooded my system with adrenaline. "It was you. You did this." My mind raced, everything falling into place. "You damaged Greg's trachea to force the surgery. You got us all here. And—" I pointed at his phone—"you just told him how to find me. But why?" I searched his barren eyes.

"For my brother. There is a fate worse than death, Kate. Have you looked at him? Greg would never want this. I did this for him."

"You did this for yourself. Impersonating him to get the house wasn't enough?"

Adam's eyes flickered. "Greg's been dead for a year; he just needed someone who loved him enough to help him go." His words twisted the knife in my gut.

"God would have taken him when it was time," I said, tears hot in my eyes, the words heavy on my heart.

"God tried to take him, Kate." His voice rose. "He tried a dozen times, but you always stepped in. Antibiotics, tube feeds, surgery to fix his trach."

"You would have him starve to death?"

"No! That's exactly my point. No one should have to suffer. When Bryce called me, I knew God had given up on you. He sent Bryce to me instead. To someone who would follow through. He has it right. Let them die humanely, with dignity."

"*Dignity?*" Shaking uncontrollably, I struggled to control my voice. "You went to med school, Adam. How humane is suffocation? Desperately seeking the next breath?"

"That's not what it's like. They die quietly in their sleep."

"Oh, come on." I had to get through to him. I moved closer. "Think about it. No one sleeps through suffocation. Jenn sat with one of Brad's victims as he died, and my aunt Irm did the same for her brother. Both described panicky movements and terror in their eyes."

Adam's face clouded briefly, but he blinked it away. "Greg was in a coma; he felt nothing. He's free and I know he's grateful."

The tears broke through. "It wasn't your decision to make."

"No, it was yours," he said, spat, really, "and you made the wrong one, over and over. My brother was an athlete, a brilliant doctor, a hero. Because of you, he's now a shriveled . . ." His voice broke. "I'll never forgive you for that. And neither will he."

Adam admired his brother? Why had I assumed him capable only of jealousy? Was he right? Had I been selfish? BJ contacted him? How did he know? A rush filled my ears, tears blinded my eyes.

At a tap on the door, Adam grabbed my arms too tightly. "Open your eyes, Kate. He's doing a good thing—helping people finish dying." He shoved me into a chair.

BJ squeezed into the room.

My mind cleared instantly. That face was burned into my memory. I jumped to my feet, but Adam restrained me. "You bastard!" I yelled, leaning around Adam. "You killed Jenn. She'd done nothing to you! And my husband!"

"Ah, no, you killed your husband. Jenn was . . . unfortunate." It was the cold voice from the simulator room, deep and ominous. He straightened a picture on the wall, wiping at a mark on the frame. "The odds of her crossing my path twice." He shook his head. "But when you're doing God's work, sometimes there are sacrifices." He turned.

I pushed back against Adam, face aflame. "God's work? God would never attack an innocent young woman."

"I beg to differ, Dr. Downey. The Old Testament is replete with murders of the innocent to further God's agenda with the Jews." He pulled a length of leather cord from his pocket. "He has called me to be his instrument, to assist those who are imprisoned in purgatory by the misguided."

I felt my first real panic. How do you reason with the irrational?

"Leave us," he commanded Adam.

Without a backward glance, Adam opened the door. My yell for help earned a backhand across the face. I tasted blood. Brad stretched the leather cord, wrapping it tightly around his right hand. With his left he spun me around, my back to his front, the garrote across my neck. Struggling only tightened the pressure.

Time slowed. Greg was dead. He might be holding Emily right now, in heaven. Could I join them? Would I be forgiven for causing his death? For keeping him alive?

No! Raw fury pulsed through me. This man had ruthlessly killed. No denying that the image appealed, the three of us together, but I wouldn't let Brad win. I shifted my hips forward to reach into my back pocket; the garrote tightened. I couldn't breathe; stars shot through my peripheral vision. I pulled out the syringe and fumbled to release the needle cap. He was talking close to my ear, but I could no longer make out the words. My vision began to darken around the edges. I swung my right arm out, then plunged the needle into Brad's thigh. His hold loosened, allowing me a hungry breath.

"What the hell?" he said as I compressed the plunger.

As he reached for his thigh, where the empty syringe bounced like a demonic metronome, the pressure on my neck relaxed enough for me to take another gasping breath. I flung my elbow back, connecting with something hard, maybe his chin, then reached up and grabbed the cord around my neck, wrenching one end from his hands. He shoved me, hard, against the wall. I stumbled against a chair, lifted it, and spun to put it between us.

"Succinylcholine," I said hoarsely. "Let's see how humane you find it."

His eyes changed then, from feral, to shocked, to angry, to terrified. Did he understand what was happening? He grabbed the chair and shoved me back against the wall. The back of the chair slammed into my chest, knocking out what little breath I'd regained.

The muscles around his eyes twitched.

"You feel it? It's starting to work." I sounded evil to my own ears, but I didn't care.

More twitching of muscles in his face and hands.

He reached for the door and stumbled out. His exertion and rising blood pressure increased blood flow to his thigh, speeding the drug's onset.

He fell in the hallway just steps from the consultation room, twitching all over with fasciculations, unique to succinylcholine. Each muscle fiber fired once, chaotically, then stilled. The more muscle, the more violent the response. But only skeletal muscle, including the diaphragm. The heart was immune. Until he suffocated to death, he would be awake and paralyzed, just like his victims. I stood over him. I wanted to see the fear in his eyes, and it was there, but gave me no satisfaction.

The hall was empty. I could walk away now. Who would blame me? A life for a life, a life for many lives. But I wasn't a murderer. I turned my back on Brad and returned to the consultation room, where I picked up the phone and dialed 0. "Code Blue, OR consultation room. And send security."

CHAPTER FIFTY-TWO

IT WAS OVER.

Back in the hallway, BJ had stilled, his chest barely moved, but I wasn't offering mouth-to-mouth. Not this time. Not for him. The code team would arrive soon enough. Even after he stopped breathing, he had several minutes. When I knelt to check his pulse, I noticed movement in my peripheral vision, someone hurrying away. I stood and yelled to him, but he continued around a corner and disappeared.

The code team arrived from the opposite direction; the leader knelt by Brad and asked the situation.

"Just ventilate him," I said. "It was succinylcholine. It'll wear off in a few minutes."

"No pulse," the code team leader said. "Start chest compressions."

"What? No." I knelt on his other side and felt Brad's wrist. A weak pulse accompanied each compression.

"Stop compressions." The leader placed the defibrillator paddles on Brad's chest. "Sine wave. Not a shockable rhythm. Continue chest compressions." He looked at me. "Succinylcholine? Hyperkalemia?"

High potassium? The level can go up, but not enough to kill someone reasonably healthy. "It's . . . possible . . . I guess."

"Insulin, glucose." He continued with a list of medications to rapidly lower the potassium level and attempt to kick-start the heart. He was good, but within minutes the EKG further degraded. I could only watch, dumbfounded. Through the haze, I compiled a list of the drugs and diseases that could cause a lethal degree of hyperkalemia in response to succinylcholine. But the timing was wrong. His pulse was strong when I called for help.

"Stop compressions. Asystole for more than ten minutes with no return of spontaneous circulation. Call the code." Silence. A moment of silence always followed when we called a code. A reflex, an appropriate one. Usually.

Claustrophobia struck, the hallway collapsing in, no air. This man deserved to die, but not by my hand. I looked back in the direction of the retreating figure. Was it by my hand? I knelt forward over Brad's chest.

"Don't touch the body," a security officer ordered. His arrival had gone unnoticed.

I leaned closer. BJ's open shirt revealed a hairless chest, red from compressions. There was a tiny red spot on the left side, over his heart. A freckle? Only one?

CHAPTER FIFTY-THREE

QUESTIONING WENT ON for hours. After telling the story so many times, I no longer knew when I repeated myself or left out important details. I'd become numb even to Greg's death. At some point an attorney tried to stop the proceedings, but I declined his help. I wanted it over with tonight. Repeatedly reassured Aunt Irm and Christian were safe, I was desperate to see for myself.

Now I waited, alone and morose.

A new group of suits entered with the same opening salvo. "We're from the FBI and have a few questions for you." Exhausted, I'd long since given up trying to remember the names of my interrogators, but oddly, their names were Jack and Jill. This was the first woman; maybe she would have compassion.

"I'll be happy to answer your questions after I see my aunt." I'd tried this each time, and each time the answer had been the same.

"Your aunt is fine. We'll bring her in as soon as we're done with this interview."

No. No more. "Sorry, I've heard that three times and have yet to see her. I will answer your questions after I've seen my aunt." I looked Jill defiantly in the eye; she seemed to be the one in charge.

"You do realize who we are," Jack said.

"I do." I held Jill's eyes. "I mean no disrespect, but it's been a very long day, my aunt was nearly killed, and she is very old. I need to see her in person before I go through all this again." I softened my stare. "Please."

Jack and Jill spoke in low tones, and then Jack left. "Would you like something to eat or drink?" Jill asked. Was she setting herself up as good cop?

"I'm fine." I stood and walked away from the conference table, pretending to study an institutional print of a palm tree on a beach.

There was a soft knock, then Aunt Irm was wheeled in. In two strides I folded her in an embrace. "Are you okay?"

"I'm fine. You saved my life, and Christian's."

"After I put you both in jeopardy. Have you seen him?"

"Sorry, time to go," interrupted Jack. He pulled the wheelchair back toward the door.

"I haven't seen him, but they said he's okay," she said.

"We'll get you back together soon, I promise," Jill said.

Aunt Irm looked back from the doorway. "Be strong," she said as the door closed.

I looked at Jill. "Thank you."

She nodded.

"We know you've been through this several times," she said when her partner returned. "This will be the last for today."

I glanced at my watch. "Is it still today?" They weren't amused. "Where do you want me to start?"

"At the beginning."

I let my head fall to my chest—of course, the beginning. I launched in again. At this point, I felt no compulsion to withhold Ricken's involvement. No doubt he was complicit. He was hired under dubious circumstances, agreed to operate when it wasn't strictly indicated, and made reckless accusations when confronted. Finally, free to include his role, more pieces fell into place. I mentioned his history in Miami and implied that he and Brad's first victim was Ricken's own brother, to gain control of his trust fund. I admitted I had no proof, but Jack and Jill exchanged a look. A short one, but I'd surprised them.

I included all the deaths, including Uncle Max and Christian's aunt Edith, as well as Mrs. Sanderson's suicide and Mrs. Brighton's murder for changing her mind.

"I don't know how my brother-in-law, Adam, met Brad. He called him Bryce. My husband has been comatose for quite some time. Adam has battled me over withdrawing care. Recently, I learned that only Greg's death would give Adam control of his parents' estate. Somehow, Adam and BJ got together and planned tonight. Adam damaged Greg's trach to necessitate the surgery."

"Why didn't he just kill him in the nursing home?"

Good question. "I suppose he wanted him dead, but not enough to do it himself." Seemed a reasonable explanation.

I told the rest of the day's events impassively, on autopilot. I skimmed over Greg's death, still not real to me, and my efforts to save Aunt Irm and Christian. Adam's betrayal. I touched my neck as I described Brad's attempted strangulation, and lifted my right hand unconsciously as I described injecting Brad's thigh.

"His pulse was strong and rapid, just what I expected." I paused. "Then after I called for the code team, I went back." I pictured myself squatting by his chest—it still moved. "I saw someone. He was walking away, down the hall, in a hurry."

Jack and Jill exchanged a look. "You saw someone?"

"Yes, a man."

"Could you identify him?"

I looked toward the ceiling, as if I could replay the image there. "He was running away." I shook my head. "But he must have done something." Then it struck me. "Potassium. He must have injected BJ with potassium, straight into the heart. I saw the puncture wound." I pointed to the left side of my chest. My heart beat so hard it might have been visible, pounding under my shirt.

"Through his chest wall?" Jack asked. "Who would do that?"

I wanted it to be Ricken, but the retreating man had no limp. "I don't know."

Jack spoke into his cell phone. "Have the pathologist look for a puncture wound to the heart, diameter of a needle."

"Ask him to look for evidence of an intracardiac injection of potassium," I said.

Jack echoed my request, then added instructions to search for the syringe along the route of the retreating man.

There was little else to tell. Both agents asked for more detail and clarification on several points, but at long last closed their notebooks.

Thank God. I wanted a shower, and Aunt Irm, and Shadow. Poor Shadow, he'd been alone for hours. "May I go?"

"Yes," Jill said, offering her card. "Please let us know if you think of anything else or have to leave the area."

"We're going home. Where's my aunt?"

Jill nodded to Jack; he left the room.

"We haven't found Adam Downey yet, but we'll need you to officially press charges."

"Charges?"

"For injuring your husband, if we can find evidence, and holding you against your will."

And impersonating Greg, the list goes on. All thoughts of Adam vanished as Aunt Irm appeared. Christian and his brother, Luke, followed.

Christian waited for Aunt Irm and me to disengage, then he stepped forward and pulled me into a tight hug.

It was all too much. He was alive; Greg was not. My choice. My obvious but unforgivable choice.

I broke down in his arms, overwhelmed by utter exhaustion and crippling guilt.

But Aunt Irm and Christian had suffered, too. Would my grief over Greg be construed as regret over the decision?

I focused on Christian's gentle voice in my ear. "I'm so sorry. He put you in an impossible situation. I can't even imagine. I don't know what to say, except, I owe you my life. You are amazing. That bastard wanted you to choose only one; you saved two."

Not amazing enough. There were three.

CHAPTER FIFTY-FOUR

EACH TIME I surfaced from shallow sleep, more flowers greeted me. Scents mingled into a cloying bouquet. Aunt Irm recorded the provenance of each on a sheet by my bed. Floral support came from all corners of my life—from old friends like Randi, and new, from colleagues and nurses, even from the church. "See how you are loved, kindchen?"

Grateful for all the care and concern, I knew my wallowing must come to an end soon, but not yet. After the funeral. I would think about the future then.

Propped in bed, I closed the last of our few photo albums and opened my laptop against my thighs. I fast-forwarded through much of the wedding Mass video until the reception. I danced with Greg, his mom danced with his dad, and Adam drank with . . . I froze the video and zoomed on the frame, on the background. Adam had invited his own friends to the open bar reception, and they'd drunk, a lot. The bill for alcohol nearly doubled the cost of the wedding. Adam didn't bother introducing his friends to us and was far too drunk to give the best man toast when the time came. My brother, Dave, stepped up and delivered a heartfelt, hilarious toast, for which I'll always be grateful. But now, staring at the faces, there was no doubt. One of Adam's drinking buddies was Marcus Culpepper, Ricken's assistant, and the man I'd called on for help investigating the deaths.

The doorbell rang. Still, I stared, Shadow pressed against me. It couldn't be time already. Aunt Irm knocked softly. "The visitors are here." She'd warned me they were coming, the FBI and the O'Donnells.

I glanced at the clock. Noon. How self-indulgent. I'd barely been out of my room all weekend. Aunt Irm was hurting, too. I should be supporting her.

Shadow protested as I rose to wash my face. Puffy eyes testified to a morning of reminiscing. I brushed my teeth, pulled my hair back in a ponytail, and dressed in jeans and a sweatshirt. Both swallowed me whole.

Jack and Jill sat in the family room, with Christian, Luke, Lieutenant Garner, and the attorney I had declined on Friday. The men stood as I approached. Aunt Irm patted the couch next to her and nodded to a steaming mug of coffee on the end table.

"Thank you for seeing us," Jill said. "We have an update."

I met Christian's eyes—concern, and more.

"Brian Jacobs' cause of death was an intracardiac injection of potassium," she said. "The syringe was found in a garbage bin in the parking garage. There were no fingerprints."

"It was Marcus Culpepper, Ricken's PA," I said.

Jill's eyes widened. "How do you know that?"

"I just realized; he and my brother-in-law are friends. He's the link." I stared at my bare feet. I'd forgotten to put on shoes.

"Where is Adam?" Aunt Irm said.

Jill exchanged a look with Jack. "He's been arrested," she said.

Jack had an unpleasant glint in his eye. "He tried to kill his own mother."

It shouldn't surprise me. In his mind, he was probably helping her finish dying, too.

"Is she okay?" I asked.

Jill nodded and continued. "Charles Ricken left for San Pedro Sula, Honduras, right after the attack. Marcus Culpepper left that evening. Same airport."

I flashed back on my recent conversations with Marcus. Had I caused the Brightons' murder by telling him about their hospital visit?

"We're trying to have them both extradited, but the authorities have to find them first. You were right, Dr. Downey, about Dr. Ricken's involvement." She handed out small stacks of papers. "The *Washington Post* received this by courier Saturday and turned it over to us. The cover letter said it had been left with Brian Jacobs' attorney, to be delivered upon his death, so he could tell the world about the importance of his work."

I skimmed the document. It outlined everything pretty much as we'd surmised. His real name was Brian Jacobs. He developed the method to "help people finish dying" during his PhD work. He became a CRNA to gain access to the patients. While finishing training in Miami, he met Charles Ricken and learned of his dire financial situation. When Ricken's brother, Malcolm Ricken III, required a hernia repair, "Charles opined that his life would be saved, if only his brother were no longer in control of his inheritance. It was an ideal opportunity to test my method, which worked to perfection. In gratitude, Dr. Ricken became my associate, along with a PA student, Marcus Culpepper, who stumbled upon my work and recognized its import.

"Marcus or I met the suffering families through support groups for debilitating diseases, like Alzheimer's and Parkinson's, online or in person. When families recognized their loved one had suffered enough," the letter went on, "we would introduce them to the Schierling Society. Sometimes we enlisted Charles' help to facilitate scheduling numerous clients in a short period of time. Sometimes I worked alone, though not entirely alone. The employment process often required facilitation by funds directed to hiring authorities, primarily chiefs of staff at the various institutions."

Walker. He'd been part of it all along.

The scheme took an impressive amount of organization.

On the next two pages, a spreadsheet listed "clients," not the person who arranged it, but the victim, as well as their disease, surgical procedure, the date and location of the operation, and the dates and amounts of payments. Uncle Max was there—Aunt Irm stifled a sob—along with Christian's Aunt Edith and his father. Near the bottom were all the patients Jenn and I had identified, followed by the child and Mrs. McGurn in Atlanta, and an additional two names. He'd recorded only the first payment for these last victims. Greg's name was absent.

"Where will you go from here?" Luke asked the agents.

"Not sure," Jill said. "With only the victims' names, it will depend on whether we can track the money back to determine whom to charge. How hard to seek each suspect is a decision above my pay grade."

"Kind of a victimless crime," Jack said.

Jill scowled at him.

"*Victimless?*" Irm's voice cracked. "My brother was improving. I would have taken care of him. His wife had him murdered, for money. He is a victim. I am a victim."

I'd never heard her so impassioned. I squeezed her hand in mute support.

Jack squirmed.

Christian and Luke said nothing.

"I believe that's all we have for now." Jill stood. "We'll keep you informed."

"Thank you." I walked them to the door.

"Dr. Downey," Jill said, "I'm sorry for how this played out. I realize it's harder to celebrate future lives saved than to mourn those lost, but you did a good thing."

"Thank you," I said, but I didn't feel grateful. Not now and maybe not for a long while.

CHAPTER FIFTY-FIVE

GREG'S FUNERAL WAS on Friday. My secretary, Mary, offered to help with the details. She planned a small wake to follow the graveside service. I handled the funeral arrangements, with Aunt Irm's help. A full Catholic Mass, just as Greg would have wanted. The nursing home recommended against Greg's mother attending the services. My brother, Dave, and his wife, Deb, came up and stayed at the house with baby Jordan, the extra commotion a welcome distraction.

The services were well attended by Greg's friends and colleagues from the military, the department, college, and even some of his high school buddies I'd never met. Shadow was there, too, sitting at my side. It was truly a celebration of Greg's life, and I was grateful for the happy memories shared, less so for the words of comfort. I remembered after Greg's accident, people incessantly asked after me. And after Emily's death, it was even worse. I appreciated their concern, but did they really want to know? That my heart had been ripped in two? That my life, as I knew it, was over? All my plans, my future, gone in a matter of months. Instead of a blank canvas, I saw a black hole.

Now, however well intentioned, words were stale. After a year of grieving, it was time to seek the light.

Christian attended with Luke. He stayed at a respectful distance throughout the long day, but I knew he was there, and found it indescribably comforting.

When we returned home, Aunt Irm, Dave, Deb, and I shared a bottle of wine by the fire.

"Kate, I realize this may be too soon," Deb said. "But what do you think about Dave and me going through Greg's closet for you?"

I stared at her, then, to my surprise, heard myself say, "You're right. It's time. But you don't have to do it."

"Kindchen, why not let them take care of it? They can take things to Goodwill or the church, and you will not suffer so much."

"I want to," continued Deb. "I want to do something."

"And organizing is one of her many talents," Dave said, rolling his eyes.

Deb nudged him. "We won't give away anything you might want. We'll check with you first."

"Wow." I looked from Aunt Irm to Deb. "How can I turn that down?"

*　*　*

First thing in the morning, I took Shadow for a run. Dave joined me. When we returned, I showered and dressed. Deb was in Greg's closet. It took all my willpower not to tell her to leave everything where it was, it was too soon. But deep down, I knew it was long overdue. In the kitchen, Christian talked with Dave and Aunt Irm. Jordan burbled in a baby seat on the counter.

"I've been enlisted to take you to breakfast," Christian said.

"You need to get out of the house, kindchen. Go."

"Are you coming, Dave?"

"Nope, I'm under strict orders to help my loving wife." He put his arm around my shoulders. "Give us a couple of hours. Enjoy your breakfast."

And so I did. We went to The Mill and sat at the same table as before. We talked about favorite books, bucket list vacation spots, and hobbies. Christian showed me photos of his pencil drawings. He was quite the artist. Most were of people. There was one of a woman and child that nearly brought tears to my eyes. The setting was ethereal. Heaven, he told me. It was his wife and daughter.

We'd read many of the same books, remembered many of the same major sports victories for the university, and two hours passed before I glanced at the time.

"Luke and I confronted Mom," he said during a lull in the conversation, staring at his coffee mug. "It took some coaxing, but she finally admitted her role. She said that years ago, when he was first diagnosed, he made her promise she wouldn't let him become an invalid. That she would find a way to let him die with dignity."

I said nothing.

"Mike took over when she wanted to back out. She'd confided in him. I think Aunt Edith was almost a trial run." He rubbed his hands on his legs. "It wasn't perfect, and I pray he slept through the suffocation, but she followed his wishes. His and her sister's. It was torture for her. She's taking all the blame to keep Mike from being charged, and our attorney is hopeful a judge will see fit to keep her out of prison." We were both silent for a long moment. "There needs to be a better way."

I started to speak. He held up his hand. "I know, the slippery slope, but there has to be a way."

"She must have really loved him to take the risk."

He nodded. "They were inseparable. She's going to miss him."

We drove home in companionable silence for several minutes.

"I drafted a response to the Board of Medicine, by the way, demanding they drop the inquiry," he said.

I hadn't thought about the investigation in days. "Thanks."

"And rumor has it the chief of staff position is up for grabs."

Walker? Gone? "He resigned?"

"Well, it wasn't strictly voluntary."

"How do you know all this?"

"You were right about the donation to get BJ hired in the first place. Mom admitted it. The university president and the hospital CEO decided to force Walker out rather than press charges. Probably better for Mom, and Mike, unfortunately."

I waited for further explanation. He pulled up in front of the house and turned off the car.

"He denies it, but Mike was involved, and he put you in danger. He called me away so you would go to the Brightons' alone, and he tried to interfere by misleading you about Helen's death."

I nodded uncertainly, considering. "True, but, devil's advocate, could he have been protecting you rather than purposely hurting me? Maybe he thought I'd wait to go later as well."

Christian's eyes became glassy, shining as if reflecting stars not visible in the morning sky. "Only you would think that way. You were almost killed." He shook his head slowly, his eyes fixed on mine, but the corners of his mouth at last turned up. "I'm headed home tomorrow," he said. "I have a lot of work to catch up on."

Home? Right, he didn't live here. Why was this a surprise? I'd grown accustomed to his company. "Of course," I said. But my healing heart sprang a new leak. "I really appreciate you sticking around during all of this."

"We made a good team." He turned in his seat and put his hand on mine. "Kate, you are a remarkable woman. When Helen died, I didn't expect to think that of another person, to ever feel drawn to anyone again."

I looked away.

"I know it's too soon for you. I know it could be a long while before you're ready to consider a relationship. But someday, I would really like to spend time with you, and talk about something other than murders and psychopaths. I can take a rain check for as long as you need."

I smiled a small smile, but could think of nothing to say, so I said nothing.

Dave and Deb sat at the kitchen table, chatting with Aunt Irm, baby Jordan in her lap slurping a bottle. Christian said his goodbyes and gave me a warm embrace. At the door, he knelt to pet Shadow. "You take good care of her, buddy," he said softly. I found those words more endearing even than those in his car.

*   *   *

A week later, I received a large, flat package. A framed picture. A beautiful pencil sketch like the one Christian had drawn of his wife and daughter. It was Greg holding—no—rejoicing in—a baby girl—Emily. Christian had captured her just as I'd dreamed, smiling, loved, in the arms of her father.

I tried to see the world the way Greg used to. Focusing not on losses, but on blessings. Perhaps Christian was the window God was opening as he closed the door on my life with Greg.

Only time would tell.

AUTHOR'S NOTE

For unknown reasons, end-of-life issues have fascinated me since high school. I wrote an essay back then in which a compassionate and brilliant physician determines a meaningful recovery is impossible—or nearly so—for a patient. When he/she informs the family, their only job is to choose a time to say goodbye. No painful decision to be made or argued about by the grieving family—"Is there *any* chance she'll pull through?"—no days-long death watch. A lethal medication is administered to ensure a pain-free death and it's over.

Though the black-and-white clarity of youth became gray in medical school, the idea that "there has to be a better way" has remained. In *Fatal Intent*, Kate recalls a family asking how she could play God and turn off the ventilator of a brain-dead patient. That story is true and happened during my internship. It is a recurring theme—from Jack Kevorkian to Brittany Maynard—when is life no longer worth living and who should decide? And for the incapacitated with no switch to flip, is starvation the only way?

I don't have the answers—no one does—but I hope *Fatal Intent* stirs discussion and prompts families to consider Living Wills and Health Care Surrogates. The forms are available online or from your physician.

Please join the discussion at https://www.teuliano.com